BUTTERCUP

A NOVEL

BOOK 2 OF *THE BRIAR HOLLOW SERIES*

BUTTERCUP

A NOVEL

LORI WAGNER

Buttercup
Book 2 of *The Briar Hollow Series*
Copyright © 2013 by Lori Wagner

Design and layout by Laura Merchant
Cover model, Victoria Ozias; Cover photo taken by Jennifer Papuga

ISBN: 978-0-9897373-0-2

Library of Congress Control Number: 2013945934

Scripture quotations are from the King James Version.

Requests for information should be addressed to:
Affirming Faith
8900 Ortonville Road
Clarkston, MI 48348
loriwagner@affirmingfaith.com
www.affirmingfaith.com

Printed in the United States of America.

DEDICATION

As I prayed and asked the Lord to whom this book should be dedicated, my thoughts kept coming back to one of my girls. Although Ashley is a young woman now, living on her own; when she lived with us, and Daddy tucked her in each night, she always chose for her nighttime verse Jeremiah 30:17, "For I will restore health unto thee, and I will heal thee of thy wounds."

There are many types of wounds in life, and physical strength is not the only type of health that impacts a person's wellbeing. Through the experiences in the lives of the characters in *Buttercup*, you will read of injuries to health, heart and spirit; even the death of dreams. You will also read some bodacious humor, interesting bits of history, inspirational words, and of course some sweet romance.

As you read, it is my prayer that you remember the words of Ashley's favorite verse. May the balm of God's sweet Spirit bring restoration and health to you—and may you experience His joy.

Ashley, Mom loves you very much.

Of course, as with every book I write, I also dedicate this to my family and to my Lord Jesus Christ.

For Lori Wagner's speaking schedule,
booking information, and additional resources,
see the Affirming Faith website at
www.affirmingfaith.com

$\mathcal{A}$CKNOWLEDGMENTS

Special thanks to:

Alex Tyson for fact-checking the details about equine care and foaling,

Carla DePriest for the wonderful treat of a tour of Belle Meade Plantation,

and Kathy Bouren for editing assistance.

CHAPTER 1

"**M**arigold Johnson!" Penny shrieked and wrapped her pale arms around her shoulders. The slight girl shivered in the middle of an expanding skirt of ripples. "It's f-f-f-freezing!"

"Oh, bosh!" Marigold watched her companion from a safe distance. The freckled girl flashed a cheesy smile and then dove into the swimming hole. She resurfaced and then effortlessly slipped into a back float. "It's not cold at all."

"How c-c-c-could you?" Penny eked out between chattering teeth, her blue eyes fixed on the hale and hearty trickster. "I should have known better. I can't believe I let you fool me again."

Marigold ignored the cold that made Penny tremble. "How could I what? Invite you to partake of this magnificent refreshment?"

"Refreshment?" Penny shook her head, "and to think I've considered you family these last few years." Penny's gaze turned from the girl to the rope still swinging between the grassy bank and the swimming hole. It had been easy for Marigold to entice her into the creek. With the unseasonably warm weather, and the exhausting, sweaty work of cleaning the stalls in the horse barn, Penny had been more than willing to join Marigold in the stream.

"I wanted to cool off, but you were less than honest about the temperature." Penny waggled a slender finger in front of her nose—a mannerism Marigold was well acquainted with, accompanied by the familiar, "That's the truth, and you know it." She gave a firm nod of her blonde head to emphasize her words, but her effort to appear stern was less than frightening on her china doll face.

"Don't go having a blow up now, sister-sister. You're acting like an old croaker." Marigold wiggled her toes and tipped her face to the spring sun as she continued her float.

"An old croaker?" Penny gasped. "So now I'm a frog?"

"Didn't I just tell you about frogs when we were cleaning the stalls?" Marigold stood and shook her gold braids in feigned disgust. "Frogs are those triangular soft spots between a horse's heels. Their hearts aren't big enough to pump blood all the way up those long legs, so they step on those frogs and they send the blood back up to their hearts."

"I know. You told me this morning. You wouldn't be trying to change the subject now, would you?"

"Would I do that?" Marigold offered Penny a swanky smile full of teeth and teasing.

"Yes, you would." Penny climbed out of the creek and sat on a fallen log. She longed for her wrap back at the cabin. Her dirty work dress draped over the bushes would have offered some comfort, but she did not want to put it on over her dripping petticoat and chemise. A layer of cold-as-Christmas undergarments between her skin and her dry clothes would do little to reduce the shivers racing through her body.

Penny gathered a handful of fabric from her full petticoat and squeezed. A stream of water flowed from the hem and she hoped the sun would quickly dry the light fabric.

"There is a lot to know about horses," said Penny. "I never really gave much attention to all the details. Zion has always been so capable."

"He's a horseman," Marigold nodded, "to the manner born." Marigold loved horses—all animals, really. Before Zion had arrived and swept her sister Rosalie off her feet five years ago, there had not been many animals in Briar Hollow; just their milk cow Clover, a few goats and chickens, and their dog Daisy.

Their Pa, Matthias Johnson, husbanded Briar Hollow Orchards for the past two decades. When Zion and Rosalie married, Matthias had given them the family home and moved himself, Marigold, and little Lucas to the old Taylor cabin on the other side of the trees. That left her mother's beloved gardens to Rosalie and gave Zion the room he needed to reestablish Coldwell Horse Farm—his father's work begun in Virginia and lost to a tragic lightning strike.

"What are we going to do, Marigold?" Penny left off squeezing her skirts and began wringing her slender fingers. "I'm willing to work since Zion broke his arm, but I don't think we're going to be able to keep up with everything." The ache in the girl's limbs from the morning chores silently amened her concerns.

"Well, I guess we'll just hang out like a hair in a biscuit." Marigold watched as Penny worked to regain her composure and stilled her hands in a ladylike clasp on her lap. Birdsong filled the silence—throaty and rich zweets and zwracks. The sweet honeysuckle scent of the viburnum bushes drifted on spring breezes.

"It's not like you to fidget," said Marigold.

"I know that it's times like these we're supposed to lean on our faith." Penny released a soft sigh. She raised her blue eyes to Marigold's big browns and buoyed the corners of her lips in a quasi smile. "It's so much easier when things are going well."

"It's easy to get balled up when difficulties come 'round." Marigold dunked her shoulders below the stream's surface, leaving only her freckled round face in view. "Now don't you be worrying about Lucy. She'll have her foal like mares have been doing since the dawn of time. We'll work, and we'll get by. That's all there is to it."

Martins chortled in the bushes; a male gurgled his courtship song. "You know what that is?" asked Marigold.

"What?"

"That sound in the bushes." Marigold dog-paddled while Penny listened.

Penny raised her delicate brows and cocked her head. "Um . . . birds?"

"You goose! Those are purple martins, and that fella is singing a love song for his gal." Marigold lifted her toes until they peeked out of the water. "It's like Pastor Dryfus was saying at Sunday preaching. There's a time for every season, just as sure as Mr. Purple Martin is singing to find his Mrs. Purple Martin."

"You're right." Penny smiled. "It's the details I'm worrying about. With all the local farmers having to get their own fields plowed and planted, there's no free time for our neighbors to do their chores and ours, as much as they would like to help."

"Now don't go getting your faith in a fuss," said Marigold. "The Good Lord will work all this out just as sure as that purple martin is going to find his sweet lady love."

"If only life was as simple as the birds in the bushes."

Penny stretched out on her back and crossed her arms to form a pillow beneath her head. The warm sun swaddled and soothed the distressed girl. "I guess I need to work on my trusting and resting." Penny's lips turned up in a genuine smile and she closed her eyes. "I think I'll start right now."

For the first time since her brother's accident, Penny allowed herself to relax. The sounds and smells of spring filled her senses. Worry, lack of sleep, and the effects of physical labor exacted their toll on the fragile young lady. Tender breezes caressed her ivory skin, and in a few short seconds she drifted into the hazy state between wakefulness and sleep.

"Penny." A voice called to her through the fog, but she was unwilling to respond. She wanted to sink deeper into the restfulness wrapping her in its sweet embrace.

"Penny." The voice grew louder—more insistent. She recognized it as Marigold's and let out a little moan.

"Oh, Mari, please . . . ."

"Penny!" There was no denying the urgency in the call. Penny slowly opened her eyes. A shadowy figure stood before her. The bright sun challenged her focus. She blinked and turned to the creek where Marigold was submerged up to her shoulders—her big brown eyes wide as saucers.

Shock crept up Penny's insides. She blinked hard and tried once more to focus on the shadowy figure.

A man. A strange man. And look at her! She was spread out like the girl on the velvet couch painting hanging in the tavern. A mixture of fear and hot shame crept over her porcelain complexion. Penny scrambled to her feet and crossed her arms over her chest like a soldier's double bandolier ammunition belt.

"Who are you?" Penny lifted her chin and cast a bold look at the stranger.

Although still uncomfortable with her state of undress, Penny's shock faded as she examined the silent young man. In quick inventory she took in his lanky, six-foot frame dressed in fancy, store-bought clothes.

Loosed from the bowler held tightly in his hands, thick tawny hair went every which way. Full eyebrows, a bit darker than the warm, sandy color of his hair, arched widely over deep-set hazel eyes. He had a slight dimple in his chin and an interesting mouth. The top lip had a narrow cupid's bow, but the bottom was a bit fuller—at least it seemed to be. She could better tell if he were relaxed.

He looks as out of sorts as I feel, thought Penny. After her quick assessment, Penny determined the stranger was not a threat. He was more of a question—a question she might have liked to investigate if she had been fully dressed.

"Cat got your tongue?" Marigold called from the safe haven of the water.

The stranger's gaze shifted from Penny to Marigold and back to Penny. He tipped his head and then made eye contact with the girl standing in front of him. "Pardon me, miss . . . and miss . . . ." The man twisted his hat in his hands. "I was looking for Briar Hollow."

"Does this look like a briar hollow to you?" Marigold teased the befuddled man. "This is a swimming hole. You city folks don't know much about the countryside, now, do you?"

A bit of humor played in the stranger's eyes: flecks of amber seemed to shift from a light brown to a golden-green. "I beg your forgiveness," he said.

The tension in the young man eased under the affect of Marigold's playfulness. "Allow me to introduce myself and explain.

"My name is Logan Mayfield. My mother and I are staying in town where I learned of a possible need for hired help at Briar Hollow. Mrs. Matheny gave me the directions, but when I heard sounds this way I thought I would check and make sure I was on the right path."

"Hmph. On the right path?" Marigold looked down her freckled nose at Logan. "Staring at half dressed girls doesn't seem the 'right path' for a gentleman to me. I wonder what Zion will think about that?"

"Zion," said Logan, "that's who I'm looking for, Zion Coldwell. Do you know him?"

"He's my sister's husband . . . and her brother."

Logan looked at Penny. She was a mixture of fragile girlhood and bold confidence standing there in her cottons. Her arms were defiantly crossed over her chest, and a look of careful analysis played behind her cornflower blue eyes. Loosed from the single braid hanging down her back, golden wisps swept around her oval face.

He knew he was in a precarious situation. He needed a job, and here he was in a compromising position with his potential employer's family. How was he going to back out of this? *Back out? I can't back out. I have to move forward.*

"I see," said Logan. "I apologize if I frightened you. As I said, I was looking for Briar Hollow, and I thought this was the way."

"You are close," said Penny. "This creek runs between Briar Hollow and the Eldridge place you just passed."

"That's my other sister's place," Marigold added, "Pansy Joy and her husband Garth's." Marigold looked over the tall man whose shirt didn't fill out the way a working man's would. "You sure you want to work for Zion? We don't push pencils, we swing shovels around here."

A dash of color flamed up Logan's neck. He knew he wasn't as sturdy as a farm-raised man, but he did know how to work— and he needed to work. The battle between his wounded pride and reason wrestled. Neither won. "Well, if you'll excuse me, Miss Millpond Mermaid, and Miss Provincial Pixie, I'll let Mr. Coldwell decide that for himself."

Logan placed his hat firmly on his head, spun on his heel and left the girls with a crisp "good day." With firm steps and a quick gait he strode from the creek back to the road passing the bushes that served as racks for the girls' dresses. A few feet from their clothes he spotted blue ribbons on the grass. He knew they must belong to one of the girls. Better judgment urged him to pass by;

15

but his pulsing adrenalin overruled. Without missing a step he swiftly scooped up the ribbons, pocketed them, and continued his trek to Briar Hollow.

"Well," Marigold snickered, "I think we ruffled his feathers."

"Feathers? I think they were more like porcupine quills," said Penny.

Marigold laughed out loud. "He did seem a bit touchy, didn't he?"

"I can't imagine Zion will give him the time of day. He looks about as sturdy as last year's scarecrow."

"I bet he is a pencil pusher." Marigold stepped out of the creek and began squeezing water from her petticoat. "Did you hear what he called us—a millpond mermaid and a provincial pixie? Those are highfalutin words if you ask me."

"He certainly doesn't look like much of a farm hand." Penny stepped to the bushes and picked up her dress. It was dirty and smelled from mucking out the stalls. What had seemed so welcome when she was shivering, now held little appeal, but she couldn't walk home in her undergarments.

Penny slipped into her button-front calico work dress. With graceful movements she smoothed out the box pleats in her skirt starting at the gathered bodice and then let down the full, cuffed sleeves she had rolled up for choring. With nimble fingers, she loosened her still damp braid and combed through her golden tresses.

"That's funny." Penny searched above and beneath the bushes. "I thought I laid my ribbons beside my dress, and now I can't find them."

"Are you sure you took them out before you jumped in?"

"I'm very sure." Penny moved the branches to see if they had fallen into the bushes. "Whatever could have happened to them?"

"I wonder . . . ."

Penny waited for Marigold to finish her thought, but she didn't verbalize the picture in her mind. Instead, she decided to keep her speculations to herself regarding a certain tall stranger.

"I wonder," said Marigold, "if those love-struck martins didn't fly off with them. They would make a right fine lining for a nest."

"Oh, no." Penny thrust out her thin bottom lip. "You are probably right, and those were some of my favorites."

"You wore your favorite ribbons to work in the barn?" Marigold wrinkled her freckled nose.

"I know you think I'm silly," Penny admitted, "but if I have a little something pretty it makes me feel better—even when I'm doing a dirty job."

Marigold rolled her eyes. She and Penny had been friends since she first came to Briar Hollow. She had helped her sister Rosalie care for her when they thought Penny had cholera. Thankfully it had turned out to be a less serious case of flux. Almost every day since, Marigold had spent time with Penny, and she still had not figured the girl out.

Marigold considered Penny to be like a stew of sorts with all different ingredients. She was smart, educated, and pretty. She had manners and knew how to use them. She used big words too, but she never made a person feel small if they didn't.

Penny loved flowers and dainty things, but she'd go fishing, too—as long as she did not have to put the worm on the hook. Sometimes she read stories to Lucas in such a way Marigold felt she was right in the middle of them. When Penny prayed, Marigold knew for sure and for certain she was touching heaven's throne. The girl had a vibrant faith in God.

Penny could sing and sew and plant and hoe. She was practical and as hard working as her delicate constitution allowed, and she also loved to play with the little ones and her dog, Micah. The girl had a real sensitive side, too. She could be quiet for hours with nothing wrong—just to mull things over like Clover chewing on her cud. She had stacks of journals filled with her drawings and musings—poems and verses and writings of all kinds.

None of Penny's attributes puzzled Marigold on their own; it was just that she never knew which one would be coming at her next. That's why she thought of her as a stew of sorts made with all the regular stuff a person would expect like meat and vegetables, and then some hot peppers and donuts thrown in. Eat that blindfolded, and that was what being with Penny was like as far as Marigold was concerned.

By the time the girls finished fastening their shoes, Penny had forgiven the alleged thieving martins. "I'll just think of those ribbons as a house warming gift for the love birds." Penny smiled as the twosome began their walk to Briar Hollow. "When I get married, I hope I have a house full of pretty things."

"Well, you'll be the first pretty thing in it," said Marigold.

"Aw, that's a nice thing to say." The girls walked a ways in silence.

"Do you ever imagine yourself with anybody in particular?" asked Marigold. "Are you sweet on anybody?"

Penny gave a small smile and shook her head. "No. Either I haven't met him yet or I'm being a very obedient saint."

"Obedient saint? What do you mean?"

"You know those verses in Song of Solomon that say not to wake up your beloved before it's time? Well, if there is love in me for someone in this county, it's still sleeping."

Marigold chortled at the girl's response. "You got woke up today, it seems to me—by that Logan fella."

CHAPTER 2

Logan quickly cleared the first yards down the main road and away from the girls—his adrenalin still pumping after their encounter. He had not needed any encouragement to feel inadequate about farm work. A recipient of academic honors from Wesleyan University, his fine education had ill prepared him for the challenges he now faced in Washington, Kentucky. Never mind he was salutatorian of his graduating class, captain of the college glee club, and a regular contributor to *Olla Podrida,* the university's quarterly newspaper. No, none of that was important here.

Logan was tortured with questions, like why his father felt he had to move from Connecticut to the Kentucky wilds. He had proven nothing and lost everything . . . including his life. Now Logan was trapped in this Godforsaken land with no means of supporting himself and his poor mother. The small schools in the area were staffed by locals. That meant no possibility of him being hired on as a teacher. Higher education was not a consideration by most of the people in the region. If it was a pursuit of the few with means, they traveled to reputable universities in other parts of the country. Where did that leave Logan? Stuck in Washington with scant funds, no contacts, and little hope.

Logan continued down the road until he came upon a sign. In scrolled letters, not too fancy, but not too plain, the words "Briar Hollow Orchard" were painted in red on a plank made of several wooden boards joined together. Scrollwork and little pictures of fruits and flowers bordered the sign. From the large sign a board was hung painted with bold block letters: "Coldwell Horse Farm."

Logan peered down the tree-lined lane, but foliage blocked his view into the hollow. *This must be it.* He stepped into the lane and willed his elevated pulse to return to its normal pace. *Calm down. Breathe. You can do this.*

With slower steps, Logan began his walk into a quarter mile of scenic beauty. Treetops seemed to bow to one another, their limbs intertwined in an embrace that formed a luscious juniper canopy. The earthy smell of evergreens and ferns saturated the air and tiny beams of light peeked through the tree tops in brilliant shafts connecting heaven and earth.

Logan was a man who appreciated beauty and he drank in the sights and smells engaging his senses. He slowed to a stop midway in the lane, shoved his right hand in his pocket and pulled out the blue ribbons. *They must be hers,* he thought—*the blue-eyed pixie. They couldn't belong to the mouthy one in the water.*

Logically, Logan knew he could not be certain, but still he pictured the ribbons in the golden hair as he rubbed the bits of satin between his thumb and forefinger. They were soft—the way he imagined her skin would feel.

Whoa, Mayfield. Logan reined in his imaginations with harsh reminders of crossed arms and penetrating eyes. *This is business—all business.*

"This is mommy's baby; yummy, yummy, yummy." Rosalie sang to the pudgy baby on her lap. "This is mommy's baby," she began the song again, and this time stuck her upturned nose in

Mattie's soft belly, using it to tickle him as she finished her ditty, "yummy, yummy, yummy."

Mattie giggled and grabbed a handful of his mother's red hair before she could raise her head out of his reach.

"Mattie," Zion called from his seat at the kitchen table. "Let go of Mommy's hair." He winked at Rosalie and whispered, "Only Daddy gets to play with Mommy's glory."

Rosalie untwined her hair from her son's chubby fist. Surprised that her husband's words still affected her like a schoolgirl, Rosalie felt the flush on her cheeks rise under his playful admiration. "Now, Zion."

"Now what, Mrs. Coldwell? Do you think he understood what I said?"

"Probably not, but Dahlia could walk in any minute, and then how would you explain yourself?"

"Hm. I'd say something like, 'only I get to pay for Mommy's story.'"

A look of bewilderment crossed Rosalie's heart-shaped face. "What are you talking about, Zion Coldwell?" She shook her head at this man who never ceased to surprise her in one way or another.

"Then she'd ask me about Mommy's story, and I'd just say, 'Ask your mommy.'"

"Oh, you." Rosalie dangled the baby on her knee and laughed at the man she loved. "You are just downright silly sometimes."

"You know what the Good Book says, 'a merry heart doeth good like a medicine' . . . and I could use a good dose here lately."

"Are you in pain?" Rosalie asked. She rose from the rocking chair, placed Mattie on a quilt on the floor and crossed to the table. "I could make you some willow bark tea."

With practiced ease, Rosalie adjusted the sling around her husband's neck. The young woman had a knack for nursing. After her mother had passed giving birth to her brother Lucas, Rosalie had devoted much of her time to learning the medicinal properties in plants and herbs.

Dr. Byerly had an office in neighboring Maysville as well as in Washington. He ministered to the needs of the city folks and those in the surrounding areas like Briar Hollow as much as one man could. Folks held the good doctor in high regard, but when they needed herbs and tending, or the doctor was not available, they often sought out Rosalie. She had a sweet blend of know-how, compassion, and a consoling touch that soothed a body inside and out.

Zion watched his wife fuss over him with tender appreciation. Rosalie moved with grace and purpose, the same way she had when he had first injured himself helping his brother-in-law Garth with the new steam tractor. Garth had been so successful with his Racine threshing machine he had decided to make a traction engine plough out of his old Clayton & Shuttleworth portable engine. The machine did a good job, but it had to be hauled by horses. Garth rigged it to be self-propelled by fitting a long driving chain between the crankshaft and the rear axle. Things were going well until he and Zion started riveting in the strakes, diagonal strips attached to the wheels to provide traction on unmade ground.

Garth had inserted a shank and held it in place while Zion worked to form the head on the opposite side that would fasten the strake to the wheel. One moment they were both standing; the next Zion was on the ground moaning and clutching his left arm. His wrench had slipped while he worked on the rivet. He lost his footing, twisted and crashed awkwardly into Garth's open tool box.

One look and Garth knew to stop snickering and start praying. He hollered for Pansy Joy who had been preparing rows for planting in the kitchen garden beside their cabin. Pansy Joy ran for her sister who rushed to the scene with her nursing bag while Pansy Joy stayed with the children. When Rosalie saw her husband's injury, shock registered in her brilliant green eyes; but she managed to disconnect her spousal concern and take charge.

22

Rosalie surveyed the scene. The bone had pushed through the skin, and she set to work applying firm pressure with a clean cloth. She gave orders like a field marshal, sending Garth for the doctor and Marigold to the Matheny's for ice.

By the time Dr. Byerly arrived, the bleeding had stopped. Rosalie thankfully stepped aside and yielded her husband-patient to the physician. Dr. Byerly removed the ice, pleased that Rosalie's treatment had kept the swelling down, and swiftly reset the bone. Once in place, he wound Zion's arm with lengths of cotton bandages soaked in a mixture of gypsum and water that hardened to form the plaster bandage Zion would wear for several weeks.

"Why don't you sit in the rocking chair where you can lean back and lift your arm above your heart?" Rosalie suggested. "It's good for your circulation, and that will help you heal faster."

Zion knew it was in his best interest to take his wife's suggestion when it was made. Rosalie was sweet—no doubt about that—but when it came to healing matters, she would not take any guff, even from him. Zion ruffled his good hand through his thick chestnut hair and unfolded his six-foot-three frame from his seat at the kitchen table. "Yes, Nurse Coldwell."

Zion grinned at his tireless attendant and then forced a deadpan expression on his tanned face. "Right away, Nurse Coldwell." He tipped his head in surrender. "Whatever you say, Nurse Coldwell."

"Oh, you." Rosalie shook her head and moved to the stove. "I don't know anyone who can say something with such agreeable words and yet be so cantankerous." Rosalie opened the stove and inserted a piece of wood, dipped some water from the pail into the kettle, and set it on the burner. "Am I going to have to put you down for a nap with Dahlia?"

Pangs of conscience pricked Zion. He had been teasing, they both knew, but he was also aware that he had been out of sorts since his injury. How could two days seem like two months? And what would six weeks do to him? To his family? To their farm? Hours seemed to last longer when they were filled with worry.

How would they keep things going on the fledgling Coldwell Horse Farm? With a mare ready to foal and his plan to purchase stock from Belle Meade, they desperately needed the new barn. The supplies were on-hand, but what good were plans and supplies if you were not able to work them?

His father-in-law, Matthias, had offered to help with the building project, but he was none too sturdy from his war injury. All the farmers were busy preparing their fields for spring planting. The seed had to get in the fields, or everyone would be hurting come harvest time.

As Logan neared the end of the lane, thinning foliage opened to a circular clearing between woodland on the west and a stream to the east. The wildflower garden, abloom with colors from every spectrum of the rainbow, filled the air with an intoxicating greeting.

A simple log cabin stood just past the wildflower gardens along the edge of the hollow. Capped with a steep-pitched roof, smoke curled out its fieldstone chimney. A narrow covered porch spanned its face, just wide enough to accommodate two rocking chairs and a table made of a tree stump.

East of the dwelling an enclosed rose garden and an arbor covered in a prolific vine flanked a worn path to orchards beyond. Near the cabin, a kitchen garden neighbored a hen house. A barn, two corrals, a small shed, and a dilapidated apple barn lined the southern perimeter.

Logan would have much preferred sitting on the bench under the grape arbor with a good book or journal to knocking on the door, but he braced himself to do what he had come to do. As he walked to the steps, a black and white shepherd with brown markings loped to the front yard from the back of the cabin. He looked at Logan and noiselessly sauntered over to meet him. *I hope everyone is this friendly.*

A knock sounded at the cabin door. "Who could that be?" Rosalie looked at Zion to see if he was expecting anyone.

"There's one way to find out . . . or two." Zion lifted his eyebrows and a playful smirk played on his face. "Do you want me to holler from here, or do you want to go see?"

"I'll get it. I'll get it." Rosalie moved to the door and opened it to a tall stranger.

"Hello. Can I help you?" She studied the young man's features, unable to read the expression on his drawn face.

Logan removed his Pullman-brown bowler. "Yes. Pardon me, ma'am. My name is Logan Mayfield. I was wondering if Mr. Coldwell would be willing to speak with me."

"Sure," Zion called from the rocking chair, "come on in."

Rosalie opened the door wide. Logan entered the cabin and Zion placed his right hand on the arm of the rocking chair to push off to his feet.

"Oh, please, don't get up on my account," said Logan.

"Here, Mr. Mayfield." Rosalie wrapped a long arm around the ladder-back of a kitchen chair and moved it next to her husband. "Please sit down. I was just making some tea. Would you like some?"

"You aren't going to give Mr. Mayfield willow bark tea, are you? That's a might bitter to serve fine company, don't you think?"

Logan kept his composure but wriggled internally at Zion's observation. He wore quality store-bought clothing that gave a false impression of his current social standing. Whatever Zion might think of him, Logan knew he was little more than a beggar.

"Of course not, Zion. I'll steep him a cup of elderberry. You get the willow bark." Rosalie turned to Logan. "Excuse my husband, Mr. Mayfield. He's a bit beside himself the last couple of days."

"I wish I was beside myself!" said Zion. "If there were two of me, maybe I could get some work done around here."

"That's what I came to see you about, Mr. Coldwell."

"You know how to split off one person into two?"

Logan sensed the muscular, broad-shouldered man's frustration. He was keeping his sense of humor, but he was obviously discomfited by his lack of ability to work.

"If I had such capabilities, I wouldn't be here, Mr. Coldwell."

Zion looked over the lanky young man. He noted new calluses on hands that looked unaccustomed to hard labor. His mannerisms, language and eyes spoke of intelligence and education.

"What brings you here, Mr. Mayfield?"

"Please, call me Logan."

"All right, what brings you here, Logan?"

Logan looked at his hat on his lap and then back to the blue eyes that reminded him of his recent encounter with a certain sunbathing girl. Zion's eyes were the exact cornflower blue of his sister's.

If he was going to make his request, Logan decided it would be best to do it before Penny returned and exposed his indiscretion. Why hadn't he stopped himself when he saw the girl stretched out on the log? He was raised better than that. It was just that he'd never seen anything so sweet, so angelic, real to life right in front of him.

Zion watched a tussle of emotions behind the young man's eyes and waited for him to speak his peace.

"My mother and I are staying in town. While I was at the mercantile waiting to speak with Mrs. Matheny, I couldn't help but overhear her discussion with her customer regarding your accident."

"I don't doubt Mrs. Matheny is doing her best to keep the good people of Washington informed."

"Now, Zion," Rosalie carried a mug of medicinal tea to her husband, "I think you might need a cookie to sweeten your disposition. Would you care for a molasses cookie, Mr. Mayfield?"

"Thank you. That would be . . . sweet." Logan smiled at Rosalie and accepted a cookie from the crockery jar. Amused at Logan's pun, Rosalie warmed a bit to the peculiar young man and returned to the stove to fetch his elderberry tea.

"As I was saying, I heard of your accident, and—forgive me for being presumptuous—but knowing it's planting season, I thought you might need some help on your farm."

Zion pursed his lips and furrowed his brow, surprised and puzzled at Logan's request. He took a sip of steaming tea and gazed at the contents in the mug.

"This comes as a surprise." Zion peered intently in Logan's face. It was evident the young man was unaccustomed to farm work. *What's your story?* Zion wondered as memories flashed back to his own arrival at Briar Hollow in the not-so-distant past. He had been a man in need—a different sort of need perhaps, but a very real and desperate lack the Lord had met in this nondescript little backwoods hollow.

Grunting from a red-faced baby broke the silence that hung heavy in the room. "Oh, Mattie. I think you need some attention." Rosalie scooped the baby from the quilt and held him at arms distance as she carried him to the bedroom to change his diaper.

"Well, Logan, I have to say, I try to be an honest man, and I appreciate an honest answer. Don't take this the wrong way, because I could surely use some help, but do you have any experience working on a horse farm?"

"Horse farm?" Now it was Logan's turn to be surprised. "I didn't realize. I thought you were raising crops like the other farmers."

"We have a kitchen garden for our personal needs, but we don't farm for our livelihood. Do you have experience caring for horses?"

"I'll be honest with you, Mr. Coldwell. Until a couple of years ago, the closest I got to a horse was when I was getting in or out of a coach. Due to circumstances beyond our control, my mother and I have found ourselves alone and in a dire situation far from where we once called home."

"I see." Zion appreciated the young man's candor. Compassion kindled in his big heart.

"In the past month I've done my best to find employment as a teacher, tutor, clerk, bookkeeper or reporter. It seems my education, although quite adequate in Connecticut, is lacking for the job market in this part of the country.

"I've learned some about horses since we left home two years ago. I've been helping Mr. Cooper part-time at the livery the past two weeks, but it's not enough work to meet our needs." Logan dropped his gaze and then raised it again to the man giving him careful consideration. "I don't know what the future holds for us, Mr. Coldwell. Perhaps we'll return to the East. Perhaps we will stay and try to live out Father's dream. Regardless, I simply must find work."

CHAPTER 3

"That was a hog-killing time, ain't so?" Marigold stepped on the path between her home on the other side of the orchard and Briar Hollow.

"A hog-killing time." Penny shook her head at her dear friend and her outlandish vocabulary. "You are something else, Marigold Johnson."

Marigold had used peculiar phrases since she was young enough to talk. She had an ear to pick up the unusual, and tucked away what she heard in her memory banks to bring out on just the right occasions. An avowed tomboy, shocking folks was one of Marigold's favorite pastimes.

"Well, thank you," Marigold drawled. "I think you're fine as cream gravy yourself, Buttercup . . . or should I say, Pixie?"

Penny glared at her teasing friend. "You go on home now, you trouble maker."

"Yes, ma'am, Missie Pixie. I'll get a wiggle on and be home faster than you can say 'missing hair ribbons.'" Marigold flashed a mischievous smile and darted down the path.

What is up with that girl today? Penny wondered.

"Hi, Micah." Penny scratched her dog between the ears. "You are a good boy, aren't you? You never talk back, do you?" Penny climbed the wooden steps and opened the door to the cabin. Inside Zion and Logan Mayfield sat, deep in conversation.

"Hi, Penny." Zion greeted his sister. Logan stood to his feet, once again taken by surprise at the girl's appearance. She was fully dressed this time, but her hair—it was fabulous. The sun back-lit golden tresses that flowed freely around her delicate oval face and hung gloriously down her back.

"Hi, Zion." Penny took her time closing the door behind her, and then turned to acknowledge their company. "Hello."

"Hello," Logan tipped his head in greeting.

"Logan Mayfield, this is my sister, Penny. Penny, this is Logan Mayfield." Zion made introductions from his seat in the rocking chair.

"Mr. Mayfield."

"Miss Coldwell, a pleasure."

"I have to brush my hair." Penny started for her bedroom. "If you'll please excuse me."

Zion watched his sister disappear into her room and close the door. "That's peculiar."

"What's that, Mr. Coldwell."

"Nothing, I guess." Zion shook his head. "I don't think I'll ever understand women, even my own flesh and blood."

"Is something wrong?"

"I don't think so." Zion shrugged. "She's just usually a mite friendlier."

"I see." Logan wondered what was on Penny's mind, and if she would tell Zion about the swimming hole incident. With great mental fortitude, he pushed his musings aside to pursue the reason for his call.

"About working for you, Mr. Coldwell?"

"I tell you what," said Zion, "I appreciate the urgency of your affairs. Thank you for being upfront with your work experience and your family situation. I'd like to discuss this with my wife and make it a matter of prayer. If you'll tell me where you're staying in town, I'll get an answer to you tonight or first thing in the morning."

"That's fair enough." Hope ignited in Logan's heart. "We're staying at the Goheen sisters' boarding house."

"All right then. You be praying with me."

"I'm sure Mother already has that covered." Logan stood and held out his hand. "Thank you for your consideration."

"You're welcome."

Logan turned to go, but stopped a few feet from the door. "Oh. I almost forgot." He reached in his pocket and pulled out two envelopes. "I was in the Post Office earlier. When Mr. Jenkins was giving me directions here, he asked me to give these to you."

"Thank you." Zion stood. He was tired of sitting. Surely he had elevated his arm long enough to satisfy Rosalie. He received the letters and walked Logan to the door.

"I appreciate your time, sir."

"You can call me Zion. Give your mother my regards, and I'll get with you as soon as I have a clear answer."

Rosalie entered with the baby in her arms as the men said their goodbyes. "Oh, let me send something for your mother. There's nothing like fresh strawberries in the spring. Penny and I picked the last of them yesterday, and they are so juicy and sweet."

Logan liked Zion, but noted a special connection with Rosalie. There was an openness about her and a kindness that made him feel like it was perfectly fine that he, a complete stranger, knocked on her door today and she was sending him off with fresh fruit like an old family friend.

"Thank you, Mrs. Coldwell. I know she will appreciate your thoughtful gift." Logan took the basket of berries and made his departure.

"What a nice young man," said Rosalie.

"What makes you say that?"

"Nothing in particular, really." Rosalie carried the empty mugs to the sink. "There's just something about him—his demeanor, his expression. He seems like an honorable person."

"What would you think about me hiring him to help out around here while my arm mends?"

Rosalie considered Logan's tailored clothes and refined manners. "Hire him to do what, exactly?"

"Hire him?" Penny emerged from her room with a scowl on her face. "You've got to be kidding, Zion. Did you see those scrawny arms? What good could he possibly be around here, on any farm for that matter?"

Rosalie and Zion stared at Penny, taken aback by her brash comments.

"Penny," Zion moved to his sister's side and studied her with narrowed eyes, "is something wrong with you? I've never seen you act so rude—when Logan was here and just now. Is there something I need to know?"

Penny grimaced and clamped her eyes shut.

"Penny?" Rosalie moved to Zion's side and stroked the distraught girl's arm.

Penny blinked and opened her eyes to the two most important people in her life. They deserved the truth. "I'm sorry. Can we sit down? I'll tell you everything."

"Sure. Sit here." Rosalie motioned to the chair Logan had used.

"No. Not there." Penny pulled out the footstool next to the chairs and plopped down on it in less than her usual ladylike fashion. Zion and Rosalie exchanged puzzled glances and took the remaining seats.

"First, I have to say that I know my emotions have been running wild for the last week. President Lincoln was shot. You had your accident. I've been worried. I don't think I slept more than a half an hour last night. I'm just plain exhausted."

"That's understandable," said Rosalie. "We're all concerned."

"I want to help—really, I do. You know I mucked out the stalls with Marigold this morning."

"I have to say you surprised me on that one, Buttercup," said Zion.

"I surprised myself." Penny held out her hands, palms up and studied the matched sets of blisters on them. "It was harder than I thought it would be. Marigold swung twice as much as I did, but I just couldn't keep up. My arms were aching by the time we finished. That's when Marigold asked if I wanted to cool off at the swimming hole."

"I remember." Rosalie nodded. "Oh, you didn't have any lunch yet. You must be starving."

"I'm too tired to eat. Maybe later."

"Are you sure? I can get you a biscuit with some ham."

"That's too heavy. Maybe I'll have some strawberries, but I'd like to finish telling you what happened first."

"Oh, I'm sorry, sweetie," Rosalie said. "I sent those with Mr. Mayfield for his mother. They're staying at the Goheen's, and I'm sure the sisters haven't been able to pick strawberries for years."

"Of course you did." Penny rolled her head back and stared at the ceiling.

"Penelope Hope Coldwell," Zion's tone shifted from concerned to confounded, "you are one odd stick today. For goodness sake, what has gotten into you?"

"Zion." Penny clamped her lips together and furrowed her brows. Her small nostrils flared for quick moments while she fought to rein in her emotions and search for the right words.

"Zion," Penny drew in a long breath and released it slowly, "I don't know how to tell you this except to tell you. I don't care for Logan Mayfield, not one whit."

"Penny, this isn't like you." Concern poured from Rosalie's expressive eyes. "You just hardly met the man."

"No. That's not exactly the whole of the story, Rosalie."

"Out with it, girl," Zion bid.

"I'm trying, Zion, but I keep getting interrupted."

With his good hand, Zion pulled his bottom lip over his top lip and turned the "invisible key" that locked his mouth. This was the same gesture Penny had used when she was a little girl begging to know her brother's secrets.

A smirk found its way to Penny's pursed lips—followed by an unexpected snicker. Zion's use of her childhood pantomime diffused the tension in the girl, and a real smile spread across her face.

"Let me start over," Penny began in a lighter timbre. "When Marigold and I were cooling off, the honorable Mr. Logan Mayfield happened to be walking toward Briar Hollow. I had stretched out on that old log by the rope swing and must have dozed off. This fine man you're thinking about hiring scared me half to death and didn't have the decency to turn away when all I was wearing was my chemise and petticoat—and they were wet, at that!"

"Oh, my." Rosalie's slender fingers flew over her mouth.

"Oh, my, is right. He stood there dumb as a stump staring at me like I was the tattooed lady on display with the traveling circus—the boarish brute!"

"That is out of line," Rosalie verbally sided with her sister-in-law, but was unable to hold back her amusement at the girl's outrage.

Being a man, Zion easily conjured up the scene. When he was single, the sight of a half-dressed girl as pretty as his sister all laid out on a log would have dumfounded him as well. Still, with Logan's obviously cultured upbringing, he should have known better than to stare, and definitely not stand there in conversation.

Zion wondered what to do. He needed help. Logan needed a job. Sure, Mayfield was a bit on the spindly side, but a measure of need mixed with a dash of character and a pinch of ethics could turn out a good worker if a body kneaded it just right and gave it some rising time. He was willing to give Logan a try, but what about Penny? She was knocked into a cocked hat by the man. It was clear to Zion that he needed to take this to prayer and talk with his wife.

"Penny, I understand you're upset. I haven't decided one way or the other about Logan, but I'll be honest and tell you I am going to be praying about it." Zion ruffled his hair, a clear indicator he was deep in thought.

"Do you remember what our life was like when we left Virginia?" Zion asked.

Penny hadn't thought about that in a long time. The period after their parent's death had been the most difficult time in her life. The calamity had been bad enough, but what it had done to Zion had been almost more than Penny could bear. Not only had Zion lost his parents, his home, and his livelihood; he had also lost his faith in God at a time when Penny dearly needed to lean on it with him. Penny had mourned, but her faith had given her peace while Zion struggled with anger and skepticism.

"Yes, Zion. How could I ever forget?"

"I don't know all the details of Mayfield's situation, but when I look in his eyes and hear what part of the story he gave me; it takes me right back to that time." Zion looked tenderly at his wife. "If it hadn't been for the good people of Briar Hollow, I don't know where we'd be today. Don't you think you could at least join us in praying about this?"

CHAPTER 4

L ogan passed through the juniper-lined lane oblivious to its scents and scenery. He and his mother were in a difficult situation, but a ray of hope now offered a bit of light amidst the questions that darkened his mind and heart.

When Logan came to the place where the girls had been swimming, his emotions swirled like dancers doing the *Cotton Eye Joe*. An image of Penny looking like an angel resting in the sunshine twirled with a picture of an arm-crossed she-bear defending propriety with all the battle her lithe limbs might wage. Penetrating, questioning blue eyes filled his thoughts that shifted from the swimming site to the memory of a haloed beauty standing in the door of the Coldwell cabin.

What was it about this girl that engaged his thoughts so, he wondered. Unconsciously, he reached in his pocket and ran his fingertips over the soft blue ribbons. He continued down the macadamized road lost in thought, barely noticing the Eldridge farm, and then the Comfort Lodge as he made his way back to town.

Washington, the county seat of Mason, Kentucky, until 17 years previous in 1848, was a well established settlement with rope-lined walks leading from building to building. Its limestone courthouse was a venerable structure with a steeple that looked like a pencil writing in the sky. Logan passed the Paxton Inn, a two-story white clapboard building with black shutters on its many windows and a front door with an arched window set in above. As he passed, Logan thought about the well-to-do travelers enjoying the inn's hospitality in its finely appointed rooms.

Resentment tugged at Logan's heart, but he willfully refused its entrance and hmphed at his thoughts of not long ago. When he had first seen the Paxton Inn, he had considered its accoutrements, furnishings and refreshments less than suitable. What a proud young man he had been; and what had his mother said so many times? "A haughty spirit leads to a fall." Well, fall, they had, the entire family. Now the question remained: where would they land?

Logan continued down the walk to the Goheen sisters' boarding house. His thoughts turned to the stories the elderly ladies had shared with him and his mother about the secrets inside the Paxton Inn. They said it had been used as a stop on the Underground Railroad before the war, publicly housing auctioneers and slave auction patrons with hospitality, while at the same time rescuing runaways in hidden staircases.

The irony struck Logan. It seemed to him there were parallels between his family's story and the history of the Paxton Inn. The opulence seen by the outside world did not tell the entirety of their tales. In the hidden places of those secreted inside the Paxton Inn, as in the depths of his father's spirit, souls had longed for freedom and a new life.

Of course, Andrew Mayfield's longings had been of a different sort. He had been raised with opportunity and resources; but his life had its own restraints, and he had longed to be free of them. It was this longing that placed Logan's feet on the path he now walked. He couldn't fault his father for having a dream and pursuing it. Andrew Mayfield could not have anticipated the challenges he had faced.

Both of the Mayfield men knew that life comes with risks—opportunities for gains and losses. Logan was a rational, logical man. He understood these realities. He accepted them. What he had a hard time accepting was his mother's simple faith. She had a Bible verse for everything, and sometimes he just got tired of hearing about how he needed to accept that from the same hand came forth both blessings and testings. The one that really got him was when she said, "All things work together for good." That was taking things just a little too far in his opinion, especially given their current circumstances.

Millicent Mayfield watched her son's approach from her seat in a cushioned rocking chair beneath the shade of the boarding house's spindle-lined porch. As she watched, she wondered what thoughts were playing behind the ever-changing hazel eyes of her only child.

She had spent the morning praying and reading from the book of Psalms, encouraging herself in the Lord, like the Good Book said. With the death of her dear Andrew, she had lost much joy, yet she clung to the Word and did her best to make melody in her heart and bless the Lord at all times. When Logan had returned from the mercantile with the news of possible employment, she had encouraged him to go without delay and see what the Lord had provided for them through His merciful providence. She felt as if something had shifted during her morning devotion and had spent the time Logan was away rocking and whispering thanksgiving to the Lord who promised to hear the cry of the widow and the fatherless.

Millicent watched her son's stride and the tilt of his head and tried to prepare her heart for what he would report. Something seemed different. She couldn't read him, and that was unusual. A mother knew her child, especially a mother who had only one offspring to learn.

Logan pushed open the picket fence. "Hello, Mother." He gave a half smile as he approached the porch and sat on the twin rocker next to Millicent.

"Hello, Son." Millicent covered Logan's hand with hers and looked into his eyes, still unable to discern by his actions the news of his morning's inquiry.

"Have you been here since I left?"

"Yes, I have. It's so pleasant here in the shade. When I rock and sing and close my eyes, it's just so peaceful." Millicent stopped herself from sharing all that was on her heart. Her close walk with the Lord was something her son did not fully understand, and she was careful not to overload him, especially now. She prayed he would come to share the faith that gave her such peace, but knew that he was at a point in his life where he was teetering. She didn't want to push him away by being insensitive to his struggles.

"How was your meeting with Mr. Coldwell?"

"I'm not sure." Logan matched the pace of his rocking to his mother's and considered how he might answer her in a way that didn't build false hope or dash what hope he held.

"You're not sure?"

"Yes." Logan looked from his mother's face to the colorful pansies lining the walkway, their petals fluttering like butterflies in the spring breeze. "I'm not sure." Logan worried his bottom lip. As a university student, he had broken himself of this childhood habit. The fact that he reverted to it now let Millicent know he was feeling a bit off his game. She watched him with concern, but could not help admiring the dimple in his chin she had always considered adorable.

"Did you meet Mr. Coldwell?"

"I did."

"And?"

"And, Coldwell Farms is a horse farm, Mother." Logan leaned back in the rocking chair and stretched out his long legs.

"Horses? I never imagined."

"Me, either." Logan and his mother both knew his experience with horses was minimal. Stable hands and drivers had stood between Logan and horses most of his life. It was not so long ago he learned to drive a wagon. When his father had moved the family from Connecticut to Kentucky, he taught Logan his newly acquired skill. Because Logan's hands were tender, even with driving gloves, his palms reddened and became sore. Andrew had done most of the driving as they crossed the states to their new home.

Andrew's agricultural studies had prepared his mind for the tasks ahead, but his body was unaccustomed to labor. He invested a goodly amount of his financial resources in acquiring land and then hired a man to oversee the business of farming, contracting help as needed. Andrew worked alongside his foreman, Angus Carver, determined to prove to himself he had what it takes to become a successful farmer and work the land.

While his wife supported his decision, Andrew had not wanted her to lack the comforts she had always known. Compelled to provide as lovely a home in Kentucky as he had in Connecticut, he poured resources into building an estate for Millicent.

After months of construction, Mayfield Manor had finally been finished; the rugs placed and the curtains and paintings hung with particular care. Men hired to transport the family furnishings had left only days before the disastrous events began to play out that forever changed the future for the Mayfield family.

The weather had cooperated and the corn crops were bountiful. Andrew hired a crew to help him and Angus bring in the harvest. Millicent, a slight woman with a history of illness, had been running a fever that caused her to toss in her bed in the days

41

leading up to the scheduled transport of the crops to market. She felt so poorly that Andrew could not bring himself to leave her. In a quick decision made the day they were to leave, he sent Angus to market alone.

Angus Carver never returned.

Andrew had been taken aback, tortured by thoughts of his lack of judgment concerning Angus' character. They had worked side by side for months, and Andrew, not for one moment, had questioned Angus Carver's integrity.

While Millicent's health improved, Andrew had spiraled into depression. Many nights Logan retired for the evening while his father worried over ledgers and accounts. He must have fallen asleep and knocked over a lamp—at least that is what Logan reasoned. Millicent's cries had wakened him to a house filled with smoke. Mother and son escaped through the back servant's entrance. The fire originated in Andrew's study. He was lost along with the house and all their fine furnishings.

After the funeral, Logan met with their local banker and discovered his father had mortgaged the property to build Mayfield Manor. The land was forced to auction in order to pay off the note, but their 200 acres went below market value leaving the Mayfields with minimal resources.

"Your father trusted Angus," Millicent had told Logan several days after the fire. "He was never wrong before about giving his allegiance in business relations."

"Until now," Logan muttered. "He was wrong about everything, it seems to me." With mixed emotions Logan uttered the words he knew to be untrue. Pain skewed his perception. Grief and anxiety built a prison around his heart that he did not know how to escape.

Andrew had been generous with Logan. While his father had worked the fields with hired help, Logan had been free to pursue his writing career. He had almost completed his first manuscript—another of the fire's casualties. Now Logan was not sure he would ever pick up a pen and attempt to write again.

Raised by an agnostic father, Logan had learned early in life to question a faith that was so easily accepted by others. After years of speaking about how, in his logical estimation, it was impossible to prove there was a God; Logan watched his father's beliefs transform. As Andrew Mayfield planted seeds in brown earth and watched them sprout, mature, and bear fruit, faith had grown in his heart. He had started talking with his wife; and before Logan knew it, Andrew had begun talking like Millicent on matters of creation and faith. The two were closer than Logan had ever seen in their family home in Connecticut.

As for Logan, his spiritual convictions vacillated between a logical, "educated" approach to life and the undeniable results of a life of faith.

"I can't explain it, Logan, but I still believe in your father's dream."

"Oh, Mother." Logan had stirred from the storage chests he had been foraging through in the barn. "All we have left are these few things that weren't transferred to the house after the furniture came. I'd like to believe with you, but it seems we have nothing to base those dreams upon in the real world."

"What's real isn't always what's seen." Millicent looked with compassion at her son. "What's seen isn't always what's real."

"I don't want to hurt you, Mother, but we must face the realities of our situation."

"I know that seems best to you, Logan; but I want to be like Ezekiel. He was looking at some terrible realities, but do you know what he said?"

"I'm sure you told me before, but perhaps you should refresh my memory."

43

"He said, in the middle of chaos, that 'from this day forth the city shall be called The Lord is There.'" Millicent looked across the grounds to the ruins where her lovely home once stood. "I see ashes, but I will choose to look beyond them. I want to be like Ezekiel and say from this day forward, regardless of what I see or am experiencing, I will say 'the Lord is there.'" Millicent placed a palm over her heart. "The Lord is here, Logan. He was there with your father. He's here with us now, and I know He's going to make a way."

"I have to say, I admire your strength, Mother."

A smile played across Millicent's thin lips, and the expression behind her eyes gave Logan pause. An unexpected laugh escaped that startled Logan. Millicent saw his surprise and tried to explain.

"I'm not laughing at our situation, Logan. I'm laughing at your perception of me." Millicent knelt beside her son who had ceased shuffling through the storage chests. "I laughed because I know how very weak I am. It's just that I've learned I don't have to be strong when I'm in the Lord's strong hands."

A month had passed since that conversation. Logan had sold the last of their belongings to pay for room and board with the Goheens, but their funds had dwindled to more of a dry nest than a nest egg. Logan's search for work had come up with odds and ends, but he knew the severity of their financial situation.

He looked at his mother's delicate features and realized for the first time the similarities between her tender oval face and the face of the blue-eyed beauty that had filled his thoughts since their meeting earlier in the day. Perhaps the similarities between Penny and his mother were what drew him to the girl.

"So you spoke with Mr. Coldwell about work?" Millicent's words called her son back from his musings.

"Yes. I did." Logan recalled the tall, toned man and their conversation. "The farm is in a beautiful location adjacent to orchards and flower gardens. I'm not sure how many horses they have or the details of their operation, but I did speak with Mr. Coldwell, and he said he would give me an answer tonight or tomorrow. He wanted to talk it over with his wife and pray about it."

Memories of Andrew flashed through Millicent's mind that caused an ache to rise in her chest. Mr. Coldwell's words reminded her of the last wonderful months she had shared with her husband discussing their dreams and plans and praying for the Lord's blessing and direction. Andrew had always been a moral man, a good provider and attentive husband; but the Andrew who had become a new creature in Christ had delighted Millicent in ways she had never known.

"Next to a 'yes,' that's the best answer I could hope for." Millicent closed her eyes and set her chair in motion. "There's something special about today, Logan."

"How do you mean, Mother?"

"I can't put it into words; but I know what I feel." A breeze lifted wisps of Millicent's flaxen hair that had escaped the knot she wore high and loose on the crown of her head. With graceful movements she used one slender finger to brush the flyaways off her forehead and then rested her hands one over the other in her lap.

The peace that oozed from his mother's countenance was both enviable and disconcerting to Logan. He wished to have it for himself, but it made no sense. Things that seemed illogical ruffled Logan's usually even temperament. For his mother's sake, he worked to keep his irritation to himself. "What do you feel, then?" he asked, biting off the "and how will feelings fill our stomachs and provide a home?" comment that had jumped to his lips and fought to free itself.

Millicent sensed the struggle in her son and silently asked the Lord to help her express what was in her heart. "I can't exactly explain it, Logan, but I feel today is a day of new beginnings."

CHAPTER 5

Rosalie smoothed the wrinkles from the strips and pieces of fabric she had placed on the table. "What do you think, Penny?" Rosalie turned to her sister-in-law and lifted a piece of lavender material dotted with tiny purple flowers.

"It's going to be a scrap quilt, for sure, with all those colors." Penny eyed the cloth Rosalie had saved over the past few years. She saw pieces from clothing still being worn and some she didn't recognize. "You have several long strips of dark colors that would make some nice edges. It almost seems a shame to cut them. Is there a pattern you know that uses small pieces and long strips?"

A pattern immediately came to mind, and a smile filled Rosalie's heart-shaped face. "Yes! I do!" She clapped her hands together and tucked them under her chin. With a spring in her step, she hurried to her room and opened the chest at the foot of her bed. "It's in here," she said as she lifted familiar quilts and sheets and set them on the ground beside her. "I know it's in here somewhere."

"What are you looking for?" Curiosity set Penny on her feet, and she joined Rosalie in the bedroom.

"It's the first bit of piecework I ever set my hands to." Rosalie lifted the last of the bedding from the chest and pulled out a piece of muslin. "I think this is it." She unfolded the rectangle and let out a happy giggle. "Oh, yes. This is it!" Delighted with her find,

Rosalie clutched the fabric to her chest and giggled again like a schoolgirl with a secret.

"What is it?" Penny watched her sister-in-law's animation with amused curiosity. Rosalie was always pleasant, but she wasn't usually so boisterous.

"This, my dear Penny, is a gaggle of geese—*Flying Geese* as a matter of fact." Rosalie spread out the piecework on the floor between them. "Do you see them?"

Penny examined the pattern. Three triangles, one of "goose" and two of "sky" were sewn together in straight lines from the bottom edge to the top edge between strips of solid colors.

"Yes. I do see them." Penny lifted the edge and saw the date sewn into the backing. "How old were you when you made this?"

Rosalie shook her head and broke again into a broad grin. "I'll never forget it. It was my tenth birthday. Momma made chicken and dumplings for dinner and Daddy made ice cream we ate with strawberry syrup. It was a great birthday dinner, but all the while we were eating, I was eyeing this package on the hearth. It was a small package wrapped in grey fabric—this grey fabric." Rosalie ran a finger over a dark strip that separated the rows of flying geese.

"I knew we didn't have extra money, and I wondered what in the world could be in that package that just had to be my birthday present." She looked Penny in the eye and asked, "Can you guess?"

"I have no idea."

"I confess, I wasn't very excited about it at the time. I opened the grey wrapping and found scraps of material inside."

"That's not a very exciting gift for a ten-year-old."

"No, it wasn't. But Momma had been saving up pieces; and she said that since I was ten, I needed to start filling my hope chest. She said it was time for me to learn how to make things a young lady would need for her home. She didn't give me a gift of leftover fabric. She gave me the gift of learning and the gift of her time."

"Oh." Penny smiled as she caught the sweetness of Rosalie's recollection. "That was a special gift."

"We spent hours together working on it. She taught me how to lay out the fabric and cut the pieces. Of course I already knew how to sew seams and do some embroidery, but I'd never done any piecework or quilting. It did make me feel like I was growing up and doing something special. That's better than any gift she could have bought at the mercantile."

"Yes, it is."

"And there's more," Rosalie beamed.

"More?"

"Yes. This is special in more ways than just the memories of the making. The *Flying Geese* pattern was used as a signal for the Underground Railroad. I didn't know it at the time, but Momma used this to give direction to runaways. Sometimes they stopped here, and sometimes it signaled them forward to the next station in Maysville where people would help them cross the river at night."

"Really? That's exciting!"

"To be honest, it was scary; but Momma was never one to sit by when someone needed help." Rosalie picked up the small quilt and stood to her feet. "Let's go look at that material and see what we come up with."

The girls returned to the table and Rosalie began shifting fabric into piles. "We'll split off the sky pieces from the geese and start cutting triangles. We have enough to make a bed-sized quilt; and with spring here, you just never know who'll be announcing a summer wedding. There's hardly a nicer gift than a covering made with love."

"That's true."

Rosalie continued sorting fabric into piles. As she watched, Penny's thoughts turned to the letter she had just received from Henry Coventry. In the five years since they met, when Zion escorted the Coventry family to the Nevada Territory, Henry had faithfully written. It had begun as little P.S.s at the bottom of his sister Rachel's letters. Over time, his notes became more personal and required envelopes all their own.

The Coventry family had prospered in their move, and the desert air had done wonders for Henry's asthma. Henry had written often, and many times mentioned his hope that Penny would join him in the West. His letter last fall had contained a serious request to come for an extended visit; but in the past few months, she sensed a distance between them greater than the miles separating them.

Penny cared for Henry. She adored Rachel. She respected his father and honored his mother, yet she had wondered many times what it would be like to marry into the Coventry family. She would never experience want, or, for that matter, ever have to weed a kitchen garden or clean a chicken coop again. Before the lightning bolt ravaged their home in Virginia and claimed her parents' lives, the Coldwells had been a family of comfortable means. Penny had adjusted to their change in social status, and was content in the little cabin in Briar Hollow. She loved being with Zion and Rosalie and their children.

The thought of being mistress of a staffed home had once appealed to Penny, but it seemed the possibility was fading. The surprising thing to Penny was that she did not truly understand her own heart in the matter. She cared for Henry, but did she love him? Would she be willing to lie beneath a *Flying Geese* quilt with him? Would the coverlet meet Coventry standards? Would she?

"Where did you go?" asked Rosalie.

"Hm?"

"You went somewhere just now. Where did you go?"

"Oh, I was just thinking about someone." Penny turned from her sister-in-law's scrutiny and focused on the fabric pieces.

"A certain male someone?"

"Well, yes, a male."

"I see." Rosalie lifted a scrap of cerulean blue calico with a lattice pattern of miniature navy polka dots and put it with coordinating fabrics that would make a blue-toned strip of *Flying Geese*. "Mr. Logan Mayfield, perhaps?"

Pink flashed across Penny's cheeks, and her eyes brightened as she fixed her gaze straight on Rosalie. "I was *not* thinking about Mr. Logan Mayfield."

"Oh, pardon me." Rosalie was taken aback by the girl's strong reaction. "I just thought . . . "

"Well you can stop thinking about him, because I certainly have."

"Now, Penny," Rosalie gentled her tone but kept her words firm, "you promised your brother you would be praying with us about the possibility of Mr. Mayfield working here while his arm healed. Did you forget?"

"I've been trying," Penny shook her head and scrunched her nose, "trying to forget, that is."

"Penny." Rosalie turned squared shoulders at the defiant girl. "I'm surprised at the way you're acting. The Mayfields are in need and so are we."

"Yes, yes, I know all that. I also know Mr. Mayfield is a cad. I'd rather have the Matheny twins tripping over themselves around here than him."

"That's not very kind, Penny, and so unlike you. You know Ethan and Evan have responsibilities in town. Where's your Christian charity?"

"Charity!" Penny snapped her fingers. "That's a great idea. Doesn't the church have a benevolence fund? Why don't you tell Mayfield to go to the parsonage for help?"

Zion caught Penny's last words as he walked in the door with Dahlia on his shoulder. "Who needs help?"

"It looks like this little girl needs help getting down. How did you get her up there?" Rosalie lifted Dahlia and set her on the ground.

"She climbed on the workbench from the stool, and then we just made it happen."

"It was fun, Momma." Dahlia beamed and Rosalie ruffled her burnished hair.

"I'm glad, baby girl, and I'm glad you didn't lose your balance. You could have fallen and gotten hurt." Rosalie shot a stern glance at her husband. "Maybe next time you should walk, at least until Daddy's arm heals."

The girl's lower lip protruded in a pout. She looked from her mother to her father who nodded his head in agreement. "Yes, Momma."

"That's a good girl." Rosalie crossed to the cookie jar and broke a molasses cookie in half. She held it out to her daughter who brightened at the offer of a treat. Rosalie pulled her hand back, and confusion played in the little girl's hazel eyes.

"It's broken. Do you still want it?"

"Sure I do."

"It's still good, even though it's broken?"

"Gimme a bite and I'll tell ya."

"I'll give you a bite all right." Zion reached for his daughter's arm and pretended to bite it.

"No, Daddy. I wanna bite of cookie."

"Here you go." Rosalie handed the half cookie to her four-year-old. Dahlia took a bite and gave her head a firm nod that sent her mahogany braids bobbing.

"Yep. It's good."

"Even though it's broken?" asked Rosalie.

"This part is good."

"Well, we have to look at Daddy's broken arm like we are looking at this cookie. Right now we don't get the whole Daddy, like you didn't get the whole cookie, but what we have is still good. Right?"

"Right."

"And in just a few weeks, you'll be able to play horsey with Daddy again. Until then, I don't want to take a chance on either of you getting hurt. Do you understand, baby girl?"

"Ok, Momma." Dahlia took another bite of cookie and smiled at her mother.

"And we'll be thankful for what we have," Zion added.

"Yes, Pa. We be thankful."

"You want some milk to wash that down?" asked Penny.

"Yes, pease."

"Let's go see Clover. It's time for her milking and you can get some fresh from the source." Penny grabbed a tin cup from the shelf and ushered her niece to the door. "We'll be back in a few minutes."

"Thanks, Penny." Zion cast an appreciative look at his sister as the twosome left the cabin. She had always been helpful, but the last couple of days she had gone above and beyond pitching in around the farm in new ways.

"That's my Buttercup."

"I know you have a bad arm," said Rosalie, "but are your eyes and ears working?"

Zion furrowed his brow. "What do you mean?"

"I mean Penny's been acting strange all day. When you came in she was telling me we should send Logan Mayfield to the pastor for a handout instead of hiring him to help around here. Maybe that's why she's so anxious to help with the chores."

"That's so unlike her." Zion stroked his fuzzy chin. "I wonder what's got into that girl?"

"Me, too."

"Maybe it was the letter from Henry?"

"What letter?"

53

"I forgot to tell you. Jenkins sent a couple of letters out with Logan Mayfield. One was from Henry."

"I can't imagine a letter from Henry riling her up so."

Zion pulled out a chair and lowered his large frame into its seat. He placed his hat on the table, and his wife sat next to him on the bench.

"You know," said Rosalie, "I don't think it was the letter. She has been acting peculiar ever since she went swimming with Marigold. Ever since . . ."

"Ever since she met Logan Mayfield." Zion finished his wife's dangling sentence. "I've never seen her react so strongly to anyone."

"Me either."

"If Jenkins trusted Mayfield with our mail, that says something for him. Jenkins has a good head on his shoulders and is a right good judge of character."

"I agree." Rosalie traced the triangles of the quilted sampler with the tip of her finger.

Zion watched his wife, observing her thoughtful expression as she studied the quilt top. "What's that you have there, Mrs. Coldwell?"

Rosalie lifted the fabric so her husband could see its detail. "This is my first effort at quilt making. It's a *Flying Geese* pattern I made when I was ten years old. Penny and I were thinking about making the same pattern out of these scraps and strips I've been saving."

"Waste not, want not."

"True." Rosalie began stacking the sorted piles to move them from the table. "This pattern makes me so mindful of all my blessings."

"How's that?"

"It reminds me that I'm not searching, like so many others are. I'm so blessed to be here in Briar Hollow with the people I love, doing what means the most to me." Rosalie finished moving the fabric to a basket and brushed the straggling frays that had slipped loose from their pieces into a small pile.

"This quilt is a symbol of direction. I know we need direction about important things right now, but we're not floundering." Rosalie lifted the quilt so that its geese were pointing upwards. "See these geese?"

Zion nodded.

"They are pointing to heaven. That's where our direction comes from."

"That's right, love." Zion cupped his wife's chin in his hand and stroked her fair cheek with the back of his thumb. He loved everything about his Rosalie, including the light smattering of freckles that dotted the tops of her cheeks—freckles she so often fretted over. "We can't look to the left or to the right when it comes to making decisions. We have to look up."

"And when I look up," said Rosalie, "I feel we can't do anything less than give Logan Mayfield a chance. We both need help. It seems like Providence to me."

"I know what you mean. I got a letter today, too, from Belle Meade. Bob Green, the hostler, sent word that the colts and fillies for this fall's yearling sale are outstanding. Even with the fighting still going on, Belle Meade is producing handsome horses. If we're going to grow Coldwell Farms, I need to get that barn ready and follow through with our plans. If I can't make the purchases and take delivery this fall, we'll be set back an entire year."

"I'm sure once Penny gets over her initial shock of their meeting at the swimming hole she'll warm up to Mr. Mayfield and see this is the best decision for everyone, don't you agree?"

"I sure hope so." Zion scooted his chair back from the table and patted his knee with his good hand. "I don't think there's any danger you might fall off my knee while I'm sitting here in this chair. Do you agree to that, Mrs. Coldwell? You won't even need to climb up on a stool."

"You're incorrigible, Mr. Coldwell, just plain incorrigible."

CHAPTER 6

"So I hope you'll be able to look past getting off on the wrong foot and see that this is what's best and what's right." Zion walked Penny through the lane toward the main road to town. She carried a basket of lotions Rosalie had made to be delivered to Martha Matheny at the mercantile.

Resignation weighed heavily on her slight shoulders. It seemed no one cared about her opinion or her feelings in the matter. Zion had already talked with Logan Mayfield the night before and he would be coming out that very afternoon to begin working around the farm.

"I understand, Zion." Penny offered a lackluster wave and began the mile trip to town. A walk would do her good, she thought. Her mind was jumping like sparks from a campfire: on thoughts of Henry's letter, Zion's injury, and Logan Mayfield in particular. Three men, three problems. What was a girl to do?

Penny made the trip to town in good time—her pace a bit quicker than normal as her thoughts raced. She delivered the jars of lotions to Mrs. Matheny, thankful she was helping a customer and was too busy to chew the fat. She knew all too well the "fat" would be her family and the new people in town.

"Just put a credit on our account, please," said Penny as she lifted the empty basket off the counter and turned to leave the mercantile.

"I'll do just that, Penny. Thank you!" Martha Matheny returned to her customer who was thumbing through bolts of fabric that had recently arrived from Lexington.

Not yet ready to return to Briar Hollow, Penny decided to take a bit of time for herself and walk through town. She passed the court house, then the post office, and Cooper's Livery. As she neared the Paxton Inn she heard a commotion in the alley next to the building. A man vaguely familiar to Penny held a gun to the back of L. C. Yates, the owner of the Washington Bank.

Both men saw Penny, and for the longest second of her short life, everyone and everything froze. The banker had his hand open with something in his palm. The attacker grabbed the item and then lifted his gun and struck a vicious blow to Mr. Yates' head.

The plump that sounded as the gun impacted hard against the man's skull was both undeniable and unreal to Penny who watched in shock as the banker fell to the ground.

Logan observed Penny's walk through town from across the street. From the look on her face when she stopped at the alley, there was no doubt she had seen something frightening. He hurried to her side, afraid she would swoon before he could catch her.

As Logan arrived at Penny's side, her shocked silence transposed into a terror-stricken scream. He looked down the alley and saw a man crumpled on the ground and a second man running in the opposite direction. The gunman reached the end of the lane and looked over his shoulder at Logan and Penny before disappearing in a clean escape.

Penny collapsed in Logan's arms.

"Help! Somebody help!" Logan cried into the street. "A man has been injured!"

The doorman on duty at the Paxton Inn called inside and several men and women poured out onto the walk.

"I'll go for Doc Byerly!" A man ran for medical help, while another flew to the victim's side. He pulled out a handkerchief and applied pressure to the gash on the banker's head in hopes it would stop the bleeding.

"Hurry, Alf! He's bleeding like a stuck pig."

Sherriff Nash's badge shone in the morning sunlight. He had just finished a pleasant business lunch with Yates at the Inn. After their discussion of security issues at the bank, Yates had slipped out the side door to take the shortcut back to work. The unexpected turn of events confirmed the need for additional policing in their growing town.

"Did you see anything, Son?" Sherriff Nash asked Logan.

"Yes. It was one man. I didn't see what happened—just him making a dash out the back end of the alley."

"Is the girl hurt?"

Logan looked at the slight figure draped across his arms and shook his head. "No. I was watching her the entire time. She was coming down the walkway and stopped at the alley. I assume she heard some commotion. She looked into the alley and turned white as a ghost. I got to her just before she fainted."

"I'll send word out to Zion. Seeing she's not injured, you take her on across the street to the Goheens and let her rest up. I'll be by in a bit to talk to her."

"Yes, sir."

"Do you need help?"

"Not with this featherweight." Logan lifted Penny easily and carried her across the street. His mother, along with Eleanor and Ollie Mae Goheen, were watching the commotion from the boarding house porch. The trio moved as one to usher Logan and his charge inside.

"Put her on the davenport, Mr. Mayfield." Eleanor bustled ahead of the young man and moved the velvet cushions off the seat.

"Oh my, my, my." Ollie Mae shook her grey-crowned head. "Poor, dear Penny-girl."

"Gertie! Come quick!" Eleanor called. A middle-aged, apron-clad woman emerged from the kitchen and peered through the doorway. "Yes, Miss Ellie?"

"Fetch a cool cloth, please, Gertie. This girl's in a faint."

"Yes, ma'am. I sure will." The woman disappeared and returned with a damp cloth she handed to Eleanor.

"Poor, dear girl." Ollie Mae shook her head and wrung her hands.

"She'll be fine, sister. Don't fret so." Eleanor applied the cloth to Penny's forehead.

"Do you have smelling salts?" asked Millicent.

"Yes." Eleanor gingerly wiped Penny's face with the cool cloth. "I don't think we need to use them. She's just had a fright. No need to startle her any more with an abrupt awakening."

Logan stood back near a papered wall in the ornate boarding house parlor and watched the ladies fuss over Penny. Her still figure unsettled him more than he cared to admit.

"Mother, this is Penny Coldwell."

"Yes, poor, dear, girl." Ollie Mae wrung her hands. Her eyes, filled with sympathy, bounced from face to face. "Poor Penny."

"Coldwell as in Coldwell Farms Coldwell?"

"Yes," said Logan. "This is Mr. Coldwell's sister."

A stirring on the davenport set the room in motion. Penny blinked and fought to focus on her surroundings, but confusion was evident in her cornflower blue eyes. "Miss Goheen?" Penny looked from Ellie to Ollie Mae. "And Miss Goheen?"

"Yes, Penny. You're at the boarding house," said Eleanor. "Are you feeling well? Do you remember what happened?"

Penny scanned the room. Her eyes landed on Logan standing next to a woman she did not know. Images of the scene in the alley flittered from a smoky corner of her memory into a clarity made plain to all by the wave of fright that swept over her delicate face.

"Logan," Penny stretched out her hand. Logan quickly crossed the room and took it in his own, delighted to hear her use his given name and the feel of her cool fingers tucked in his. Millicent watched in silence, pondering the connection between the pale girl on the davenport and her son.

"I'm here." Logan dropped to one knee and looked deeply into pools of cornflower blue where fear and confusion swam together.

"You . . . you were there. You saw . . . ."

"I saw only you. I had just crossed the street when you were coming down the walk. You stopped at the alley."

"It all happened so fast." Penny lifted the back of her hand to her forehead and squinted. "That man. I don't know his name, but I've seen him before."

"The man who was struck?"

"Everyone knows Mr. Yates. It's the man with the gun. I can't place him, but I know I've seen him before—somewhere."

"Well, no never mind now, my dear," said Eleanor. "We just want to make sure you're well. Would you like a cup of tea? A drink of water?"

"Gertie!" called Ollie Mae. "Oh, Gertie!"

"I'm right here, Miss Ollie Mae."

"Oh, yes. Yes, you are, dear. Would you please get a drink for poor, dear Penny?

"I'm fine, thank you. I'd just like to sit up."

"Let me help you." Logan offered Penny his free hand. She held tightly as he eased her from her prostrate position to upright and then tenderly shifted her legs so she could rest against the backside of the seat.

Just like he's done for me so many times, observed Millicent, proud of her gentle son and the tenderness he displayed.

Sheriff Nash knocked on the door and then opened it before anyone could answer. He tucked his burly, hat-adorned head in the frame. "Is Penny awake?"

"Yes," Eleanor answered, "come in."

"Yes. Come in. Come in, Sheriff," echoed Ollie Mae.

"Well, now, little lady," Eudell Nash crossed the plush Oriental rug in long strides, "it looks like you had yourself quite a fright."

"Yes, sir." Penny offered a flaccid smile.

"Are you up to telling me about it?"

"I'll be happy to tell you what I remember."

Sheriff Nash seated himself in an armed chair next to Penny and settled in to hear the story.

"Would you like some refreshment, Eudell?" Eleanor asked.

"That's a right kind offer, Miss Ellie, but I'm fine, thank you. I just had lunch with Yates before all these shenanigans played out." Eudell turned his gaze back to Penny. "Now, if you'll just tell me what you saw, please."

"It all happened so fast." Penny shook her head hoping to jostle her thoughts back in line. "I was walking. I had just delivered some lotions to the mercantile and was coming up to the Paxton Inn when I heard a noise in the alley. I looked and saw this man with a gun drawn on Mr. Yates. Mr. Yates had some item in his hand he was giving the man with the gun. It was like everything froze. Both men looked at me. I looked at them . . . and then the man with the gun bashed Mr. Yates on the head." Penny winced and closed her eyes to erase the scene, but it replayed in an ongoing loop that made her tremble.

"I'm sorry you had to witness that, Penny." The timbre of Sheriff Nash's voice soothed the girl. Penny felt safe for the moment, yet still troubled.

"I need to ask you just one more question."

"I'm ok, Sheriff." Penny nodded. "Go ahead."

"Did you recognize the man with the gun?"

Penny's eyes narrowed. She tried again to remember. "There was something familiar about him."

"So you think you've seen him before?"

"I do, and it bothers me that I can't place where."

"You've had quite a shock today, Penny." Sheriff Nash rose to his feet and mashed his hat back on his head. "I want you to go home and rest, and do whatever you usually do. If you try too hard to remember, you'll just upset yourself. That memory will be gone nigh as a jackrabbit with a mountain lion on its tail." The sheriff once again conquered the rug in a confident gait and opened the door.

"You go on home now, and try not to dwell on it, and I'm a thinking it will come back to you in time. Meanwhile, I'm going to Doc Byerly's and check on Lars. He took a hard blow and lost quite a bit of blood. He was unconscious the last I heard."

"Oh, we'll be praying for him, Eudell," Eleanor called after the sheriff.

"Yes. We'll be praying." Ollie Mae closed the door behind the sheriff. "Poor, dear Lars."

CHAPTER 7

S tabbing pains plunged through Harley Crawford's chest as he worked to take in air. He had not run like that in years. Recurrent chest infections and a recent bout of pneumonia had weakened his breathing capacity, but the run had been worth the effort. It seemed his luck had turned 180 degrees. He had been at the right place at the right time when he overheard the sheriff and the banker make their lunch plans. He had seen the banker use the alley before, and his assumption had been right. Yates used the shortcut today, as well.

Now Crawford had not only the man's wallet, but the key to the vault. He had not planned to clock the guy with his gun, but when the girl showed up . . . that girl. He had thought about her so many times since he first laid eyes on her last fall at the Germantown Fair.

The flaxen-haired beauty had been at the fair with a group, her family he assumed. From his seat in the middle of the carousel, Harley had watched. As the calliope played and the girl went round and round, he could not keep from staring at this lily among thorns. His eyes followed her with each lap of the painted horses. Up and down, round and round she went just out of his reach.

When the ride finished Harley had jumped up and offered her assistance to dismount. A look of surprise had filled her beautiful blue eyes, but she had placed her small hand in his and allowed him to help her from her perch on the painted steed. Harley Crawford had never forgotten the feeling of her hand in his. Visions of her sweet oval face filled his dreams and drew him back to Washington.

He knew she was out of his arena. That's why he needed some resources and why he devised the plan to nab the banker's vault key and raid the bank when the town was sleeping. He had planned to take Yates with him and tie him up until he could get out of town, but when everything happened so fast in the alley, he realized he could not walk down the street in the middle of the day with his gun to the banker's back. At the same time, the chance to have him alone in the alley had been more than he could resist.

Harley had taken his chances, and this is how his hand had played out. He could not change the cards now. The question was how to play them.

She had seen him, his little china doll. This unexpected twist could definitely complicate things. Getting her alone could prove to be harder than it might have been before. *If she sees me, she'll probably scream or run or both.*

First things first, Harley schooled his thoughts. *First, I have to get the money from the vault; then I'll plan how to get my dolly.*

With the sheriff gone and Penny looking better, Logan wondered about getting the girl back to her home. If things were different, he would have made arrangements to hire a carriage. It was challenging, to say the least, knowing that such a small expenditure would put a painful dent in his purse.

"Would you like me to walk you home?" Logan offered.

Penny looked into the hazel eyes of the man before her. They were unusual, with flecks of amber that appeared to shift in color from a light brown to a golden-green; and they were filled with tender concern. Logan Mayfield was not as tall as her brother, but he did stand a full six feet. He wasn't as filled out as Zion, but there was something about the way he carried his lanky frame that spoke of dignity and character.

His tawny hair, the brownish yellow of tanned leather, was thick and coarse, a bit lighter than his bushy brown eyebrows. Among his strong facial features was a notable dimple in the middle of his chin. It was not prominent, but Penny allowed her thoughts to drift and remember what he had looked like when she had first noticed it at the swimming pole.

Penny's blue eyes iced over. "I can make it home fine on my own, thank you, Mr. Mayfield."

Logan watched. He saw it happen, but he did not know what caused the change in Penny's expression or the curt tone of her reply. One moment she was reaching out to him and calling his name, and then, well, he did not know what to think. Who was this girl, and what power did she have over him to befuddle his thoughts and send his emotions swirling?

Martha Matheny kept her finger on Washington's pulse and knew what had happened immediately after the incident occurred. When she saw the sheriff leave the Goheen sisters' boarding house, she sent her sons to rescue the damsel in distress. From her vantage point at the mercantile, she watched the twins drive down the street in a fringe-canopied surrey, hop from their conveyance, and move as one to the porch.

Eleanor bustled to the door in response to Evan's percussioned knock.

"Hello, boys."

"Howdy, Miss Goheen," said Ethan. "Me and Evan done come to fetch Miss Penny and take her on back to Briar Hollow."

Penny rose to her feet and smoothed her skirt. "Why thank you, Ethan. Thank you, Evan." Her voice was sweeter than maple syrup. She dipped in a slight curtsy before the red-headed twins. "That's so kind of you. Can we leave right away?"

"Sure thing, Miss Penny." Evan stepped forward and held out an elbow. Penny slipped her hand through and allowed him to escort her to the door.

"Let me help, too." Ethan followed the twosome out the door and offered Penny his arm as well.

Penny walked between the two men. When they reached the surrey, she looked over her shoulder and lifted her chin ever so slightly in Logan's direction. Then she turned and offered a smile to Eleanor and Ollie Mae. "Thank you, ladies."

Ethan and Evan helped Penny into the surrey and sent the horse trotting down the street in the direction of Briar Hollow.

"Thank you, boys." Penny waved goodbye to the Mathenys. She knew she should have invited them in, but she wanted to be alone. Of course, there was no avoiding telling Zion and Rosalie what had happened, but afterwards she hoped to escape for some time alone in her room.

Penny took a deep breath and opened the cabin door. Inside, she found Rosalie in the rocking chair nursing Mattie while Dahlia played with her ragdoll on the rug near her mother's feet.

"Hi, Rosalie. Is Zion here?"

Rosalie turned from her baby's face to her sister-in-law's. Penny was pale and clearly disturbed.

"No. He's over at Pa's helping him and Marigold with the spring fertilizing. Are you alright?"

Penny exhaled deeply and seated herself in a ladder-back chair at the table. "I am, but I did have a bit of a scare earlier." Penny deliberately folded her hands in her lap to keep them from shaking. "Actually, I passed out in town."

"You what?" Concern filled Rosalie's green eyes. She wanted to get up and see to the girl, but Mattie was not finished with his meal.

"I really was hoping to tell you and Zion at the same time so I could get it over with."

"Well, you better tell me, Penelope Hope Coldwell."

"Oh, now you sound just like Zion." Penny rolled her eyes and slowly shook her head. Suddenly, she was very tired. All she wanted to do was lay down. "Rosalie, I'm exhausted. I just want to lie down. I'll give you the short story, and then if it's all right with you, I'd like to go to my room for awhile."

"That's fine, Penny. I just want to know you are ok."

"I am," Penny nodded, "I'm just tired."

"Tell me what happened, sweetie." Rosalie gave a soft smile.

"You know I went to the mercantile with your lotions. Mrs. Matheny put a credit to our account."

"Thank you."

"You're welcome." Penny placed her elbows on the table and dropped her chin into her hands. "I felt like taking a walk through town before heading home. When I got to the alley by the Paxton Inn, I heard a noise. A man had Mr. Yates at gunpoint. He saw me, hit Mr. Yates on the head with his gun and ran off. I passed out, but I'm fine. I'd just like to lay down now."

"Oh, you poor thing. Of course." Rosalie looked to the little one still filling his belly with warm milk. "I'll be done here soon. Can I get you anything?"

"No, thank you." Penny walked to her room and closed the door, thankful to be alone. She unbuttoned her shoes, slid them off, pulled back the quilt and slipped into bed. With shaky fingers she tucked the quilt under her chin and hoped to lose herself in dreamland.

When she closed her eyes, events replayed. She willed them away, but they continued to haunt her. Fear grew, and the harder she tried to rest, the more troubled she became. There was something unsettling about the day's events, and she knew it was more than witnessing an assault upon a kind man. Something niggled inside and caused a growing alarm within her.

What time I am afraid, I will trust in Thee. Penny's eyes opened wide. She was alone, but it seemed as if her mother was there speaking to her. When Penny was a little girl she had been afraid of the dark. Every night after prayers, her mother had recited Psalm 56:3 over her as she tucked her in bed.

"What time I am afraid, I will trust in Thee." Penny closed her eyes and repeated the beloved psalm aloud several times until a familiar peace descended and settled in her spirit. She drifted to sleep with a soft smile on her lips.

CHAPTER 8

"Right here in Washington?" Zion ruffled his hair and paced inside the small cabin.

"I'm afraid so," said Rosalie, "but lower your voice, dear. She's resting now and you don't want to wake her."

"Wake her? This better wake up the law around here. I'm going to town to talk to the sheriff."

"Don't you want to talk to Penny first?" Rosalie watched her husband's face as a host of expressions played across his handsome features. Anger turned to concern and then to discouragement. He ran a hand through his coarse brown hair a final time and then dropped into a chair.

"I don't know, Rosalie. That old saying seems to be true."

"What saying is that?"

"When it rains, it pours." Zion looked at his wife who sat in silence and watched him stew. "I hope that other saying doesn't come true."

"What's that, Zion?" The steady sweet voice and loving expression on his wife's face calmed Zion, but he remained unsettled.

"That bad things happen in threes."

"Oh, I don't think that's true," said Rosalie. "It's just an old wives' tale."

"Old wife. Young wife. Whoever said it, I've seen it come to pass more than once."

"Well, I'm not going to borrow any trouble. I have enough to put my mind to right now." Rosalie opened the oven door. The comforting aroma of baking bread filled the cabin.

"Just look at this. Not long ago this bread was a lump of dough that was kneaded and then punched down, but look at it now. It's raised up high, golden brown, and smelling delicious."

Zion stood to his feet and grabbed Rosalie with his right arm. She shut the oven door and turned to face her husband who locked her in a single-armed embrace. "You are one fine woman, Mrs. Rosalie Coldwell—smelling good and looking delicious yourself."

"Mr. Zion Coldwell," Rosalie laughed, "if Pa was here he'd say you are a conniption."

"I meant every word." Zion nuzzled into his wife's hair, enjoying its scent and her sweetness. "Life knocks me down, and you raise me up. What would I do without you?"

Penny bolted upright in the bed. Cobwebs loomed as unconsciousness attempted to regulate with the conscious world around her. What had she dreamt? Why had she awakened with such a start? There was something there—something in her dream she needed to remember, but all she recalled was the sound of music.

Music was one of Penny's great joys in life. Hearing melodies in her dreams should have been soothing rather than upsetting. The song had not been a sad one, like a funeral march. The tune had been bright and happy, but still Penny was shaken by the memory.

Not ready to face the world, the jittery girl collapsed on her mattress and pulled the covers over her head. A knock on the cabin door followed by conversation in the living area invaded her sanctuary. Reluctantly, Penny left the comfort of her bed and

72

smoothed her skirts. She brushed and rebraided her hair, all the while wishing she could ignore the voices outside her door, but keenly aware of each word.

"You were there, too?" Zion shook his head and ruffled his good hand through his hair. "That's the first I've heard about this." Marigold sat at the kitchen table holding Mattie who was gnawing on a piece of hard bread. Dahlia stood on a stool at the sink next to her mother, the duo washing and drying dishes from their midday meal.

Logan stood just inside the cabin door holding the empty basket Penny had left at the boarding house and the one he had used to carry Rosalie's gift of fruit home the day before. "Yes, I was outside and had just crossed the street. Your sister was coming down the walk in my direction, but she didn't see me. She looked a bit distracted, and when she stopped at the alley, her entire expression changed. I couldn't tell if it was shock or fear or a mixture of both, but I was worried I wouldn't make it to her before she fell over in a faint."

"I'm so glad you did." Gratitude spilled from Rosalie's green eyes. "Here, let me take those." She reached for the baskets as Penny opened her door.

"Penny, look who's here," said Marigold, "your knight in shining armor."

Penny attempted to restrain her eyebrows from lifting in a catty arch, but her efforts were less than successful. She knew she should be thankful, but the thought of Logan Mayfield being considered her champion sent her over the edge. Marigold bit her tongue as she watched Penny's usually impeccable manners follow her raging emotions.

"I am thankful I didn't land on the walkway, but I would hardly bequeath Mr. Mayfield such a valiant title as 'knight in shining armor.'"

Pale from the stress of the day's events, the pink that rose in Penny's high cheekbones caused a dramatic effect on her porcelain face. She drew a deep breath and tried to settle her shaking hands.

"Girl, your nostrils are flaring like Lucy's after a long run," said Marigold.

Penny gasped and her eyes grew large as Marigold's words spun around her already befuddled thoughts.

"Marigold," Rosalie made a verbal dash to stop any further fireworks between the girls, "Penny has had a trying day. Don't you think it would be more fitting to be a comfort to your best friend than a tease?"

With appropriate remorse, Marigold quieted. "You're right, Rosalie." She turned to Penny. "This sure has been your week for adventures. Are you all right, sister-sister?"

With concerted effort, Penny stilled her emotions and kept her words even. "Yes, Marigold, I'll be fine." Anxious to deflect herself from further scrutiny, Penny attempted to change the focus of conversation. "Speaking of Lucy, how is she?"

"I was just going out to check on her," said Zion. He looked at Logan who had remained mute at the girls' exchange. "What do you say, Logan? Do you want to go out with me and check on the mare? She's about to foal here in a couple of weeks, and I'm keeping a close eye on her."

"Yes, sir, Mr. Coldwell. I'm ready to start work whenever you are."

Zion pulled his hat off the peg and mashed it down over his coarse brown hair. "All right then. Let's do it." Zion opened the door, and he and Logan made their way to the red barn. Four stalls lined the back wall of the wood building. In each stall was an area for feeding and watering. Outside the stalls, tack hung on hooks; and a bin contained grain for the three horses and cow that called the barn home.

"I've converted this barn into a make-shift stable. It's been serviceable. We started out small, but I'm itching to get the new one up. I have all the wood and supplies just waiting to get started. I planned to buy two yearlings this fall, and I need a place to keep them. In the new stable I'll be able to house more horses and store more hay, grain, tack and so on." Zion scanned the walls of the barn while visions of his new building danced in his head like sugarplums the night before Christmas.

"A good stable gives a horse a feeling of comfort and security. The new horse barn will have a corral attached and a special enclosed stall inside for foaling or if a horse has any special health concerns we need to monitor or isolate."

Zion walked to a stall where a beautiful bay stood. Her black mane, tail, and ear edges contrasted her richly colored reddish brown body. Zion reached through the opening and gave the horse a soft, but firm pat. "This is Lucy."

Zion switched from patting to scratching the mare on her back. The beautiful animal had a well-chiseled head on a long neck, high withers, and a deep chest. A Thoroughbred, she had good depth of hindquarters and long legs. Her usually lean body was heavy with the weight of the foal inside.

"This is Lucy's maiden pregnancy and I'm keeping a close eye on her." Zion checked the manger and noted the mare had not eaten well.

"It's not unusual for a mare's appetite to drop off when she is heavy in foal. There's just not as much room for food. What I'm keeping an eye out for is to see if she has any sudden changes in her behavior or goes off her feed entirely."

"I see." Logan approached the stall and attempted to pat Lucy's face. The horse shook her head and drew back. "I don't think she likes me."

"It's not a question of liking or not liking. She just doesn't know you yet." Zion called to the horse and she responded, sticking her head outside the opening in the stall door.

"First of all, how would you like it if a stranger came and stuck his hand in your face?"

"I guess I wouldn't like that myself." Logan smiled.

"Right, and neither does a horse. The first thing you do when you're meeting a new horse is reach your hand out, palm flat and up, and let the horse sniff your palm. You try it."

"Ok." Logan followed Zion's instructions. Lucy remained calm at his approach, stuck her nose in his palm, and sniffed.

"Now start talking to her and reaching that same hand she just sniffed on down the base of her neck where it meets the withers. That's where she likes to be patted the best."

"Hi, Lucy. How are you doing today, little lady?" Logan spoke calmly and moved his hand down the horse's side. Lucy stood still and Logan's confidence buoyed as the mare allowed him to pat her.

"Now move on down to her back and give her a good scratch."

"How would you like a little scratch, Lucy?" As Logan itched her back, Lucy stretched her body encouraging him to reach for the places she could not.

"Look at that, now, would you?" Zion said with a smile. "You've done won her over. I think you've made a friend."

"I'm pleased to make your acquaintance, Lady Lucy."

"Just make sure you keep away from her sensitive areas. She doesn't like to be touched on her flanks, rear end, face, or ears. If you pat her on her neck, back, withers or hips, you'll both be happy."

"Happy horse; happy me." Logan turned to Zion with a capricious grin spread across his face.

"Me, too," said Zion.

"Now, to take care of her needs, we need to make sure she has forage and water available at all times. She needs to be able to eat as she pleases and keep hydrated before and after the birth or she could lose her milk."

"Got it."

"She's been out in the bigger paddock, but she's getting close now. Her belly used to be in more of a hanging position, but now it's filling out her flank area."

"I see that. She looks a bit uncomfortable, I have to say."

"No doubt about that," agreed Zion. "Her belly shifted a couple of days ago, and that means she should foal in the next couple of weeks. Her udders will likely get bigger in the next few days—another sign she is getting closer to having her baby."

"You sure know a lot about horses."

"I was raised on a horse farm, and I confess, I think it's in my blood. There's nothing else I'd rather do for a living than raise horses."

"It must be a good feeling," Logan rubbed his dimpled chin between his thumb and forefinger, "knowing what you want to do, and being able to do it."

"What do you want to do with your life, Logan Mayfield?" Zion studied the young man and wondered if he would share more of his story.

"I used to think I would be a writer." Logan recalled the awards he had earned and the positions he had held in school and university. "I'm not sure anymore."

"What changed your mind, if you don't mind my asking?"

Logan considered the big man in front of him. Zion had gentled him the same way he had taught Logan to approach the horse. Logan felt safe. "I've been writing all my life and was working on my first full-length book. The publishing house had already approved it for publication based on the first three chapters and outline. I was working on the last chapter when it was lost in the fire, and I just don't know if I have the heart to start over."

"That is a terrible loss," said Zion. "I've never written a book and lost it, but I do know what it's like to lose your dream . . . and people you love."

"You look to me like a man who has everything he could ever want."

"I do now, and I thank God for it every day."

CHAPTER 9

"I've been thinking." Zion passed his empty bowl to Rosalie.
"Thinking about what?" Rosalie ladled up a second helping of white bean soup with bits of ham swimming in a savory peppered broth.

"I had a good day with Logan. He's not experienced with horses, but he's bright and willing to learn and work. Lucy warmed right up to him after a bit."

"I'm thankful the Lord sent him our way." Rosalie passed a plate of cornbread to her husband who took a piece and crumbled it in his soup.

"I can't explain it exactly," said Zion, "but I feel a connection with him and his family. Maybe it's because we share a similar loss."

Penny listened to the conversation on high alert, but kept her thoughts to herself. Throughout the afternoon she had spent time praying and reflecting on the events of the last two days. The more she thought about it, the more she questioned herself. She vowed to keep her mouth a bit more closed and her heart a bit more open; but for some reason when it came to Logan Mayfield, she had a hard time keeping either in check.

Her thoughts wandered to the time following her parents' deaths and the loss of their home in Virginia. It had been hard on her, but it had shaken Zion to the core. She wondered about women being the "weaker vessels," and then decided that must not be talking about every aspect of life. Zion could certainly lift more weight physically, but bearing the weight of grief had been more difficult for him. Perhaps, she decided, it was because he felt not only the loss, but also the weight of caring for both of them and Balim, who had been a part of their little family at the time.

How she wished Balim was near. Next to her mother's skirts, there had been no place she felt as safe as when she had burrowed her head in the big man's chest. He smelled of the familiar mix of horses and leather and Balim—a scent more comforting than Rosalie's sweet lavender soaps and lotions.

Balim was a stabilizer: a rock and a fountain—offering strength and refreshment to Penny and Zion. He had always been more family to the Coldwells than servant. At the request of their cook, Balim's aunt Liddy, Zion's father had brought the boy into their home when his parents were sold off from a neighboring plantation. Liddy had been the Coldwell's cook for years and had mourned for the little boy left all alone.

Penny had been thinking about Balim, and she knew he would be disappointed in the way she was acting with such flightiness and unkindness. She could almost hear his deep baritone repeating the words she had heard so many times: "The Good Book says, 'be ye kind one to another,' Missy Penny."

"What do you think, Penny?" Zion looked at his sister. She sat across from him but seemed far from the conversation around the supper table.

"I'm sorry, Zion." Penny dabbed the corners of her lips, folded her napkin, and placed it on her lap. "I'm a bit distracted today. What did you say?"

"I said that it seems a good thing to offer the loft to the Mayfields. They lost just about everything, and if they don't have the boarding house expense to pay, it would help them get back on their feet a mite quicker."

"Stay here? In our house?" Penny blinked and worked at keeping her lips from blasting out unkind or selfish words.

"I'd like us all to be in agreement before I make the offer. Nobody is using the space now. What do you think?"

Be ye kind one to another, Missy Penny. Balim's words replayed in Penny's mind. She knew what was right, but did not know if she was willing to do it. She looked to Rosalie with a forced blank expression on her face. "What do you think, Rosalie?"

"I know it's hard to have people in your home for an extended period of time. We would have to adjust a bit, but I'm willing. It's not forever—just while Logan works for us and your brother's arm heals."

"The Mayfields aren't sure where they are going from here," said Zion. "They may stay on in Kentucky, or they may head back East once they raise the money for the fare."

"They don't have enough money to go home?" Penny was surprised at how desperate the Mayfield's situation truly was. They had nice clothes. Logan seemed educated and his mother very polished and high society. The realization that they had lost everything but a few personal belongings eked into Penny's resolve. Compassion cracked her resistance.

"It would just be for a few weeks?"

Zion smiled at his sister, pleased to see she had softened toward the Mayfields. Her response to Logan had surprised him. Penny was usually sweeter than clover honey and considerate to a fault. Her deep faith motivated her to all sorts of kindnesses few knew about. She had a secret he had uncovered only last December. For the last three years people around Washington had been blessed with unexpected gifts. It wasn't just at holiday times or special occasions; but when folks were in need, they often discovered baskets left anonymously on their porches. Inside they would find either just what they needed or a little something to boost meager supplies and uplift downturned spirits. On every basket a little tag was tied on with purple ribbon that said, "Trust in the Lord."

"There's my Buttercup!"

The corners of Penny's thin pink lips turned upward at her brother's response. A pang of remorse coursed through her spirit when she realized her poor conduct had added to her brother's recent challenges. She knew better than to behave like she had been. Her life verse was Micah 6:8. She had even named her dog Micah to reminder herself to always do justly, love mercy, and walk humbly with her God.

"I'm sorry if I've made things more difficult, Zion. I don't know what's gotten into me lately." Penny rose from the table and began collecting empty bowls. Still a bit shaky about the assault she had witnessed, she was sure of one thing: Logan Mayfield was just a stranger passing through. She was going to do as her mother had taught her. The Bible said to be hospitable to strangers because you never know if you might entertain a very angel from heaven. She was going to do it—even if the cad had the bad manners to stare at a girl in her underclothes.

Penny turned to the sink with the dishes in hand. A real smile filled her oval face. Yes, Logan had stared, but for just one moment she wondered what had been going through his mind when he stumbled upon the girls swimming and sunbathing. Surely he had never run across such a sight in his proper Eastern community. He must have been befuddled, "fo sho and fo certain," as Balim always used to say.

"I'll wash these up, if you like, Rosalie." Penny shaved some soap into the washtub and poured in hot water from the kettle on the stove.

"Thank you, Penny." Rosalie wiped Dahlia's face and helped her from her seat talking to Zion over her shoulder as she worked.

"I'll help you saddle up West so you can ride to town and back before it gets dark." She patted her daughter on the top of her head. "You be a good girl for Auntie Penny, and listen for your baby brother. I'll be back in just a few minutes."

Zion checked on Lucy and greeted Penny's horse, Absalom. All had been groomed by Logan that afternoon, but still he checked West's coat to make sure it was free of any mud, dirt, or hair clumps that could become irritating under the saddle. He gave a customary check for sores on his back and cinch area before putting the saddle blanket well forward on his back and then pulling it down just in front of the withers.

He placed the right stirrup and cinch over the seat of the saddle and raised it high so none of its flaps hit the horse as he gently lowered the saddle on West's back.

"Put your hand here, Rosalie."

"There?" Rosalie looked puzzled. "Why do I need to put my hand on his rump for you to saddle him?"

"I'm going to walk behind, and keeping a hand on his backside as you circle around keeps the horse aware of your presence. With my bum hand, I need you to do it."

"If you say so, Mr. Horseman."

"I say so." Zion lifted the front part of the saddle pad to create an air pocket between the blanket and the horse's withers and then reached under the horse's belly for the cinch. He ran the tie strap through the cinch twice and tightened it just enough so it was up against West's belly. "Can you make a knot here, please?"

Rosalie pulled the tie string to one side of the cinch and knotted it.

"That's good." Zion patted West and spoke in calming tones. West was a purebred. He was powerful, and not usually temperamental, but he was also used to Zion saddling him. Zion wanted to make sure the massive animal remained calm as he and Rosalie worked together to prepare him for the ride to town.

"Now slowly tighten the cinch so it's nice and snug around his belly just behind his front legs." Rosalie did as she was told while Zion checked to make sure the blanket stayed centered and the cinch was straight.

"Perfect. I'll take it from here." Zion took the tie strap and secured it through the front of the saddle. "Let's see how that feels. Come on, West." Zion walked the horse through the barn door and checked the stirrup length. All was in order.

"Will you be able to mount with one arm?" Rosalie had watched Zion mount his stallion many times with grace and agility. He had an upper body strength that made the task seem easy, but that was with the use of two good arms.

"Watch this." Zion grabbed West's leads and moved to a more open piece of ground.

"Bow." Zion tapped West on the shoulder with his whip. The horse responded with a deep bend of his front legs.

"Good boy, West. You remembered." Zion used the whip again to tap West firmly on the rump. "Down, West. Down."

The massive animal lowered himself to a recumbent position on the ground. Zion stretched a long leg over the saddle, lowered himself into the seat and then grabbed the reins in his good hand. "Up, West."

Zion was no featherweight, but the muscular animal was able to lift to his feet with his owner atop. "That's a good boy." Zion beamed and patted the stallion. "Give him an apple, Rosalie. It's been a long time since we've done that, and he was incredible."

"I'm impressed." Rosalie lifted the lid on the box that housed the animal's treats. "Here you go, West. Such a strong boy you are. And you, Zion Coldwell, never cease to amaze me."

With a tip of his head and a mischievous gleam in his blue eyes, Zion agreed with his wife. "I am pretty amazing, if I say so myself." Zion pressed his legs into West's sides and pulled the reins in the direction of the lane. "A surprise now and again keeps the mystery of love alive, don't you think? I wouldn't want you to get bored with me."

"I don't see that happening," said Rosalie. "Now you be careful and keep yourself on the back of that horse. I don't want you breaking your other arm, or worse a leg. I'd never be able to carry you around."

"We could have some fun trying."

"Oh you. Get going now so you can make it back before dark."

"I love you, Rosalie."

"I love you, too."

CHAPTER 10

"Come, Banjo." Logan waited for the dog to join him on the porch. "Look what I have for you." He offered the sorry looking creature the bone Gertie had given him, a leftover from their evening meal.

Never one for pets, Logan had surprised himself by his response to the stray who found his way to the barn the day he and his mother sorted through the storage chests. They had so little, but he couldn't turn him away. Where the name Banjo came from, he wasn't altogether certain, but it seemed to fit the dog with its wiry black and brown coat.

"I don't know who your momma or daddy were, but what a couple they must have been." Logan laughed out loud as he examined the little dog with deer-like legs that seemed such an odd match with his small body and long nose.

The sound of a horse coming down Main Street drew his attention from the dog happily gnawing on his bone. Logan recognized West before he made out the man in the saddle. Surprised to see Zion riding with his arm in a cast, he rose to his feet and stepped into the yard to meet him.

"I apologize for not dismounting, but it's a bit of a challenge getting up here, and I won't be long."

"That's no problem. I sure wasn't expecting to see you on horseback."

"Well, it's my first time. I don't think Doc Byerly would be any too happy with me, but I wanted to come talk to you before the morning."

Logan's heart sank deep in his chest. He knew he wasn't a horse farmer's "dream hand," but he thought he and Zion had worked well together. He reasoned in himself that the only motivation Zion could have had to ride into town in his condition was to tell him to stay home in the morning.

Zion watched Logan's face and read the distress he saw flash across his features. "I've come to make you an offer."

"An offer?" A flicker lit in Logan's downcast eyes. Maybe he had been wrong about Zion's motives.

"Yes. The whole family has talked it over, and we want you and your mother to come stay with us while you're getting back on your feet."

The stranglehold that had gripped Logan released in a warm flood of pleased confusion. "Really?"

"Really." Zion looked down on the young man. A knowing came to him—a confidence and peace that the Lord had purposely crossed the two men's paths. He saw Logan as a reflection of the man he had once been, and prayed God would use him to help the young man through the transition life had brought his way.

The two men stared at each other. Thoughts flitted through Logan's head like hummingbirds dancing around a syrup-filled feeder. Zion's proposition was so unexpected, but what a wonderful surprise.

Logan refused to entertain the thought of rejecting the offer. His pride taunted him, but his logical mind shooed it away. There was so little left in his purse, the money he made working for Zion would be deeply cut into by living expenses. With lodging provided, he could save his earnings and they would have a little something to work with. His mother still held out hopes for

Angus' return, but Logan knew the truth. He should have been back months ago.

"It's nothing fancy, but we have a loft at our place no one is using right now. You and your mother are welcome to it."

"That's such a kind offer. I'm sure Mother will be pleased."

"We'd be right pleased to have her—have you both, for that matter."

The screened door of the boarding house opened. Millicent saw the man on the horse talking with Logan and crossed the yard to join them.

"Mother, this is Mr. Coldwell, my employer."

"How 'do, Mrs. Mayfield?"

"I'm so pleased to meet you, Mr. Coldwell. What a blessing you've been to us."

Zion looked in the face of the delicate woman. "Well, there's a saying, Mrs. Mayfield: one hand washes the other. Logan and I had a good day in the horse barn and there's much to do yet while this arm of mine mends. We're helping each other out, like the Good Book says."

"That's what it says, indeed." Millicent's slight stature and the way she tilted her head when she smiled up at him reminded Zion of his mother—and Penny, who was, as Balim had so often said, her "spittin' image."

"Mother, you'll never guess what a kind offer Mr. Coldwell has made."

"I can see you're excited. Why don't you tell me?"

"He's invited both of us to stay in his home while I work for him." Logan could almost see the dollars marching back into his purse. A "little boy" grin broke out with a delight Millicent had not seen in far too long.

She knew that since the tragedy Logan had felt incredible pressure to see to their financial needs. She was also well aware that her dear son struggled with trusting God as their provider. Millicent knew that trusting God was not something that comes naturally to a man; but when a person walked hand in hand with the Lord as long as she had, it was simply a way of life.

Millicent extended a hand to Zion, still seated on the horse. "Thank you, Mr. Coldwell. You're very kind."

"Forgive me for staying seated, ma'am. I haven't forgotten my manners; it's just a challenge to get up and down with my bad arm."

"That's quite all right. No need to explain."

"If you can be ready in the morning, I'll have my brother-in-law, Garth Eldridge, come by with a wagon to fetch you."

Another of Logan's needs had been anticipated and answered. Maybe his mother's prayers were working after all. "But we haven't talked about any of the details," he said.

"No need. Just load everything you have on Garth's wagon and we'll take care of the details when you arrive."

"If you're sure, then," said Logan.

"Oh, I'm sure." Zion peered to the west and the array of pinks and purples washing across the evening sky. "I'm sure I better get back home before Rosalie sends out a search party."

"What time shall we expect your brother-in-law?" asked Millicent.

"What would you prefer?"

"Is 7:00 a.m. too early? I know you need Logan out for work."

"That will be just fine." Zion tipped his head and directed West to turn toward the street. "See you tomorrow."

"See you tomorrow!" Millicent waved and Logan gave a tip of his head that matched Zion's.

"See, Logan!" Millicent clasped her hands together and her blue eyes sparkled. "I knew the Lord would make a way."

With the breakfast dishes washed and put away, Rosalie pulled out the fabric for the *Flying Geese* quilt. She and Penny had already sorted the most complimentary colors into piles that would be pieced into blocks then stitched into rows with the dark strips between them. "You start cutting these into triangles." Rosalie handed a stack of lavender scraps to Penny. "I'll work on the muslin."

"Sounds good." Penny picked up the top piece of calico and rubbed it between her fingers. It was a purple with a small lavender floral print; a remnant from a dress Rosalie had made for her when she and her brother were first married. "I love working with fabric."

"Me, too," said Rosalie, "and I loved making dresses for you before you became so skilled with a needle."

"I had a good teacher." With the template in place, Penny finished the first snip at the calico. The sound of an approaching wagon snapped her attention from pleasant memories.

"There they are." Rosalie placed her scissors on the table. "Let's go greet them."

"Ok." Penny followed her sister-in-law out the door into the glorious sunshine. The sweet honeysuckle scent of viburnum, mingled with fragrant blue phlox and wildwood violets, greeted the girls as they stepped off the porch and into the yard.

"Whoa." Garth reined in the team just in front of the house. Logan stepped down and reached to assist his mother. Banjo jumped from the wagon bed. Micah spotted him and barked a greeting that launched a tail-wagging, sniffing square dance in the yard.

"Look at that," said Rosalie.

Penny watched carefully, a bit on edge with the presence of the interloping varmint. A sassy retort flung forward in her mind, but she captured it and watched the dogs in silence. They seemed to be getting along. She wasn't sure how she felt about that, but decided to be thankful. She could be breaking up a fight, and that was not the way she wanted to spend this beautiful spring morning.

"They seem to be making friends." Logan moved to Penny's side. The couple quietly watched the dogs together for a moment.

"Yes," Penny agreed, "it looks like they are. Zion didn't tell me you had a dog."

"I tried to tell him last night, but he said to load everything on the wagon and we'd work out the details when we got here. So, here we are."

Penny nodded slowly. "Yes, here we are."

Dahlia dashed to the wagon, her mahogany braids flapping behind her. She carried a handful of wildflowers that she extended to Millicent. "For you."

"Oh, you dear!" Millicent was touched by the girl's sweetness. Her eyes moistened at the kindness of the good people of Briar Hollow. Surely the Lord had led them to this place. "Thank you so much."

"Let's get these things inside." Garth handed down a chest to Logan who jostled it to the ground.

"I can take that." Millicent reached for a sewing basket—a gift from the Goheen sisters who said every lady simply must have her own place for her needlework and sewing items.

All that remained on the wagon was a carpet bag which Zion lifted with ease. Garth and Logan each took a side of the chest, and the party made its way into the Coldwell home. Millicent paused to take in the surroundings. The flower gardens were breathtaking: one filled with wildflowers in every hue, height and shape; the other with a lovely variety of roses. Grape leaves spanned the sides and top of the arbor near the entrance to the orchards promising a plentiful harvest yet to come.

The log cabin was a welcome sight. While not grand like her home in the East or the beautiful Mayfield Manor that was no more, its pitched roof and fieldstone chimney held a charm of their own, as did the covered porch that spanned the cabin's face.

Inside, the furnishings were simple. The main items were a cast iron stove, a rectangular wooden table with two ladder-backed chairs on the ends, and benches on the long sides. Two rocking chairs graced the front of the large stone fireplace.

"What a lovely home you have," said Millicent, "and thank you so much for having us."

"It's our pleasure, Mrs. Mayfield." Rosalie motioned the woman to a rocking chair. "Would you like to rest a bit after your trip from town?"

"Thank you, Mrs. Coldwell." Millicent realized she was tired. A few minutes rest and she would be all set to unpack.

"Please, call me Rosalie."

"Only if you call me Millie."

Millie? Logan wondered at the nickname he had never heard his mother use before this very moment. His father had certainly never called his bride the name in his hearing, but somehow in this place it seemed to fit.

"Ok, Millie and Rosalie it is. Can I get you a cup of coffee or cool mint tea?"

"Oh, no, dear. I'm fine. I don't want you waiting on me. I'll just rest up a few minutes and then you can show me where to unpack."

"Rosalie?" Penny called from her room. "Could I see you for just a minute, please?"

For a moment, Rosalie worried that Penny had a change of heart about the Mayfields, but her expression put her at ease. "If you will, excuse me a moment." Rosalie headed to Penny's room.

"Do you want this up in the loft?" Garth asked Logan.

"Wait just a minute, please," Penny called from her room.

"Yes?" Rosalie eyed her sister with open curiosity.

"Rosalie, I don't think it's fitting for Mrs. Mayfield to climb the ladder to the loft. She's frail and older, and I'm just worried she might lose her footing on the rungs."

A small sigh escaped Rosalie. "I know what you mean. I had thought of it, but it is our only extra room."

"I'd like her to use mine."

"That's so sweet, Penny." Rosalie kissed Penny's cheek and then studied her features. "Are you sure?"

"I'm sure."

"Then why don't you go tell Garth and Logan to bring the chest in here?"

Penny pulled her dresses from their hooks and reached under the bed for a bag for her undergarments and sleepwear. "Would you, please? I'll just gather my things and be out of here quick as a wink."

CHAPTER 11

O nce the unpacking was completed and dinner consumed, Rosalie offered Millicent a tour of Briar Hollow.

"Your mother must have been very special," said Millicent. "These gardens are beyond lovely."

"Thank you, Millie." Rosalie scanned the wildflower garden filled with blooms and sweet memories. "She loved flowers, and she also loved planting things that helped people. She made tonics and teas to help people from all over with one ailment or another."

The duo moved from the wildflowers east of the cabin to the enclosed rose garden to the west. Rosalie stopped and picked a handful of dandelion greens. "She taught me that some things we take for granted, like these dandelion leaves. They have hidden value if we take the time to learn about them. These common greens that many just pass by or consider weeds have anti-inflammatory properties. They can help people with asthma, arthritis, digestion and even rashes."

"I never imagined." Millicent's appreciation for Rosalie was growing by the minute. One whom her society friends would consider a simple farm girl, had much wisdom.

"It's true, and Momma said there are life lessons to learn from plants. One of them is that God made things with purpose. She thought it was a waste to not investigate what that purpose was.

"Momma didn't like to waste anything. She said God didn't waste anything and neither should we." Rosalie lifted a spatula-shaped leaf for Millicent's inspection. "See these grooves?"

"Yes," Millicent ran a long finger over the shiny leaf, "I never noticed them before."

"God put those there on purpose. They funnel rain to the root of the plant." Rosalie pointed to a plant still firmly rooted in the ground wearing a bright yellow flower on elongated stem like a jaunty cap. "And did you know the flowers aren't out all the time? In the evening and in gloomy weather, they close up. When the sun comes out, there they are, bright and cheerful as the dawn."

"Rosalie, you are a delight."

A blush tinged Rosalie's lightly freckled cheeks, and a felicitous pleasure settled in her spirit. "It's a delight sharing my mother's garden with you, Millie."

The younger woman smiled at the older. Rosalie was happy, but she never forgot the times life had stripped her of loved ones and almost of hope itself. She felt a fellowship with the elegant lady beside her. Her Pa called it "the fellowship of sufferings." Matthias had taught her that through suffering people can either become bitter or learn compassion, and her heart went out to Mrs. Mayfield.

"God doesn't waste anything," Millicent rehearsed the line.

"No, ma'am. He sure doesn't."

"That's an encouraging thought, isn't it?"

"Yes, it is." Rosalie plucked a yellow dandelion and handed it to Millicent. Memories of a toddling Logan rushing to her with a bouquet he had picked himself came to mind, and with them, a reminder of the simple pleasures of love and family.

"Would you like to sit on the bench under the arbor?" asked Rosalie.

"That would be nice." Millicent and Rosalie moved to the bench near the creek. Beneath the shade of the grape arbor, the women sat in a comfortable, quiet companionship.

Millicent admired the orchards that lay in neat rows beyond the cabin. She noted the kitchen garden and henhouse.

"What's that little building over there?" Millicent pointed to a small shed along the southern perimeter of the hollow.

"That's one of my favorite places." Rosalie smiled as she pictured the interior of the little building. "Pa built that potting and drying shed for Momma. She loved it, and so do I."

"And that building?"

"That's our old apple barn," said Rosalie. "Pa built a new one on the other side of the orchard. This one's in bad shape, but that's because we haven't used it for the last four years. It wasn't too sturdy before then."

"Really?" Millicent was surprised. "Everything else looks so well maintained."

"Some of the wood has needed to be replaced for years. My Pa has limited mobility from a war injury, and he just never got around to fixing it. He thought sheltering the animals and tending the crops were more important."

"I see."

"Anyway, we haven't used it at all the past four years. Zion had plans to tear it down this very week." Rosalie pointed to a large pile of lumber near the barn. "See all those building supplies?"

"Yes. That's quite a pile."

"That, someday, is going to be the new barn." Rosalie looked at the building supplies and grieved a bit for her husband. "We had some delays with the delivery, and then Zion got hurt."

"Oh, dear." Millicent understood the disappointment Rosalie felt for her husband. She knew firsthand how hard it is for a woman to stand by and watch her man feel helpless and disappointed.

Millicent covered Rosalie's clasped hands with one of hers and gave a slight squeeze. "I'm so sorry for your difficulties, Rosalie." She looked in the young woman's tender eyes and offered a knowing smile. "I did hear a very wise person once say that God never wastes anything."

Rosalie broke into a full grin beneath her floppy straw hat. "No. Of course, He doesn't."

From their seat on the bench, the women watched as Micah and Banjo circled from the back of the cabin to the barn.

"It looks like those two are fast friends already," said Rosalie.

"I'm glad for that."

"I know we are just getting to know one another," said Rosalie, "and I would never say this to anyone but family otherwise, but I do confess I am a bit bewildered by the sparks that fly between Penny and your son."

"I've never seen anything like it myself."

"Penny is such a good-hearted Christian girl. I'm truly befuddled."

"Logan has never had an enemy in his life." Mrs. Mayfield raised a hand to shield her eyes from the bright sun as she watched the dogs saunter around the property like sentinels on duty. "Just look at those two, Rosalie."

"The dogs?"

"Yes. They are an unlikely pair, aren't they?"

Rosalie chuckled. She hadn't expected such a refined family to have a dog that looked as pathetic as poor, wiry Banjo. "Well, yes. They are."

"If the two of them can become fast friends, we'll just have to pray Penny and Logan do the same."

"I do believe in prayer, ma'am."

"Then that's what we'll do. You and I will pray."

Rosalie gave a firm nod. "Yes we will; and we will see what God will do."

Sweat dripped between the blades of Logan's shoulders. A bead dropped into an eye and he wiped at it with the back of his gloved hand. Mucking out stalls: he tried to be thankful for his employment. He was, in one sense; but he could not deny the dueling thoughts of feeling inadequate and at the same time overqualified for such work.

"In everything give thanks." That's what Zion had read from the Bible after breakfast that morning. It wasn't as if the big man was sitting on top of the world. He had plenty he could grumble and complain about. What got to Logan was that the man with the broken arm and struggling farm actually chose to give thanks when the natural response would be to worry and whine.

Once the soiled bedding had been removed, Logan used a pitch fork to fluff the new straw. Zion had explained that fluffing separates the straw flakes and creates more cushion and absorbency. Once he spread the new bedding, Logan banked the edges of the stall. Banking, Zion had said, can prevent a horse from getting cast, or stuck close to a wall in a position where he can't get his feet under him to get up. If a horse gets cast, he might panic and injure himself.

It is interesting, Logan mused, how many details are involved in what he had always assumed was the simple process of cleaning a barn. He had never considered how many small things could affect the health and welfare of the animals inside.

"Looking good." Logan turned to see Marigold watching from the barn door.

"Thank you, kind lady."

"Oh, kind lady is it now? Not 'millpond mermaid?'"

Logan took off his gloves, stuck them in his back pocket and wiped the perspiration from his palms on his trousers.

"Which do you prefer?" Logan asked the animated girl.

"I get to pick, now, do I? Aren't you the flannel-mouthed dude?"

"Flannel-mouthed?" Logan prided himself on his excellent vocabulary, but this girl's jargon was expanding his lexicon of rural lingo.

"Yeah, a fancy talker, smooth with the words."

Logan laughed out loud, his chin dimpled in amusement. "I do like words," Logan admitted, "and I'm getting quite an education from you on some new ones."

"Glad to oblige." Marigold plucked a blade of clean straw from a bale stacked inside the barn and spun it between her fingers. "There is a lot to learn around a farm. Take this straw, for instance."

"I know what that's good for. I just cleaned it out of the stalls where it was fully used for its intended purpose by your brother-in-law's horses."

"Straw's good for bedding, right so." Marigold continued to twirl the blade, enjoying the feel of its tickle on the pads of her fingers. "It can also be used for making hats, dolls, baskets, bricks, and even roofing."

"I'm sure that's all true," said Logan, "but I'm also sure you don't want to use any that I just cleared out of here for such endeavors."

"You got me there. That would be rich, wouldn't it?"

"Rich, as in rich fertilizer?"

"You're not so bad for a shave tail city fellow."

"Well, thank you kindly." Logan lifted the pitch fork to its hook on the wall. "I'm glad we're getting along so famously."

"You and Penny fight like Kilkenny cats," said Marigold. "I have never seen her act the like. You get her back up like no one else."

"I can honestly say I'm sorry about that." Logan lifted the dipper from the water bucket and took a long draw. "I know we got off on the wrong foot. I wish I could go back and change that, but I can't."

"Nope. There's sure enough things we'd all do differently if we could go back and change them. I'd erase a blow up or two myself, that's for sure." Marigold twirled the straw between her thumb and middle finger and then looked up to study Logan's features. He wasn't hard to look at, she decided. And he did seem to be a pleasant sort of fellow once you got to know him.

"I don't think she'll be down on you forever," said Marigold. "Some folks' feelings just take a bit longer to mend once they've been upset." The memory of Penny rising off the bench by the swimming hole made the girl chuckle. "I think we'd both agree Penny was a bit upset at your first meeting."

Logan shook his head with remorse. "I know, but like you say, we can't go back." He looked at the dancing brown eyes in Marigold's freckled, heart-shaped face. "What's a dude like me to do?"

Marigold threw her head back and let out a hearty laugh. "You are picking up on the local terminologies, aren't you?"

"Working on it," said Logan. "I'm working on a lot of things."

"Well . . . ." Mischief took hold of Marigold's better judgment. Life on a farm lacked for amusements at times, and there was something in her that could not resist blowing on the sparks that flew between Logan and Penny. "I might have some advice for you."

"Really?"

"Penny has a nickname she is right partial to."

"Not 'Provincial Pixie?'"

"Definitely not that." Marigold tossed down the piece of straw she had been playing with and headed to the barn door. "It's Buttercup. She just loves to be called Buttercup."

CHAPTER 12

Logan rambled on a meandering path from the barn to the water pump. Penny opened the cabin door and walked out into the sunshine. She looked fresh and lovely in her simple choring dress with an egg basket dangling on her arm. Logan had seen many handsome women in his days who wore elegant outfits and carried beaded bags and feathered parasols; but they had never captured his attention like this young, calico-clad girl. There was no denying that something in Logan very much hoped to make a better connection with this Washington beauty.

Logan took off his hat, placed it over his heart and gave a slight bow. "Hello, Buttercup!"

Shock darted through Penny's emotions like a lightning bolt in a spring storm. Her eyes grew large at the same time her lips all but disappeared in a taut pink line.

"B-Buttercup?" Penny sputtered, her gaze transfixed on the garish and impudent man. This interloper who intruded on her home and her already frazzled emotions had once again stepped way off the path of good manners. That he dared use a family pet name in such a familiar way caused heat to rise up her neck and into her hairline as fast as a locomotive with full steam. Even the Matheny brothers knew better than to speak to a lady with such familiarity.

The realization that Marigold had played him for a fool dawned quickly on Logan as Penny spun on her heel and stomped back in the cabin. The sound of the door being deliberately shut fell just below slamming level, but definitely made the point that the one closing it was quite decisive about returning inside.

"Marigold Johnson," Logan moaned, "how could you?"

"What in the world?" Rosalie watched Penny storm into the house only moments after she asked her to collect the eggs. "Is something wrong?"

"Wrong?" Penny's blue eyes flared with indignation. "Wrong, you ask?" A thump from the basket landing hard on the kitchen table accentuated her outrage. "Whatever could be wrong?"

Rosalie knew words were useless and determined to hear the girl out before interjecting more.

Penny made long strides toward the sink, clenched her fists and turned in what became a serious pacing back and forth. She stopped in front of the rocking chair, tried to speak, but instead stomped her right foot and started pacing again.

Dahlia emerged from her nap rubbing sleepies from her hazel eyes. Her aunt's energetic march had wakened her. She watched Penny traverse the floor in an uncharacteristic stalking and fluttering that reminded her of the time her pa brought home a new rooster. Roo had been outraged, and Zion said he was going to change his name from Roo to Stew if he didn't stop marching around the chicken run, sharpening his spurs on the rocks.

Bare footed and tousle haired, Dahlia clasped her pudgy fingers behind her back and did her best to lock-step with her flustered aunt. Side-by side the twosome made their course. Penny trod on, muttering occasionally under her breath and shaking her head, oblivious to the little girl beside her.

Dahlia took two steps to Penny's one, and when they reached the fireplace the second time, in her efforts to keep up with her aunt, Dahlia turned so sharply her braids spun out. Rosalie did her best to contain her mirth. One hand covered her mouth and the other her stomach, but her amusement crashed over her manners and a hearty laugh stopped both the girls in their tracks.

Penny shot a quarrelsome look at Rosalie who pointed to her daughter in her defense. Dahlia had diligently flanked Penny's side on her vexatious rounds like a lieutenant alongside his commanding officer. The little one turned innocent eyes to her aunt's face, fully expecting to receive her approval.

Penny's thoughts were spinning. She wrinkled her nose and blinked hard in an attempt to refocus on what was actually happening in the room.

Dahlia broke the silence. "Were we practicing for sumpin'?"

"Practicing?" Penny shook her head. "What do you mean?"

"You know . . . like the p'rade at the fair?" Dahlia studied her aunt's features and watched as they transitioned from puzzled to bemused.

Penny looked at Rosalie who barely contained a gut-busting guffaw and finally broke a smile of her own.

Like cold water poured over the edge of the cast iron cooker, the little girl's sweetness released the pressure building in Penny. For a moment she forgot why she was upset and laughed with her sister-in-law.

Dahlia's smile stretched across her darling face. "I like the fair. I got a b'loon there."

"Yes, you did," said Rosalie. "You had a lot of fun with that balloon, didn't you?"

"Mmhm," Dahlia nodded, "and on the car'sell."

"Carousel." Rosalie bent at the knee and motioned her daughter to her side. "You sure remember a lot of big words for such a little one."

Dahlia hurried into her mother's arms. "I 'member the car'sell. I rode a pretty painted horsie . . . and there was music."

Penny's thoughts raced back to the fair. Dahlia had loved the carousel. She rode it three times, and each time she asked Penny to ride with her. Rosalie had been in the early stages of her second pregnancy. With her stomach already churning from the effects of her condition, riding in circles held no appeal; but Penny had been happy to oblige her niece.

Pleasant pictures replayed in her mind, but when joined with the remembrance of calliope music, something unsettling crawled up Penny's spine and made her shiver. Her demeanor turned dour as she searched for the source of her discomfort.

"Would you please excuse me?" Penny asked Rosalie. "I'm not feeling well, and I think I need to lie down for a few minutes."

"Of course," said Rosalie. "Can I get you anything? A cup of chamomile tea? Or lavender?"

Penny rubbed her forehead with a shaky hand and then dropped it to her side. The look in Rosalie's green eyes revealed her concern. "Why don't you use my bed? I don't think you need to go up the ladder right now."

"Oh . . . that's right . . . Mrs. Mayfield."

"I'll tuck you in, Auntie," Dahlia offered.

Penny gave a faint smile and tugged lightly at one of the girls' reddish-brown braids. "Thanks, 'Dollya,' but I think I can manage."

Dahlia placed the back of her chubby hand on her aunt's cool cheek. "Your face was red and now it's white."

Rosalie watched with appreciation as her daughter attempted to diagnose and nurse her aunt. "Auntie Penny will be fine, sweetie. Let's just let her rest for a few minutes."

"Yes, ma'am."

Penny slipped off her shoes and stretched out across *The Rose of Sharon* quilt on Rosalie and Zion's bed. She fidgeted and then rolled to her side, pulling the edge of the bedding over her back and shoulder. Since she and Zion had moved to Briar Hollow, her life had been ordered and pleasant, if somewhat routine. The last few days she felt like her normally cheery world could be compared to a dandelion flower that had turned to fluff and was now blowing in the wind in all different directions.

What's going on, Lord?

Anxiety had never been Penny's close companion; and was now an unwelcome intruder. Fragments of images accosted her mind tumbling like bits of glass in a kaleidoscope that made abstract pictures but nothing precise or specific. A distant music accompanied the chaos that haunted her.

Amidst the jumble, the memory of Balim's rich baritone broke into her thoughts: "Trust in de Lawd, Missy Penny. He's gwanna make all things beautiful in His time. We's just gotsta trust Him."

Harley Crawford patted his trouser pocket to make sure the key to the bank vault remained safely in his possession. From his hideaway, a triangular hunter's lean-to attached to a mature sassafras tree, the jaundiced man looked out on the woods about a half mile off the old buffalo trace outside Washington. Shaky fingers ran over his mutton chop beard as he considered his options.

With Yates still unconscious, he reckoned his chances of accessing the bank vault were either improved or riskier than ever. It had never been his intention to beef the banker. He had never killed anyone.

Despite the new twist, Harley was hopeful, confident even, that he could euchre Yates out of the goods in the Washington bank. And when he did, he would find a way to fetch his blonde-haired, blue-eyed dolly girl and whisk her away on the first steamboat leaving from Maysville, just four miles north of town.

A twinge of remorse panged Harley. He had not planned to hurt anyone, but things just didn't work out the way he had planned. Life just wasn't fair. It hadn't been fair his whole life long. It was not right that some folks were flush with money and fine houses while he had no home. His ma, a saloon girl from Surry County in North Carolina, had passed from some kind of illness when Harley was halfway between hay and grass, neither man nor boy. He was considered too old to adopt, but was too young to make a respectable living. His health had never been favorable. Poor living conditions and lack of nutrition aggravated a chronic respiratory condition. Recurrent chest infections and pneumonia left Harley weaker than most young men his age. What was a boy to do?

Fritz, the bartender, allowed Harley to pick up some odd jobs around the saloon. An unusual character, Fritz was a German immigrant with a thick accent who tended bar in leather bundhosen and suspenders. He put on no airs, wearing finery like other barkeeps. He said his workwear from "the motherland" was sufficient for his work in the new country.

Fritz kept a loose watch over Harley, who, after his mother died, never had his own room. When business closed down each night, and the last patron passed through the bat-wing doors of the saloon, Harley fashioned a bed of sorts near the single, wood-burning stove. He had a roof over his head and sparse meals, but little more.

Harley, by observance, learned to play Faro, Poker, Brag, and Three-Card Monte. The players who downed Fritz's rotgut paid no attention to the spindly young man lurking in the dimly lit saloon. From the shadows, Harley watched the hands play out. Over and over he saw how loose and foolish men became at the gaming tables, the more oh-be-joyful they consumed.

By the time Harley was 15, Maxwell, a regular dealer, engaged him as a shill. When playing Three Card Monte, Harley would pretend to play the game to give the illusion to unaware patrons, or marks, that it was a straight gambling game. The mark would be drawn in, thinking he was capable of winning. Maxwell usually let the new person take a hand or two; but then, once his confidence was high and his bets raised, with sleight of hand, the evasive "money card" was manipulated around the mark's bets.

Harley's first run-in with the law came when a customer, full as a tick, lost a big pot and called Maxwell out as a chiseler. Quick as lightning, the inebriated man drew a gun on Maxwell. Everything happened so fast, and then time stood still. Harley knew someone was fixing to take an unexpected trip to the bone orchard. His thin lips, barely visible under ordinary circumstances, all but disappeared while he made quick deliberations. With no weapon of his own, Harley used the only thing he had in his possession— his empty hands.

Harley had sat out the round and watched the game with his hands resting on his thighs. When the mark drew his gun, quick as a whip, Harley flipped the table. Cards and drinks went flying. The gunman fired.

A shot ran through Maxwell's upper arm. It tore through his humorous, but cleared the brachial artery, which saved Maxwell's life, but ended his card dealing days.

The law was called in. Harley was questioned and warned by the deputy about his associations and the path they were leading him down. By the end of the day, Harley decided to move on and left Fritz and North Carolina on a meandering, undetermined path that eventually led to the East Coast.

Harley never maintained permanent employment. With recurrent health issues, including blackouts and seizures, he floated from place to place for several years without putting down stakes. In 1850 he happened into Germantown, Pennsylvania, at the same time Gustav Dentzel arrived from Germany with a full-sized carousel. His father, Michael, had sent him and his brothers to America to test market the family business.

Previously, Gustav, along with his father and their entire family, had spent their summers traveling around southwest Germany. They shared their carousel ride at fairs and carnivals across the country. Building on his father's dreams, Gustav began the work of carving out a business creating flying horses and menageries that he hoped would find their way to locations around the United States.

Harley Crawford connected with Gustav Dentzel at a transitional time in both of their lives. Harley garnered favor with Gustav for no obvious reason. He simply happened to be available and on site when Gustav arrived from Germany with his business plan, carousel, and dreams. In Harley's favor, his years with Fritz had provided a few German phrases and an ease in dealing with a foreigner lacked by some.

Harley worked with Gustav doing everything from sweeping shavings and painting the saddled creatures to installing gears and cranks. When a portable model was ready, Harley was on the team of operators who took it out on the summer fair circuit. He knew everything about the carousel and the calliope that whistled cheerful melodies as steam blew through its pipes.

It was the carousel that brought Harley to the Germantown Fair in Maysville last year; and it was the dream of a doll-like girl that compelled him to return. Since the previous summer, Harley had spent his spare time carving a music box. Meticulously, he fashioned a tin musical roll that duplicated the song the calliope had played when the girl had ridden the carousel. It was his intention to give it to her as a gift.

Seated inside the hunter's lean-to, Harley opened the music box and listened to the song that made memories of a blonde-haired, blue eyed angel dance in his dreams.

CHAPTER 13

The sun washed brilliance over Penny's beloved Briar Hollow. Morning drops of sparkling dew displayed a spectrum of shimmering colors on blooms and foliage in the wildflower garden. Wafting ambrosial scents mingled, transcended at times by the heavy, potent smell of honeysuckle or the sweet aroma of bluebells. Soft winds swept graciously through the hollow sending the birch trees' delicate leaves fluttering in a wave offering of early morning praise.

With so much on her mind, Penny welcomed the morning quiet. Roo's crack-of-dawn prattle had come and gone, but the cabin dwellers were not yet out and about. Penny watched as a black swallowtail caterpillar worked its way along the tender outer edge of a leaf of Queen Anne's lace.

"How is it you can eat those leaves, but they give me a rash?" The banded larva gave no reply. Penny stooped to a neighboring plant and pulled it up by the root. The distinct smell of carrots and dirt filled the air. "You eat those leaves," Penny addressed the busy caterpillar, "and I'll take this over for Lucy. I'm sure she will enjoy a little treat, too. Horses love carrots."

Penny drifted from the wildflower garden through the yard. As her feet wandered, her eyes moved about the hollow, bouncing from sight to sight until she focused on the building materials near the old apple barn. There it was, all piled up—the symbol of Zion's plans—waiting, just waiting, for things to get back to normal. It seemed waiting was what everyone was doing these days. *So much for our plans for this season*, Penny mused.

What about My plans? The inaudible impression of God on Penny's spirit was unmistakable.

"Your plans?" Penny audibly answered the silent rebuke. "To be honest, Lord," Penny's lower lip trembled and her eyes glistened, "I'm not too happy with Your plans lately."

Zion had rehearsed Jeremiah 29:11 at many family devotions. The words of the Scripture chased down the echoing chambers of Penny's heart. *For I know the thoughts that I think toward you, saith the Lord, thoughts of peace, and not of evil, to give you an expected end.*

Penny shook her head to strew the words away. God's promises weren't matching up with her reality at the moment. Life was simply not making sense.

Penny opened the barn door to find Lucy in her stall, lying down on her sternum with her muzzle to the ground. Her entrance caused the horse to waken slightly, but after a few moments, the pregnant mare drifted into deeper sleep, swaying and twitching her legs slightly. A snuffly whicker eked out her muzzle that was smashed against the ground.

Logan watched from the haymow. He did not know what to do. Should he be as still and quiet as possible, or should he make his presence known? His recollection of the first time he made a surprised encounter with the girl made his decision for him.

Logan stretched and feigned a loud yawn Penny was sure to hear. Noisily, he stomped into his boots and descended the ladder into the lower level of the barn.

"Good morning, Miss Mayfield."

With the initial sound of Logan's yawn, Penny realized she had forgotten a key piece of information. Logan Mayfield was sleeping in the haymow. How she hoped he did not think she had entered with the intention of a morning rendezvous.

Sleep lingered in hazel eyes handsomely adorned by bushy brows, and a warm smile broke out above a dimpled chin. Logan smoothed his tawny hair before mashing his Pullman-brown bowler over its thickness. Six feet tall, the young man was certainly trim, but not gangly. He lacked the muscular build of the laborers in Penny's life, and yet she had to admit there was something compelling about his looks.

Logan Mayfield carried himself with the mannerisms of the wellborn, but without an elitist attitude or haughty spirit. Yes, as much as she tried to delude her own thoughts, her own emotions, there was something about him that stirred her in ways she had never before experienced.

Logan's black terrier-mix mongrel stood on his hind legs, entreating his master's attention. "Good morning, to you, too, Banjo."

Penny sucked in her bottom lip and searched for the appropriate response to the situation she had placed herself in unawares. Her morning routine had certainly been abbreviated in her rush to get outside for some quiet time. She had hastily slipped on her shirtwaist and skirt, but forsaken her shoes and hairbrush.

A slender hand tucked silken tresses behind a dainty ear and then slowly trailed to the end of a long, golden strand. She twirled the bit of hair between her fingers before she released it and crossed her waist to clasp the elbow of her opposite arm. In vain Penny wrestled with the knowledge that bare toes tucked out beneath her calico hemline, and she cast a furtive glance at the offending digits.

Logan followed her gaze and noted her discomfort. "You're up early today. Is everything ok?"

Penny's pale cheeks flushed under his scrutiny. Deliberately she schooled her timbre and replied with a calm that belied her galloping thoughts. "Yes," Penny raised her cornflower blue eyes to connect with Logan's amber-flecked orbs. "I was in the wildflower garden." She raised the hand that held the plant. "I thought I'd bring Lucy a treat."

Concern made its way across Logan's handsome features. He hesitated to say anything. After all, Penny had been raised with horses; but his concern for Lucy and her foal compelled him to speak. "Have you given Lucy wild carrots before?"

"No." Penny shrugged. "Why do you ask?"

"I'm not a horseman, as you know." Penny nodded her head. The corner of her thin pink lips began a turn upward as she watched Logan search for the right words.

"I've done a lot of reading, Miss Mayfield, and it comes to mind that I read in the *Farmer's Almanac* that wild carrots could be injurious to horses."

"You read that? In the *Farmer's Almanac*?" Penny could hardly believe Logan's library included such a provincial publication; nor could she bring herself to believe she might injure Lucy or her foal due to her own ignorance.

Logan maintained a humble posture, but confident in his recollection, nodded his head at the girl. "Among other things: like how the Chippewa Indians board their babies; and quite the tale of a Frenchman and a skunk."

"I see." Penny carefully studied the wild carrot in her hand, turning it from one side to the next as if signs of toxicity could be discovered on its surface. "I've never heard of such. I just wanted to give Lucy a little treat. She's been so uncomfortable."

114

Logan's warm smile confused Penny. Was he mocking her? Did he think she was an ignorant, silly girl? Still, she didn't want to take a chance on her brother's prize mare. "Well, Mr. Mayfield, I'll just check with Rosalie. She knows everything about anything growing in Briar Hollow."

"That's a wise idea." Logan lifted his hat with one hand and motioned to the door. "Or, ace-high, as Marigold says." A tooth-filled smile lighted the young man's face. He bowed slightly as Penny moved to the door.

Penny's befuddlement muddled Logan's thoughts. Her ethereal comeliness evoked a myriad of poetic phrases, while her words spun them with a hotchpotch parlance that was both bitter and sweet.

"Thank you," said Penny as she passed Logan and crossed the threshold.

"You're welcome."

"Oh, yes." Rosalie wrinkled her brow. "I'm so glad you didn't give this to Lucy."

"It really could have hurt her?" Penny's blue eyes filled with concern.

"Not only is Queen Anne's lace noxious to horses, it's known to cause miscarriages."

Concern transposed to horror. That Lucy or her foal might have been injured in any way caused Penny to retreat into silence.

Zion had watched the exchange. No one knew more than he how devastating the loss or damage of health to either Lucy or her foal might be to their enterprise. "Hey," he called out to the spooked girl.

Silence.

"Hey, Buttercup."

Penny slowly turned to her brother, her features staunch and expressionless.

Zion stepped to the girl, stretched out his good hand and twisted the invisible key over her mouth. With his index finger he tickled her bottom lip. "There, you're unlocked," said Zion. "You can talk now."

"Oh, Zion." Penny shook her head, her fine golden hair sweeping back and forth with the motion. "What if . . ."

"What if nothing." Zion took his sister's small chin in his work-roughened hand and tipped it upward. "The Good Lord was looking out for us again."

"That's right." Rosalie took the offending plant from Penny's hand. "Now, let me put that to good use."

"What are you going to do with it?" Penny regarded the plant as an interloper in her otherwise safe home.

"We can eat the root. It's the leaves and seeds we don't want for dinner." Rosalie snipped off the top of the wild carrot. "I do make tea from the leaves. It's a diuretic. And the leaves and seeds when used properly can help people with digestive issues."

Rosalie pinched the stem and caught the thick sap that oozed from it in a saucer. "Even this is good for something. It makes a remedy for cough and congestion. The key is knowing how to use the things God's given us."

Logan admired Rosalie's knowledge and insight. He thought back to the times in his past when he had previously considered farming families simple. He had been wrong. Living simply was not the same thing as being simple minded.

"What a wonder you are," Millicent had watched the interchange from her vantage point in the rocking chair, "and what wonders our God has made."

"That's right." Zion thumped his chest with his fist. "You know, I always thought I was wonderful, but lately I've come to know it for a fact."

"Is that right?" Rosalie shook her head at her capricious husband.

"It is indeed, fair lady. I read it in the Good Book."

"I know the Bible talks about Zion and wonders, but I don't think the Scriptures were referring to you personally, Mr. Coldwell." Rosalie's lilting voice revealed the mirth her husband inspired so often and so well.

"You have it all wrong. I can prove I'm wonderful from the book of Psalms. Chapter 139 and verse 14 says, 'I will praise thee; for I am fearfully and wonderfully made.'" Zion slapped his knee with his right hand. "See that?"

"Why don't you enlighten us?" asked Penny.

"You heard it. The Holy Word of God said I'm wonderfully made. That means He made me wonderful. Right?"

Penny rolled her eyes. "Ok, Mr. Wonderful. Didn't King David write that? How can you say that applies to you?"

"I think I know the answer to that," said Logan. "We studied the Psalms in one of my Wesleyan University classes."

"You always did so well in school," said Millicent, happy to see her son join in the conversation.

"Professor Merrick spent considerable time on Psalm 139. He said there was no other place in Scripture where God's greatness was so strikingly set forth and that 139 was considered by some to be the 'crown of the Psalms.'"

"The 'crown of the Psalms,'" said Zion. "I never heard that before, but I can't disagree. It's always been one of my favorites."

"It is beautiful." Millicent swayed back and forth in her chair as content as a little one its cradle. "What else did Professor Merrick say?"

"That's what I was leading to," said Logan. "Yes, the Psalm was written in first person by King David, but he addressed it to the chief musician for everyone to sing. His words were meant to be sung by every member of the congregation."

"And if they were singing it saying 'me' and 'I' that's the way it was meant to be," Zion added.

"It's like when we sing 'Amazing Grace,'" said Rosalie. "John Newton wrote the words, but they apply to all of us."

"That's the gist of it." Logan smiled. It seemed a lifetime ago he had so enjoyed a conversation.

"So you went to seminary?" The thought struck Penny as peculiar. Logan was knowledgeable enough on this particular Psalm, but he lacked the peace and strong faith she and her family shared.

"No. Wesleyan University is the first academic institution named after John Wesley who founded the Methodist church, but it's not a seminarian school. I took some religious courses, but the curriculum included many other areas of study. In particular, I concentrated on modern languages."

Millicent rose from her chair and threaded a small hand beneath her son's elbow. "Logan's a writer."

"Oh, really?" said Rosalie. "Have you written anything we would know?"

Logan forced back a scowl. "No. Nothing you would know, Rosalie."

"His book was lost in the fire while he was putting the finishing touches on the last chapter." Millicent patted Logan's forearm. "It was fine work, too, Son."

Compassion swept over Penny as quick as a spring shower crossed the hollow, softening the soil of her heart for the young man.

Penny considered herself an overcomer. She had experienced heartbreak that could have made her a bitter, wounded young lady; but she chose to live above the tragedies of the past, not beneath them. At times, however, memories rushed in like unexpected waves that crested with frothy spumes of emotion.

Loss. Raw pain. They no longer tortured or taunted, but they were undeniable parts of the quilt of Penny's days. That's how she considered life—like a patchwork quilt in the hand of God. Each day, each season, each event made up a piece. Some were cheery florals or bright patterns; some were dark, and some were just plain old boring beige. Yet each fragment belonged. Every scrap had passed God's inspection, she knew, because she believed His Word.

In the Bible she read that every trial Job had endured had been first presented to the Lord and allowed by Him. They had been terrible tragedies, to be sure, but Job's end had been greater than His beginning.

Penny took particular comfort from Paul's letter to the Romans. He had written that all things worked together for good to them that loved God and were called according to His purpose.

Besides the beloved Scriptures that brought her such reassurance, Penny had a special thought that had seen her through many dark days. When she felt distraught by the heaviness of life, she would close her eyes and picture herself sitting cross-legged right in the palm of God's hand. Whenever she felt she wasn't strong enough to carry what life brought her way, she reminded herself that she didn't have to be strong as long as she remained in God's strong hand. Such consolation she experienced when the God of all comfort lifted her above her struggles and filled her very soul with His comforting Spirit.

Penny looked at Logan in a new light. She realized she had been judging him by one scanty patch of his quilt. He was more than a singular incident at the swimming hole. Logan Mayfield was a complex young man dealing with tremendous challenges who had risen to do everything in his power to care for his widowed mother.

Her perception of Logan changed from an awkward, inept intruder, to a vigilant, determined survivor. As surely as the momma of that black swallowtail caterpillar had transfigured from a creeping worm to a flying beauty, a transformation occurred in Penny's heart. Mercy and forgiveness eased in where indignation had been roosting. She felt resentment lift off and fly away.

Mattie's whimper broke the silence. Rosalie moved toward the bedroom door to retrieve her son from his cradle. "It looks like it's time to get the troops moving. Marigold is coming by with Lucas to take Dahlia berry picking this morning."

Zion lifted an invisible bugle to his lips and blew out a rendition of *Reveille*. Dahlia emerged from the bedroom dragging her ragdoll by one arm. Tendrils of coppery hair escaped the confines of the little girl's braids, and light danced in her hazel eyes. "Daddy! Daddy! What's going on?"

"Major Mommy ordered the troops rallied. I was just giving the wake up call."

Logan lifted his hand in salute and stood at attention. "Your orders, sir?"

"Assemble the saddles and tack and everything we need to clean them: buckets, water, soap, sponge, and oil. Then meet back here for vittles in half an hour, Private Mayfield."

"Yes, sir." Logan bowed to the ladies then spun on his heel, making a crisp turn before heading out on his assignment.

Dahlia danced on tiptoes and mimicked Logan's salute. "What 'bout me, Daddy? What 'bout me?"

"You, Private Dahlia, are ordered to put on your choring dress and gather your berry picking gear. Aunt Marigold will be here with Lucas soon, and you want to beat the birds to the red mulberry trees, don't you?"

"Mulberries!" Millicent was delighted. "I have a lovely receipt for Cook's mulberry sauce. It was Andrew's favorite."

"Wanna come berry pickin?" asked Dahlia.

Millicent beamed at the invitation. "May I?"

"Sure," said Dahlia, "just put on your choring dress like me."

Millicent looked down on her costume. The wide pagoda sleeves of her mauve morning dress would certainly be in the way for berry picking. The lace collar could be removed, but the projection of her very full, crinolined skirt would definitely create an obstruction.

"If you don't mind, you can wear one of mine," Penny offered. She and Millicent were close to the same size. Although not a perfect fit, one of her dresses would suit for a berry picking adventure.

"You're so kind." Millicent reached for Penny's slight hand and wrapped it between hers. "Thank you, dear. On behalf of the mulberry sauce I'd like to share with everyone, I accept."

CHAPTER 14

Marigold arrived at the cabin with her usual flush and fanfare. On her way down the orchard path, she met Penny coming from the chicken house with a basket of eggs dangling from her arm.

"Hey, Penny. I see you have the girls' daily contributions to Rosalie's kitchen."

"Good morning, Marigold." Penny lifted the basket. "I sure do. They are laying nicely this spring. Do you need any eggs at your place?"

"Not today, thanks. Pa and Lucas wanted flapjacks this morning, so we still have plenty."

"Just let me know. The girls are outdoing themselves. Lavinia's gone broody, though, sitting in the nesting box all the time. She won't get out for much of anything, and she's been fluffing up at me whenever I try to look under her."

"Stick a burr in her box," suggested Marigold. "That'll get her going."

"That's not nice." Penny shook her head at the incorrigible girl. "She would peck at me, for sure if I did that."

"Who said anything about nice?" Marigold cocked her head and gave Penny a sideways glance. "Speaking of 'not nice,' how's Mr. Fancypants?"

"Logan?"

"Logan, is it? Not Mr. Mayfield . . . or that mudsill?"

Penny shook her head. "I've never called anyone a mudsill, Marigold Johnson."

"Hey," a dangerous spark lit Marigold's big brown eyes, "speaking of burrs and mudsills, that gives me an idea."

"Uh-oh. You have that look."

"I heard Logan say he was going to have your pale-faced hired hand exercise West today."

"That may be. They're working on cleaning the tack this morning."

"Perfect." Marigold rubbed her hands together in anticipation. "That means he'll take him out this afternoon. We'll be back from berry picking in time for dinner. I'll take care of everything."

Butterflies flitted in Penny's midsection. Foreboding or premonition, she knew not which, but she watched with apprehension as the spunky girl dashed inside the cabin.

"I see you've forgotten your hat again." Rosalie pulled four straw hats from pegs by the door and passed them out to the eager berry pickers. "Here, Millie. You take this. You don't want to get your lovely bonnet caught in the trees."

"Rosalie, I don't see why you're so down on sunshine." Marigold reluctantly tied the straw hat over her golden hair. "I know God made Adam and Eve robes to cover their nakedness, but I never read anywhere that He made them wear hats."

The rambunctious girl let out a sigh and turned to address Mrs. Mayfield. "Be that as it may, my sister is sound on the goose about your bonnet, Miss Millie. Those flowers are so pretty you might have a run in with some of my bees."

Laughter filled the cabin followed by a flurry of activity as Marigold hurried her berry pickers with all their berry picking paraphernalia toward the door. "Get a wiggle on, Lucas."

"Let's move on to the saddle, now." Zion ruffled his hair with his good hand and worked hard at being patient with his temporary disability.

Logan positioned himself next to West's saddle rack.

"First, take off the stirrup leathers and stirrups." Logan loosened the three-inch straps that connected the supports to the saddle.

"Good. Now take the leathers off the stirrups and put them in the bucket of water. Just set the leathers aside. We'll start on the saddle while those soak."

Logan was an excellent student and followed Zion's directions to a tittle. He submerged a cleaning sponge in a bucket of water until it was saturated and then squeezed most of the water out of it so that it didn't drip. Zion handed him a bar of saddle soap. "Rub this into the sponge until it's nice and soapy, and then lather up the saddle."

"Yes, sir." Logan worked meticulously, making sure he cleaned all the leather parts of the saddle and then wiped off the excess lather with a rag.

"Good work." Zion nodded. "Now use this sponge here for the neat's foot oil. Put just enough on it to make it slightly damp and rub it all over. Make sure you get the bottom and all the nooks and crannies. It's humid today, so we'll let that sit overnight."

"Neat's. Isn't that another name for cattle?"

"It is," Zion answered. "This oil is actually made at the slaughterhouse by boiling the feet of butchered cattle. The feet are boiled just a few minutes at first—long enough to loosen the hooves. Once the hooves are pulled off, the feet are boiled another eight or ten hours. The oil is skimmed off the top, screened, dried, and filtered until you get this yellow stuff here that works wonders on keeping up leather."

"That's a lot of work for one saddle."

"Saddles do lots of work for the folks who use them. It pays to keep your tack in good condition." Zion examined Logan's work once more and indicated his pleasure with a nod. Satisfaction in a job well done sat well in Logan's spirit.

"All the saddles deserve the same attention, but I confess I am a bit partial to this one. It belongs to West. I'm counting on him to make Coldwell Horse Farms an institution in these parts. He comes from a fine line of Thoroughbreds sired by Epsilon from Belle Meade."

"I've heard of Belle Meade Plantation," said Logan. "Harding, isn't it? William Giles Harding from Tennessee, if I remember correctly."

"That's right," said Zion. "He knows how to make a prime combination of sire and dam to produce a quality Thoroughbred. West is evidence of that."

"And the fact that he has amassed the largest collection of silver trophies and cups of anyone in America," said Logan.

"A body can't argue with silver trophies and cups now, can they?"

"No, sir."

Zion shook his head at the young man. "It's Zion, remember? You don't need to call me sir."

Logan eyed the big man and then slowly nodded his head. Everything was so different in Briar Hollow. In Connecticut he had been raised in an environment where an employee always addressed his employer with a title that showed deference. It was a change for him in Kentucky; but when he considered it, he liked the friendly feel of relationship and mutual respect. Since his first meeting with Zion Coldwell, Logan had felt accepted and valued as a person, regardless of the depth of his need or his abilities as a farm hand.

"You know," said Zion, "Harding's success has been attributed more to his hostler, Bob Green, than his knowledge of horses."

"I never heard of him." Logan looked up and gave Zion his full attention.

"It's a fact. Harding brought Green in as a slave when he was just a whippersnapper. He grew up working with the horses and eventually became his right-hand man. Green's just about famous for his horse smarts, at least among horsemen."

Zion stroked his fuzzy chin as he pulled up some old memories. "I remember Green. I met him several times over the years on trips with Dad. He always wore a white apron. It was like his signature. He was a character, ole 'Uncle Bob'; and many a gentleman in the horse business can attribute his success to Green for his help, especially at the yearling sales."

"I guess it takes more than just an investor to run a thriving operation."

"That's so," said Zion. "It's not a man's position that makes him, it's the difference he makes in the lives of others." Thomas, the barn cat, moved in one quick motion from the sunny spot he had occupied by the barn door to a ground-hugging crouch. Patiently he calculated the distance and the right time to pounce on a rodent who dared consider his barn a place to find a meal.

Zion and Logan watched Thomas give a quick shake of his yellow head before pouncing with amazing accuracy.

"Good job, Thomas." Zion applauded the cat and then turned to address Logan. "Now all you did for the saddle, you need to do to the stirrup leathers. We'll put everything back together tomorrow when it's good and dry."

"I'll get right on it." Logan reached for the leather strips and his soaping sponge. "Anything else?"

"That's it for now. After dinner we'll saddle West with Absolom's tack. His saddle isn't a perfect fit, but we'll use a thick wool felt pad that will absorb the pressure points. It will be fine for a quick run."

"Yes, sir . . . I mean, ok, Zion."

Zion waved his goodbye and with long strides crossed the yard. He pushed open the cabin door to find Penny and Rosalie bent over the table. "What's this? A party? In the middle of the day?"

"Oh, bosh, Zion Coldwell. We're working." Rosalie pushed back from the table to show him the *Flying Geese* blocks she and Penny had been arranging on the big tabletop. "We want to lay out the colors in order before we start sewing strips together. We just haven't decided which we like best: light to dark or alternating light and dark strips. What do you think?"

"I think that's women's work," Zion hooked his good thumb on a suspender strap, "and speaking of women's work, are you gonna whip up some grub around here, or am I going to starve to death?"

Penny read the time on the mantle clock with surprise. "It seems we just cleared the breakfast dishes. It can't be almost noon."

"It can be, and it is, and this man of the house is in need of some sustenance. Where's the victuals, womenfolk?"

"Oh, Zion." Rosalie cast a playful grimace at her husband. "You can't be that hungry watching Logan work."

"Woman, you cut me to the quick."

"Alright, you two," Penny interrupted. "Rosalie, I like what we've come up with here. What do you say I stack these in this order. We can lay everything out again this afternoon and get Millie's and Marigold's opinions."

"That sounds good," Rosalie answered and then turned to her husband. "It looks like dinner will be light today, since time got away from us. It was just so peaceful with Dahlia gone and Mattie napping. Sorry, dear."

"Oh, never you mind. I was just teasing. I'll feast on your beauty 'til the food is ready. The kids aren't back yet anyway. Can you use some help from a decrepit but ever-so-loving admirer?"

"Ick." Penny made a face at her brother. "Sometimes I think I'm going to get a cavity from all the sugar around here."

"Don't be jealous now, Buttercup."

"Ha. That will be the day." Penny placed the last strip of *Flying Geese* on the stack and set it on the sideboard. "I'm going to pick some lettuce for the sandwiches. I should have done it this morning when they were nice and crisp."

Penny grabbed a clean towel and knife and then headed outdoors. The sun shone bright overhead. For a moment she regretted leaving the cabin without her hat; but the lettuce grew in a spot that received shade until the afternoon, so she found quick relief once inside the fenced garden.

Penny planted lettuce three times a year. It added a nice touch to so many meals. Carefully, about one inch from the stalks, she harvested leaves from the more mature outside edges and put them in her towel. She left the inner to continue growing for another day. The sound of berry pickers making their way down the juniper-lined lane met Penny as she straightened herself from her cutting.

Marigold's voice rang out above the cheerful mix of happy chatter bantering about the lane. "I think you have more in your belly than in your bucket, Lucas."

"My bucket's full." Nine-year-old Lucas Johnson lifted his tin receptacle to prove his point. "How's yours, Dahlia?"

The little one clasped a biscuit tin with purple fingers and grinned with coordinating purple lips. "Mine's full, too."

"Ace high," said Marigold. "Let's get this whole kit and caboodle inside and wash up for dinner. Whatcha say?"

"I say, yes, yes, yes." Millie's eyes sparkled with pleasure. She had enjoyed her morning adventure, but her energy had waned beneath the hot Kentucky sun. The rocking chair in the cool cabin beckoned like a siren to a passing sailor.

The foursome emerged from the lane into the hollow. Penny waved to the entourage. "Welcome home!"

"Hey, sister-sister." Marigold passed her full bucket to her brother. "Lukey, will you take these inside? I'm going to help Penny. I'll be in shortly."

"Sure thing." With Marigold gone, Lucas assumed leadership of the little group. "Come on, Dahlia. Mrs. Mayfield looks played out. Let's get her inside."

Delighted, Marigold skip-walked to Penny as she closed the garden gate. "How was your morning?"

"Oh, it was just fine. Rosalie and I layed out the quilt strips in several arrangements. I'd like to get your opinion later if you have time."

Marigold checked the sun's position in the sky and thought for a moment. "We took longer than I expected. Let me see if I can get Pa to come here for dinner instead of making something at our place. Do you think Rosalie has enough fixings?"

"The time got away from us, too. We're just having sandwiches today. I'm sure there's plenty."

"I'll bring over some apricots. I picked a whole bushel of early ones and they are delicious."

Logan walked out of the barn carrying a bucket. From their vantage point in the bright sunshine, the girls watched undetected by Logan as he circled behind the building to dump the bucket's sloshing contents.

"Where's he going with that?" Marigold wondered aloud.

"He can't hurt anything behind the barn," said Penny.

"What about the asparagus?"

"I thought you knew." Penny swept a wisp of hair off her face and squinted at a location across the yard. "The bed your pa planted had run its course a couple of years ago. With the slope, there was too much water getting into it and the roots rotted. Zion started up a new bed out by the old apple barn. Do you see it?"

Marigold followed Penny's pointing finger. "Oh. I didn't know. I guess it's safe for him to dump his bucket there, then."

"That reminds me. This is the bed's second year. We should be getting some edible shoots now. It's been at least three weeks since I applied the compost tea fertilizer. I'll see if we might have some for our dinner."

"You do that, and I'll go fetch Pa and the apricots."

"All right."

"You want me to tell your hired hand it's eating time?"

Uneasiness niggled at Penny, but her desire to make a first harvest from the new asparagus bed pushed it to the back of her mind. "Fine," Penny proceeded with deliberate steps to her destination and called over her shoulder, "I'll see you in a few minutes."

Marigold launched herself towards the barn where Logan had just hung up the bucket and was wiping his hands.

"Hey."

"Hi, Marigold," Logan answered stiffly, the memory of the girl's recent shenanigans fresh in his memory.

"The barn looks good." She eyed the clean saddle on its rest. "Is that West's saddle?"

"Yes, it is. Zion and I cleaned it today. I was just setting things back in order."

"Really?" Marigold seemed disappointed.

"Is something wrong?"

"Oh, no, there's nothing wrong as far as I can see. I just thought I heard Zion say West was going to be exercised today. I was surprised to see his saddle apart."

"Zion said I could use Absolom's saddle as long as I use the thick felt blanket underneath."

"Oh." Marigold nodded her head, her freckled face registered the new information and she quickly recalculated the particulars of her prank.

"It's almost time for dinner. Do you want me to help you saddle him up now so he'll be ready to go?"

Surprised at her offer, Logan did the gentlemanly thing and accepted, albeit reluctantly. Marigold made quick work of fetching West from his stall and launched her tutelage.

"Let me show you how my pa taught me." Marigold picked up the thick wool pad Logan had previously indicated. "Fold the pad in half, putting your fingers right on the center line of the fold, like this. Next, put the pad high up on the horse's neck and then slide it down into place centering it on his back but not down on his hips."

Marigold moved towards Absolom's saddle resting on its stand. "Before you pick up the saddle, put the cinch and the opposite stirrup over the seat, so they don't hit the horse when you put the saddle on." She lifted the saddle and gently slung it on West's back.

"Put it on soft as you can and then pull the pad up into the saddle's gullet. See how that makes a point in the pad?"

"I see." Logan watched intently, hoping to pick up any new insights or tricks that might help him in the future.

"Making that point in the pad helps keep the saddle from slipping down the horse's back and puts a little air space over his withers that keeps him comfortable."

"I'm sure West appreciates your attention to details."

A twinge of conscience tapped Marigold on the shoulder, but her mischievous nature brushed it aside and kept the prankster on task. "Now we go to the other side." Marigold patted West's hips as she circled his backside.

"When you're walking behind the horse, make sure you keep a hand on him, so he knows where you are. Now on this side, you just need to let down the cinch and stirrup and make sure the pad is in the right place and all the strings are hanging properly." A second time, Marigold patted her way around West's backside and returned to the fasteners.

"All right. Now we put this stirrup over the seat while you're working and grab hold of the cinch. When you reach for it," Marigold made eye contact with Logan, "make sure you face forward. That way, if West decides to throw a kick, you take it in your hindquarters, not your noggin."

"Good point." Logan nodded. Marigold eased in the cinch.

"Tighten the cinch slowly and gently. This gives him a bit of time to adjust. Since you're not riding just yet, leave this loose for now; and then after dinner all you have to do is tighten and buckle it up, and you'll be all set to go."

Logan admired Marigold's ease and confidence. "Thank you."

"My pleasure." Marigold winked. Her freckled face bore an expression that sent merriment and pernicious misgivings tousling in Logan. "I'm off to fetch Pa for supper now. You best wash up yourself. Penny said it was going to be ready shortly."

CHAPTER 15

"I'm looking forward to our ride this afternoon." Logan patted West's handsome neck. "I bet you're anxious for some exercise."

West nickered as Logan shut the corral door behind him. He turned to the house just as Penny made her way from her plantings.

"Is that asparagus?"

Penny smiled, pleased by her first harvest. "Yes, it is. We'll have some with dinner."

"Marigold said things were ready. Should I keep working?"

"Oh, no. We'll eat these just like God made them. Spring asparagus is wonderful right out of the garden."

"I've only had it cooked."

Penny lifted her towel filled with lettuce and asparagus. "Try one. It's sweet and nutty and so tender."

Logan reached for a spear and bit off its head. "Mm. It is good." The succulence of the young shoot surprised him. "I can't wait for dinner."

"Me, too. Let's go in." Penny took two quick steps toward the cabin and then abruptly stopped. Logan valiantly tried to keep himself from crashing into the girl who had halted so suddenly and without warning right in front of him. Pivoting in a quick turn, Penny's thoughts were on a new task when she found her face inches from Logan's.

"Oh," Penny whispered, "excuse me."

Logan sucked in air that lodged in his throat. The girl's nearness made breathing difficult and talking impossible. He stood mute—paralyzed by surging emotions while thrilling in their sweet agony. She was exquisite; so lovely in every way.

Logan admired her soft, dark blonde hair that looked golden beneath the noon sun, a fitting crown for such a comely maiden. Her fine features were carved in a most pleasing arrangement of startlingly blue eyes, aristocratic nose, high forehead and thin pink lips set in a lovely oval face. At five feet six inches tall, she was the ideal height to tuck perfectly beneath Logan's chin. It would have been so easy to close the short gap between them and capture the beauty's tender delicate lips in his.

Penny's eyes widened. Her pulse quickened. The sound of the songbirds faded and the breeze no longer stroked her cheeks as she slipped into an otherworldly tunnel that drove away every imposing environ.

Heat flushed her face and a battle raged between impulse and impropriety. She collected herself long enough to take a step back and break the spell that was drawing her, calling her like the swimming hole on a hot summer day that bid her to lose herself in its sweet waters.

"I'm sorry," she whispered.

"Not at all," Logan replied in matching airy tone.

Penny grappled for words, and then thrust her bundle of vegetables into Logan's hands. "Here," she said, "will you take these inside?"

The touch of her fingers sliding across his palms filled Logan with sublime sensation. How he wished her hands had lingered in his.

Penny stared at the bundle now in Logan's hands, consumed and stormed by a surprise attack of raw emotion. Slowly she raised her cornflower blue eyes to meet Logan's gaze.

"I didn't mean to stop so suddenly."

"It's quite all right." A soft smile turned up the corners of Logan's lips deepening the dimple in his prominent chin.

"I just thought to get some mint . . . from the half barrel . . . for Mr. Johnson."

"I see."

"We grow it in the barrel."

"Mmhm."

"Rosalie said if we don't keep it in a container it will take over the yard."

Logan nodded.

"Mr. Johnson likes it in his tea. Rosalie says it helps with his digestion."

"By all means." Logan watched the girl fidget and search to put her words in order. The realization that she was as disturbed as he caused his grin to grow into a tooth-filled smile.

"Why don't I just take this in then so you can get some?" Logan gave a slight bow and took his leave. Penny watched him go, his carriage erect as his long legs made confident strides across the yard until he reached the cabin and disappeared inside without looking back.

Baffled by her response, Penny lifted a finger and ran it lightly over her bottom lip. *He wanted to kiss me.* The thought pinked at her heart. The realization that she had wanted it too wiggled its way past her emotional safeguards into a place that demanded attention.

What's going on with me? Penny wondered as she made her way to the barrel overflowing with an abundance of fragrant herb. The established planting was ready for a spring harvest and drying that would supply Rosalie's coffers for teas, treatments and treats.

Using the blade of her knife, Penny cut fresh sprigs of mint for Matthias Johnson's tea. Words slipped unbidden with each snip.

The realization that she had slipped into a minty rendition of the flower oracle surprised her. "He loves me a little; he loves me a lot. He loves me scarcely; he loves me passionately. He loves me in marriage; he loves me not at all."

Penny eyed the big barrel of mint and chuckled. "I'd be an old maid by the time I finished plucking all this stem by stem." She laughed out loud at herself. "At least I can stop wherever I want."

The thought sobered the girl. *If it was up to me,* she wondered, *how would I want this oracle to end?*

CHAPTER 16

Marigold found her Pa working on fertilizer for his beloved trees. He made his own concoction of fish parts, sawdust, and straw.

"Hey, Pa."

"Afternoon. How was the mulberry picking?"

"Fine as a fandango. Lucas and Dahlia ate about as many as they picked, but we all filled our buckets. Even Mrs. Mayfield did a bang up job."

"Good to hear. I'm not one to deprive nature of their necessities, but I sure don't want the birds to get all the berries this year." Matthias reached for a jar of molasses and handed it to Marigold.

"You're just in time to add the finishing touch." He poked a stick into his compost. "Pour that in here while I stir."

"Why are you adding molasses to fish guts and sawdust?"

"Are you questioning your pa's husbandry skills, girl?"

"Oh, no sir. I'm just wondering why you're adding molasses to that pot of rot."

"You never saw me sweeten the fertilizer before?"

"No, sir. I can't say that I have."

"Well, you pour it in, and I'll educate you while I stir."

Marigold did as her father bid and dumped the molasses in the compost.

"Now I know you've heard the term 'slow as molasses,' but molasses ain't always slow. It actually speeds up the rotting process in this here compost mixture." Matthias gave the muck a final stir and straightened himself as much as his injured leg allowed. "Helps with the smell, too."

"Don't that beat all?"

"Yep. Molasses might be slow on the drip, but it hotfoots the decaying process, and that's what we need for good fertilizing."

"Speaking of hotfooting, Pa. Since we got back so late from berry picking, Rosalie invited us for a light dinner at her place."

"That's right congenial of her." Matthias pulled a handkerchief from the pocket of his worn dungarees and wiped a bead of sweat from his brow. "I'll be ready directly."

"Sounds good, Pa. I'll light a shuck for their place and help Rosalie get the food out."

"Tell Dahlia Pawpaw's coming to eat her up."

Marigold laughed. "I will! She'll be tickled to hear it."

Marigold grabbed some apricots from the bushel basket and carried them in a towel. Hurriedly, she took the path between the Johnson and Coldwell cabins, sidestepping for a quick moment to grab a cocklebur from a tree. She made sure to get a big one covered with stiff, hooked spines and then made a bee-line to the corral.

To keep West from spooking, she slowed and caught her breath before opening the gate and calling to the stallion. "Hey, West." Marigold approached the Thoroughbred and patted him on the neck. "You don't mind if I see how our fine helper, Mr. Logan Fancypants Mayfield, stands the gaff, do you?"

With a cautious glance she surveyed the property. Everyone was inside. She hesitated for just a moment, but her mischievous spirit got the better of her and she slipped the cocklebur under the blanket beneath the saddle's gullet.

"That'll kick up a row for sure." Marigold pictured Logan mounting West with a burr under his saddle and chuckled at her rascality. "Let's see what kind of stuff the dude is made of."

"It's pert near like a holiday in here." Matthias Johnson looked around the familiar cabin at the faces of so many people he loved. "We should have invited Pansy Joy and Garth."

"I think we're going to have to expand the cabin," said Rosalie, "the way our family is growing."

"I thought many a time about bumping out the back of this place. You could have a big living area and make the loft into a regular-like second floor with a stair case and all, just like downtown."

"If your daughter keeps producing these fine young'uns, we may just have to do that." Zion winked at his wife as she refilled Matthias' tea.

"Thank you, Daughter." Matthias sipped the cool beverage. "The Good Book does say to be fruitful and multiply, now, doesn't it?"

Rosalie shook her head at her father. How he and Zion loved to get her going. "Well, I think we're off to a good start. You seem pleased with the grand-offspring thus far."

"That I am," Matthias bounced Dahlia on his knee, "but you see, I'm gonna eat up this here Dahlia girl. She looks plumb delicious."

"Papaw! Don'tchu eat me up!"

Matthias bounced the giggling girl on his knee once more. "Ole Papaw loves to eat up little girls, doesn't he Rosalie?"

"He sure does." Pleasure swept through Rosalie at the sight of her little girl on her father's lap, her mahogany braids flying and hazel eyes sparkling.

Marigold bent her forefinger so that the top disappeared beneath the bottom. "Look here, Dahlia. Papaw ate off part of my finger of this afternoon."

Dahlia's joyful countenance turned to a gaping stare of horror. She looked at Marigold and then her grandpa and then her auntie again and then squirmed off Matthias' lap as quick as her little legs allowed. "Oh, Papaw! How could you?"

Zion's roaring laughter drowned out the chuckles and snorts of the family and guests gathered around the table. "Oh, Dahlia, my girl; don't you let Marigold get your dander up. She's just fooling around."

Marigold held up her hand with the "half missing" digit and slowly extended her finger in the little girl's view.

Dahlia's eyes grew larger and her jaw dropped farther than before. "Is that a mir'cle?" she asked Zion. "Like Pastor Dryfus told about in church?"

"No, Dahlia. That's just Marigold being Marigold."

"Oh." Dahlia looked disappointed and relieved at the same time.

Logan rose from his chair, his hunger satisfied and his mind set on his next task. "Thank you for dinner, ladies. I'll be taking West out for that ride now, Zion. How long should I exercise him?"

"I don't want you to take him for a gallop on your first ride. You two need to get to know each other first. I do want him to stretch his legs good, though. I've only ridden him to town the one time since my accident, and a Thoroughbred like West wasn't made to be kept in a corral."

"He is a beautiful animal," said Logan.

"I'll walk out with you and see how you two get along, and then we'll see where that takes us."

Matthias picked up his cane and rose to his feet. "I think I'll join you fellas."

The threesome left the cabin and ambled to the corral where West waited patiently inside.

"You already saddled him up," said Zion.

"Marigold actually did the saddling. She was giving me some pointers. We left the cinch a bit loose. I'll just tighten it up." Logan opened the gate and slipped inside the corral. When he tightened the cinch, West jumped.

"Easy, boy." Zion called out to his horse. "That's unusual. Logan, take it easy when you step in the stirrup."

Logan nodded and patted the stallion on the neck. "Come on, West. I'm counting on you to make me look good, friend."

Logan placed his left foot in the stirrup, but before he could mount the horse, West bucked hard.

"Whoa, boy!" Zion sprang into action. A horse of West's stature could easily kill a man. Zion's heart pounded. West bolted to the far side of the corral and Logan fell to the ground.

"Logan, are you all right?" He scanned the young man for signs of damage.

"Oh, my backside," he moaned. "I don't think I broke anything, but it does hurt."

"Thank God your foot didn't get tangled in the stirrup. You could have landed on your head and been drug across the corral—even stomped on." Zion helped the young man to his feet. Logan tried to hold back the moan, but it escaped before he could get it under control.

"Rosalie will know what to do to ease your pain; although there's nothing that will cure a sore tailbone but time."

"What happened?" Matthias asked. "I've never seen West act like that before."

"Me either." Zion crossed the corral making comforting sounds to his horse. "Come on now, West. What's gotten into you?" He looked at the saddle and everything seemed in order. West calmly allowed Zion to examine him, until he lifted the cinch. The tautness on the strap forced the bur into his back. The big horse stomped and whinnied.

"Easy, boy. Easy." With his good hand, Zion loosened the cinch and freed the horse of the saddle. He pulled off the blanket and discovered the source of West's peculiar behavior.

"Look at that." Zion attempted to pull the cocklebur from West's back, but it was entangled in his hair. "Pa, will you have one of the girls fetch me some cooking oil and a fine toothed comb?"

"Surely." Matthias leaned into his cane and left on his mission while the two younger men considered what had happened. "You said Marigold saddled West?"

"That's right," said Logan. "I watched the entire time. There was nothing on his back; and the way Marigold handled the blanket with her fingers in the fold there, it's simply not possible there was anything like that on the blanket without her knowing it. She would have been jabbed, without question."

"That just doesn't make sense. It looks like someone did this on purpose, but who?" Zion let his thoughts wonder as the assemblage in the cabin burst through the door and moved en masse down the slope to the corral. Penny was the last of the entourage. She trailed behind with the oil and comb. Zion watched his sister. Anger rose as a hypothesis formed.

Penny had not been herself since Logan had come on the scene. Zion had never seen her act so unkindly toward anyone or anything her entire life. She had been outside getting mint when everyone was in the house and Marigold had run home to fetch her pa. As far as he could tell, she was the only one who had the opportunity or reason to sabotage Logan's ride.

"Are you all right, Logan?" Millicent hurried to her son's side.

"I will be, Mother." Logan offered a cross of grimace and grin. "I just took a hard fall to the tailbone."

"'Twas most peculiar," said Matthias. "I ain't never seen West get his back up so."

"I found the reason for it, Pa." Zion locked eyes with Penny as he addressed his father-in-law. "It seems someone planted a cocklebur right under his saddle. When Logan tried to mount, West reared and Logan fell hard on his backside."

Penny watched as her brother practically bore holes through her. *He thinks I did it!* Shock ripped through her at his unspoken, but very clear accusation.

Brother and sister maintained eye contact, each trying to read the other while Marigold clasped her hands together and watched in silence.

"Logan or West could have been seriously injured."

"I'm glad they weren't." Penny tried to remain calm as she walked toward her brother with the items he had requested.

"I cannot believe some foolhardy person would risk harm to someone or threaten our very livelihood. With a bad enough injury, West could be crowbait." Zion snatched the oil and comb from Penny's hand. "I think Logan should lie down; and if you don't mind, I'd like to tend to West alone. He's pretty shaken up."

Penny watched her brother move to the horse with a rigid back and steps of military precision. His actions let everyone know they had been dismissed.

There was no mistaking the tension between the siblings. "Ma?" Dahlia looked up at her mother.

Rosalie extended her hand to her little girl and wiggled her fingers in an invitation for Dahlia to put her small hand in hers. "Come along, baby girl. Daddy has work to do."

"Do you need help?" Millicent asked.

"I can make it, Mother," Logan winced as he stepped, "but I do confess lying down sounds perfectly wonderful."

"Rosalie will fix you up with something for the pain, boy." Matthias emphasized his point with a crisp nod of his head.

"And I will be happy to take it," said Logan. "I need to get back to work as soon as possible."

"There's no rush, Logan." Rosalie opened the cabin door. "I'll get some willow bark for the pain; and if that doesn't help, we can go to the Matheny's for some ice. That can help, too."

145

"Why don't you rest on my bed?" Millicent offered.

"Thank you, Mother."

Penny rushed ahead of the two into her room. "I'll pull the covers down for you."

Logan watched as Penny pushed back the quilt on the bed that she had so sweetly shared with his mother. He gingerly eased to a sitting position and attempted to take off a boot.

A gruff, indistinguishable noise accompanied the dropping of his foot.

"Let me help you." Penny knelt beside the bed and reached for Logan's foot before he had a chance to protest. She shimmied the first boot off and then reached for the second. "There," she rose and moved the boots out of the way, "now you can lie down."

"Thank you." Penny's humble assistance caused a swelling in Logan's heart—a sweet ache that numbed the pain emanating from his tailbone.

"Wait!" Rosalie called from the kitchen. "Let me have him take this first. It will be easier if he's not lying down."

Since Matthias first stepped foot in the cabin, Marigold remained mute. Her prank had gone up the spout, and she did not know what to think or how to act.

She watched the ladies ministering to Logan. Guilt weighed heavily, and she sought escape outside the cabin. From a safe distance she watched Zion pour oil above and onto the cocklebur. With care, he combed and gently eased the offending seed from West's coat.

She knew she needed to fess up, but considered things might go better for her if she waited until Zion cooled off. Shame hung on the girl like wisteria blooms dangling from an arbor in the springtime. As quiet as she could, she slipped down the path to her home to figure out the best way to approach her brother-in-law.

CHAPTER 17

"Thanks, Rosalie." Pansy Joy clipped off the tip of the sugar pea vine. "I've been craving pea shoots, but I didn't plant any peas this year."

"You know I always have peas." Rosalie carried baby Blythe on her hip as her sister harvested from her garden. "I confess, they don't always make it to the table. I come out with every intention of getting enough for a meal, but they are so sweet and delicious raw I nibble away at them. Before I realize what I've done, there are hardly enough left to serve."

"Since confession is good for the soul, I will admit that I came for another reason, too." Pansy Joy straightened from her work and slipped the scissors in her apron pocket. "Since Garth helped the Mayfields move into your place I've been hankering to meet them."

"I'm glad you came today instead of yesterday," said Rosalie.

"Why is that?"

"We had quite the hullaballoo here." Rosalie bounced her nephew on her hip and let her sister's curiosity simmer.

"What happened?"

"Zion was so angry." Rosalie shook her head at the memories of her evening conversation with her husband. "He's still not happy."

"Out with the details, woman!" Pansy Joy waggled a finger at her sister. "Don't keep me hanging like the wash on the line."

"I do need to bring those diapers in . . . ."

"Oh, Rosalie!" Pansy Joy stomped a foot in playful frustration. "Tell me what happened!"

"Thankfully no one was seriously hurt, but Logan has a bruised tailbone from a fall he took in the corral."

"How did he fall?"

"That's what all the hullaballoo is about. It seems someone planted a big cocklebur under West's saddle."

Pansy Joy gasped. "Why would anyone do such a thing?"

"That's what we haven't figured out. The rider or the horse could have been seriously injured; and without West, I just don't know what Zion would do."

"Oh my goodness." Pansy Joy lifted her basket and the sisters walked toward the cabin.

"Zion and Logan are out in the barn now, but poor Logan is hurting for sure."

"I imagine so. He took a hard fall?"

"I didn't see it, but from the way he's walking and the fact that he couldn't sit for dinner, I can only speculate."

"Poor fellow."

"He's handled it like a Thoroughbred," said Rosalie. "Why don't you stay for a cup of tea and you can meet Logan and his mom. Zion and Logan won't be long, and Penny and Mrs. Mayfield will be back from town any time."

Pansy Joy looked at her basket and smiled at her sister. "Since my mission is only half complete, I'll take you up on your offer."

"She's so big she looks like she could foal any day." Zion rubbed Lucy's ear. The mare dropped her head and leaned in for more.

"She looks uncomfortable," said Logan.

"You would know about uncomfortable now, wouldn't you?" Zion winked at his farmhand.

"Yes, sir, that's a fact." Logan nodded and smiled. "It's not too bad, though; and not nearly as bad standing as it is sitting."

"I'm just glad you weren't hurt worse."

"Me, too."

Zion kept his anger at his sister to himself. He had not cooled off enough to speak with her yesterday, and she seemed to have avoided him, as well. This morning he had only seen her at breakfast and had not wanted to discuss his concerns over the morning meal.

"We'll keep an eye on Lucy. She's been bagged up for over a month."

"That means her udders are enlarged, doesn't it?" Logan asked.

"Exactly." Zion reached for the cloth in the bucket of warm water Logan had carried to the barn. "This is Lucy's first pregnancy, so it's good to get her used to being handled. Her foal will have an easier time nursing if she doesn't resist because she's not used to being touched."

"I see." Logan watched as Lucy accepted Zion's manipulations without complaint.

"By doing this every day, we'll be able to tell when her udders first start to fill up here by the belly. Her nipples will thicken and hang down lower. When they get waxy, we'll know our new colt or filly is on its way in a day or so."

"You know your horse stuff, Zion."

"I love my horses." Zion surveyed his barn, a wistful expression on his face. "I had so hoped to have the new barn well on its way by now."

Logan understood Zion's frustration. He remembered how his father had worked to bring his dream of Mayfield Manor to life. He thought about the months he had personally invested in a book that was lost in one quick moment. "Sometimes life shanghais a man's best plans."

"That's right as a trivet." Zion ran his fingers through his hair and then shoved his good hand in his pocket. The big man breathed deeply, and a soft sigh slipped through his lips; his usual cheerfulness gave way to a momentary display of concern.

Not one to be defeated by circumstance, Zion purposed to chase away the mulligrubs with a word of faith. "The Good Book says 'Eye hath not seen, nor ear heard, neither have entered into the heart of man, the things which God hath prepared for them that love him.' Sometimes our plans get shanghaid because we're supposed to go a different direction than we thought."

"Do you really believe that?" Logan studied the man before him. The strength of his faith intrigued him.

"I do." Zion coupled his words with an affirming nod. "I know that particular Scripture is talking about spiritual things, but if you go down just a few verses it says that a person who is spiritual judges all things."

"And what does that mean to you?"

"That with God's help and His Spirit living inside, a man can read the proper meaning of things; that God can give him insight and understanding."

"But why does everything have to be so complicated?" Logan wondered aloud. "I mean, if God can show you now, why didn't He show you from the beginning and avoid all these problems in the first place?"

"That's a good question, Logan. You have a fine mind and your reasoning is sound on the goose." Zion patted Logan on the shoulder and motioned with his head to step outside the barn. "You see, this is a beautiful world, but it has its problems. It didn't used to be that way, but the truth is mankind is in a fallen state. There's sin in the world and because of that, bad things happen.

"God can and sometimes does help us avert hardships and trials. We have no way of knowing what He's protected us from, but sometimes we have to walk through things. It's during these times, even though I do have questions and concerns, I feel His presence with me. He's so near. And it's during these times I learn to trust Him more deeply."

Logan pondered Zion's words. They weren't easy, but there was a sincerity, an integrity in them, that resonated in his spirit.

The sound of hooves on the lane announced Sheriff Nash's arrival before he passed through the junipers and entered the hollow. He drew up his horse next to the men and dismounted.

"Hello, Zion; Logan."

"Good morning to you, Sheriff. What brings you out to the Hollow?"

"I wish it was a social call, Zion, but I want to update you on Yates' condition and my concerns about his attack."

"How is Mr. Yates?" asked Logan. The image of the man in a heap in the alley replayed in his thoughts.

"L.C. is still unconscious. Doc Byerly says it's pretty touchy. He doesn't know if he'll pull through or not."

"I still can't believe this happened in the middle of the day right in town." Zion shook his head and Nash nodded.

"What's worse is I was with him right before it happened. I'm none too happy about it, myself."

"I can imagine," said Zion. "Have you uncovered any details? Do you know who did this?"

"I can't say for sure, but it's my conjecture that robbery was the motive. L.C.'s wallet was missing, and I know he had it on him. He paid for our meal at the Paxton Inn just before this lowlife clocked him in the alley."

"Is there anything we can do to help?" Zion asked.

"I'd like to talk to Penny. I want to see if she has had any further recollections on who this rip might be."

"She hasn't mentioned any more about it to me." Zion turned to Logan to ask his opinion and then thought better of it. "Penny's actually off to town this morning with Mrs. Mayfield. I expect they'll be back directly if you'd like to talk to her."

Nash looked up at the sun. "I reckon I have a few minutes. It would be better to talk to her here than on the road."

"And I reckon my wife will have something to refresh you from your ride. Let's go inside and see what she's got cooking in there." Zion started toward the cabin followed by Nash. Logan held back.

"If you don't mind, I'm not much up to sitting inside." Logan winked at Zion. "I'll just take a little walk, if that's ok with you."

Zion had never experienced a bruised tailbone personally, but he could only imagine it was no pleasure to sit on one. "Sure thing." He winked back at Logan. "Come on in, if you feel up to it."

"Thanks." Logan turned toward the apple barn while Zion and Nash slipped inside the cabin.

"Mighty fine cobbler, Miss Rosalie." Sheriff Nash picked up the last crumbs from his plate with the back of his fork and finished them off with relish.

"Glad you liked it, Sheriff. More coffee?"

"Thank you, kindly." Nash lifted his tin cup to Rosalie who grabbed the pot with her apron and poured.

"You're welcome." Rosalie filled his cup and then her husband's and returned the pot to the warmer on the back of the stove.

"Penny hasn't talked much about the incident," said Rosalie. "She's definitely been more uptight than usual—more nervous, too; but she's really not shared any new memories or thoughts with me."

The cabin door swung open. Bright light filled the room followed by Penny and Millicent.

The men stood as the ladies hung their hats. "Howdy, Miss Penny; Mrs. Mayfield." Sheriff Nash greeted the women.

Penny's thoughts whirled with reasons the lawman might be at her home. "Hello, Sheriff." Penny's voice shook slightly. "Are you here with news about Mr. Yates? Did you catch the man who hurt him?"

"I do have news on Yates. He's no worse, but he's no better either. He's not regained consciousness or responded to pain, light or sound."

"I'm so sorry to hear that." Images played in Penny's memory. She furrowed her brow and drew her lips into a thin line.

"I know it troubles you, Miss Penny," said Sheriff Nash, "but I came out to see if you had any further recollections of the attacker. You said he seemed familiar, and often with a bit of time, pieces of memories can connect into a picture that might help with an investigation."

Nash watched Penny. She was nodding her head and twisting her hands, obviously conflicted. "I'm sorry to bring it up, but I want to do all I can to wind this up and see this doesn't happen again."

"Sit down, Penny." Rosalie scooted a ladder-backed chair away from the table and motioned to her sister-in-law. "Can I get you anything?"

"No, thank you." Penny sat rigid in the chair, her back straight as a poker. She schooled her hands in her lap, willing them to be still.

"I wish I could say I haven't given the matter any thought; but the truth is, it's troubled me greatly." Penny looked from the sheriff to her brother who offered a tender smile and nod of encouragement despite his earlier choler.

"I can't say I have a full picture for you, Sheriff."

"Anything you tell me could be helpful, Miss Penny."

Penny smoothed the folds of her dress and took a moment to frame her thoughts. "I wish I could say I didn't know anything and be done with it, but the truth is I do remember seeing that man before."

"Excellent." Sheriff Nash straightened in his chair, keen to Penny's every word. "Any physical details you recall?"

"He was average height, I would say; and he had whiskers."

"Good, good." Nash recorded the details.

"He seemed shaky and a bit hunched over, but that could have been because he was leaning over Mr. Yates when I saw him."

"Is there anything else about his physical appearance that stood out to you?"

"Just that he didn't look healthy. His eyes were sunken and he looked jaundiced."

"What was he wearing?"

"Nothing notable," Penny cocked her head and searched for the particulars, "just the usual men's apparel: wool trousers, vest and waistcoat."

"What was the quality, if you remember?"

"They looked like homespun: dark colored, a dark brown, I believe. His hat was low with a flat top, also brown."

"Miss Penny, this is very helpful information." The sheriff was pleased. He had something to work with; a start, at least. "Is there anything else that comes to mind, anything at all?"

Penny was reluctant to share the final detail. It seemed so ambiguous and unrelated; yet she didn't want to withhold anything that could help the sheriff with his investigation. "There is one more thing."

She paused and tried to bring the fuzziness into focus, but there was no image – only a sound. "It's peculiar, Sheriff, and I don't know if it has anything to do with the attack at all."

"It could be nothing, but it could be something." Nash eased back in his chair hoping his more relaxed appearance would calm the girl.

"It's crazy, I know." Penny chortled and shook her head. "It seems silly to bring it up." She shrugged her slight shoulders and let out a deep breath. "It's just I keep hearing music."

"Music?" Zion had watched from the sidelines of the conversation, but broke in with surprise at his sister's revelation. "What kind of music, Penny?"

Penny shook her head. "It's not clear to me. I just know at times when I think about the attack, I'm haunted by a song. I don't know its name and I can't place where I've heard it, but I know I've heard it before."

"That's all right, Miss Penny." Sheriff Nash rose to his feet and picked up his hat. "You've given me a lot to go on, and we'll just have to trust the Lord to help us bring all these pieces together and catch this hard case before he does any further damage."

"I'll walk you out." Zion rose, opened the door for the sheriff, and the two stepped outside.

"Zion, you let me know if anything unusual happens around here, will you?"

"Sure will, Sheriff." Zion tipped his head. "Anything else I should know . . . as the man of the house?"

"Nothing concrete," said Nash. "It's just that if Penny has seen this attacker before, that means he's seen her, too. She's a witness to his crime. If Yates passes and we catch the fellow, he'll be swinging for sure. If he thinks Penny can identify him—well, I just want you to keep an eye out for anything unusual. You might want to keep a weapon handy."

Zion looked at his arm in the sling. The sheriff sensed his vulnerability. "At least you didn't break your shooting arm," said Nash.

The sheriff mounted his horse and cantered him down the lane. Logan emerged from the side of the apple barn and stood next to Zion, staring down the lane as the sheriff disappear among the juniper trees.

"Zion," Logan called to his employer, but he did not respond.

"Zion," he called again.

"Oh, huh?" His reverie broken, Zion turned to face Logan. "Sorry. What is it, Logan?"

"I couldn't help overhearing your last words with the sheriff."

"Yeah."

"I'd like to help, if you'll allow me."

Zion eyed the young man. His countenance was earnest. "In what way?"

"In my previous life, before mucking stalls became my most favorite pastime, I had two great passions."

Zion chuckled. "And what could be more fun than mucking my horses' stalls?"

"As I said, I have two passions. You know about one: writing; the second is weaponry."

"Really?" Zion questioned aloud. "I didn't see that coming."

"A person with a build like mine needs to have some source of protection." Logan laughed at his self derision. "But seriously, Zion, I once had quite a collection of pistols and am very well trained in their use."

"So you're offering to be deputy of Briar Hollow?"

"No badge required," Logan nodded, "but I'm here if you need me. I do have one fine shooting iron left in my arsenal: my Beaumont-Adams. I had it shipped from Britain and it arrived the day after the house burned. It's a beauty; a double-action percussion revolver capable of shooting 12 rounds per minute. It's good up to 100 yards."

"It sounds like you know your arms like I know my horses."

"Every man has his interests," said Logan.

"Yes, and my most important interests are in yonder cabin." Zion looked across the yard to the structure that housed his family. For a moment he pictured an armed intruder threatening his loved ones and then shooed the images away.

"Well, now, Deputy Mayfield," Zion dropped a beefy arm around Logan's trim shoulders, "It looks like Briar Hollow has a new peace officer."

"That's just what I'm hoping for," said Logan.

"What's that?"

"Peace." Logan looked up at Zion who stood four inches taller than his six foot frame. "It's my preference not to have to shoot my fellow man."

"No good man wants to shoot another," said Zion, "but there may come a time when we have to protect those put in harm's way by men with evil intentions."

Logan threw up his hand in a salute. "Deputy Mayfield, reporting for duty, sir."

CHAPTER 18

Zion tipped his hat under the bright sun, making a bit of shade so he could better see his favorite horse in the corral. "Let's go say howdy to West. You and he need to keep on good terms, especially after yesterday's fiasco."

"Yes, sir." Logan punched his hands in his pockets and mustered the courage to bring up a subject that had been on his mind all day. "I was wondering if I could talk to you about something first."

Zion pondered what could be on Logan's mind. It was obvious he was thinking hard on something by the way he fell into calling him "sir" for the first time in days. All sorts of thoughts raced through Zion's mind.

"Why sure, Logan. What's on your mind?"

"Actually, you are."

"Me?" Logan's answer surprised him. "What do you mean?"

"I've been thinking about your barn situation."

Zion scanned the yard. His gaze settled on the old apple barn and the pile of building supplies off to its side. "Yep, we do have a barn situation. At least we have one viable building. The stock we have is sheltered, even if the milk cow is sharing it with the Thoroughbreds."

"With the new foal coming and the purchases you were planning for the fall, I don't see how you are going to fit all your horses in that barn, unless you're planning to stack them one on top of the other."

Zion snickered. "Nope, that won't work, will it? It looks like some other lucky horse farmer is going to benefit from my misfortune. I most likely won't be able to take delivery of the yearlings I've been hoping to buy from Belle Meade."

"I have an idea." Logan started toward the apple barn. "Come with me."

Intrigued by the young man's enthusiasm, Zion followed, his curiosity stirred.

When they reached the dilapidated building, Logan led the way inside and stood in the middle. "I know this barn was never meant for animals, but I was out here today thinking, and an idea came to me. This would be a great spot for a round barn."

"A round barn?" Zion scratched his head. "What made you think about that? And why do you think it would be a good idea for us?"

"First of all, the design I'm thinking of isn't really round, it's more of an octagon, which is easier to build than round."

"I can see that it would be. Tell me more."

"Did you know George Washington designed and built his own sixteen-sided round barn in Fairfax?"

"I'm from Virginia, and I never heard that before. How do you come to know about Washington's barn?"

"Reading." Logan smiled. "Remember my two passions?"

"Right: books and weaponry."

Logan nodded. His youthful face was alight with enthusiasm. "Even though George Washington implemented a round barn on his property, the design never became popular with the public. I think it's mostly a matter of custom. People build what they are used to building; however, I believe a round barn could offer you many benefits."

Zion sat down on an old crate. "Such as . . ."

"A circular structure is stronger in high winds, and Kentucky does get its share of twisters. In addition to superior stability, the inner workings of round construction can be arranged to make caring for your stock more efficient."

"I see." Zion listened carefully as Logan made his case.

"Consider this, Zion. The circular shape of a round barn has a greater volume-to-surface ratio than a square or rectangular one."

"Hold up there," said Zion, "and translate into words a man like me can understand."

"That means that round barns cost less to build. They don't take as many materials. The inner capacity of a circle is greater than a rectangle. You can get the same amount of square footage with 30 to 50 percent less expenditure."

"More barn for less money sounds good to me."

Logan's excitement rose, and he began pacing as he spoke. "Picture this: a circular design with the mow in the middle takes advantage of gravity to move hay from the loft to the stock below. You could even make a silo right in the middle of it with the horse stalls circling around."

The pictures Logan painted captured Zion's interest. He wanted more information before he took the concept to prayer and his wife. "What other ideas do you have?"

"When I was at university, a man named Orson Fowler was a guest lecturer. He spoke from a book he had written: *A Home For All*, and he had some unique ideas on the benefits of octagon buildings. He was focused more on homes, but his techniques would apply to building a barn as well. I think we could come up with a design so efficient you could work it with one hand tied behind your back."

"How about tied across my front in a sling?"

"I think we may be on to something." Zion reached for a second helping of fried potatoes. "I'd like to talk with Garth about it after supper."

"Goodness knows we've faced enough setbacks lately," said Rosalie. "Maybe this is why. Momma always said God never wastes anything. Perhaps He has been trying to get our attention so He could speak something new into our lives."

"That's a thought worth thinking." Zion sent a wave of affection his wife's direction so thick it was almost tangible.

"Perhaps He's doing that for each of us," Millicent mused aloud. "It is something how the Lord has connected us. I never would have signed on for this journey, but I know God is with me, still speaking, still teaching. And I want to keep growing and learning."

"Aren't you too old to learn new things?" Dahlia's innocent question sparked a round of chortles and laughs around the table.

"There's no age limit on learning, Dahlia." Penny folded her napkin into a triangle and wiped crumbs from the girl's face. "Are you too little to learn?"

"Nope. Today I learned to keep the diaper over Mattie while he's being changed or wee-wee goes all over the place."

"Oh, Dahlia, you're a caution." Rosalie flushed at her daughter's frank discussion during the evening meal. "I think we need to have a lesson on what makes good conversation at supper."

"Well, how about I change the subject to the gingerbread I smelled cooking in here this afternoon?" Zion rubbed his belly in anticipation.

"You, husband, might have a bad arm," said Rosalie, "but your nose is in perfect working condition."

"My keen sense of smell has led me to many a fine baked good."

"It looks that way." Penny jabbed her brother in the belly.

"That's muscle."

"Mmhm." Penny laughed and pushed away from the table. "I'll get the gingerbread."

Rosalie stood as well and began clearing the dishes to make room for dessert. "And I'll bring the coffee."

Zion and Logan made their way the half mile to the Eldridge Farm. Garth sat on his front porch reading a newspaper.

"Hello, the house!"

"This is a nice surprise." Garth stood and tucked the paper under his arm. "Business or pleasure?"

"How about the pleasure of doing business?" Zion took the steps up the porch two at a time. Logan followed. "May I present my associate, Mr. Logan Mayfield?"

"Associate, is it now?" Garth extended his hand to Logan and gave it a firm shake. "It looks like you've earned yourself a promotion since I drove you and your ma over from town."

A quick memory of Logan's pre-Briar Hollow despair flared, but was quickly replaced with a sense of purpose. His days with the Coldwell family had given him a new outlook, and he was determined to help them as much as was within his power. "I don't think I've been promoted from barn duty, but I do have some thoughts about the new barn. Zion thought we should get your opinion on a matter we were discussing earlier."

"Well, then," Garth motioned to the front porch chairs, "I invite you to my office for an official meeting. Please be seated, gentlemen."

Zion took a seat. "If you don't mind, I'd prefer to stand." Logan winced at the memory of his discomfort at the supper table not long ago."

"Logan took a fall and landed hard on his tailbone," Zion explained to his brother-in-law.

"That hurts."

"And that's a fact." Logan nodded, happy to stand, but feeling awkward about towering over the other men. "Why don't I just step off the porch so you don't have to crane your necks while we talk?"

"If you're more comfortable thataway." Garth turned to Zion. "Before we get down to business, how are Penny and Lucy?"

Zion laughed. "Do you want to know about the horse first or the girl?"

"Whichever order you want to give it to me."

"Well, Lucy's getting close. I expect her to foal any day. The poor girl looks big enough to be carrying a baby elephant, but I'm right proud of how she's handling herself."

"You're a true horseman, Zion, giving the stock report before the family news."

"The truth is they are both doing well. Penny was definitely shaken by the attack, but she seems to have come through the worst of it." Zion motioned to Logan's gun holster. "We are taking some precautions just in case the rip that clocked Yates has any notions of taking out the witness to his crime."

"Do you really think that's a possibility?"

Zion shook his head. "There's really no way to know. The sheriff stopped by and we discussed it. We don't know who this is or what kind of man we're dealing with. It's my hope he's cleared out of Mason County, but I don't want to be caught unprepared."

"That's best, I'm sure." Garth turned to Logan. "It's a good thing you showed up when you did."

Logan received Garth's words and tucked them away for further consideration when he had the time. With all that had gone so wrong in the last few months, the thought that somehow things might be coming together for good was a welcome sentiment.

"I'm glad to be here."

"Do you two want a cup of coffee or anything?" Garth looked from one man to the next. "Pansy Joy is giving Blythe a bath and

Maggie is 'helping.' Otherwise I'm sure she would have been out here passing some kind of drink or dish at you."

"We left the house right after supper, and I'm full up. Do you want anything, Logan?"

"I'm fine, thanks."

Garth chuckled softly. "You should have seen Blythe. He got a hold of his dish at suppertime and put it on his head like a hat. Food was dripping all over the place. He got it on his sister, too."

"It must have been a *bowler*," said Logan. Laughter erupted and Logan relished the feel of it. "Speaking of round containers, that's the reason we're here."

"Oh really?" Garth leaned back in his chair. "Well, let the cat out of the bag, then."

Zion took the lead. "Logan has an idea about the new barn."

"I know you really wanted to have that project well underway by now."

"I did," Zion nodded, "and I admit I've been disappointed how things have turned out, but maybe there's a reason for it. Tell him your thoughts, Logan."

"I've been looking out at the pile of building materials and the old apple barn, and the same idea keeps coming to me. Instead of a standard rectangle barn, I keep seeing a picture of a round barn."

"Round, you say?" Garth stroked his chin between his thumb and forefinger. "Why do you think a round barn would be better than a standard rectangle?"

Zion and Logan replayed the details of their previous discussion, piquing Garth's interest. With his expertise in mechanisms, efficiency continually factored in his thoughts. "It does seem like it would be easier to feed the stock—could be easier to clean, too."

Garth stood and worked up some options. "If you made a silo in the middle, with a walkway between a circular row of box stalls and the silo, you could install chutes from the haymow for hay and grain that drop at a central feeding alley. You would hardly have to move the feed at all. "

"That could save a lot of time," said Zion.

"If it was large enough, you could make an inside track to exercise the horses in bad weather or warm them up on a cold winter day." Garth stopped and clapped his hands in excitement. "Picture this: a track system along the ceiling for a manure bucket to move along the outer edges of the stalls."

"That would be easier than carting manure from one end of the barn to the other." Zion rose to his feet.

"And with this construction, I really think you could increase your capacity for storage in the haymow," said Garth.

"In bad weather," Logan interjected, "since the silo is filled from the haymow, once the feed is inside you would never have to expose it or yourself to the elements."

"That's a bonus, for sure." Zion nodded his enthusiastic agreement.

The gears in Garth's brain spun, cranking out new ideas by the minute. "How about this: if we could figure out a way to make a dome-shaped roof, we could nearly double the capacity of the haymow."

"If we build the silo up the center," said Logan, "it could act as a roof support. We wouldn't need tresses like in a standard barn. I think it's quite feasible to build an unobstructed haymow."

"And if the silo is covered by the barn, it wouldn't need to be boarded up on the outside," Zion added. "That would save even more on the building costs."

"I can picture it now." Zion closed his eyes and dreamed his dream. "On the ground floor we could build a saddle room, a veterinarian's room with medicine and supplies, a small office, and a nice-sized foaling stall."

"How about a water tank on a third floor? Putting a tank up high like that would provide water under pressure to any part of the barn. Fill the tank once, and you would have water on hand anywhere you needed it."

The advantages of Logan's idea took root in Zion. He was ready to tear down the old apple barn with his one good arm and get started right away. "This is getting better by the minute."

Garth's machinist brain was in full production mode. "How about a windmill on top to pump water to the upper level tank? And a freight elevator to move things from floor to floor?"

"Hold up, Garth." Zion looked at the long shadows cast by the evening sun. "Would you be available tomorrow to sketch out some plans? I want to get home to check on my family."

"Sure thing." Garth punched his hands into his pockets excited about the project in a way that hadn't motivated him since he purchased his portable double-blast thresher. "I might draw out some ideas this evening."

Zion stepped off the porch and stood next to Logan. Garth picked up his newspaper, ready to dash inside and find some drawing paper and a pencil. "Oh, before you go, let me tell you what I read in the paper."

"What's going on in the world today?" asked Zion.

"This is the weekly out of Lexington, Pa brought it home last week, but I've been so busy I just finished reading it. There's an article here on Lee surrendering his Army of Northern Virginia on the ninth of this month."

"What does it say?" The desire to read a paper cover to cover swept over Logan; his appetite for reading and news and learning whet by the carrot tucked beneath Garth's arm.

"It seems Lee abandoned the Confederate capitol in Richmond and planned to meet up with forces in North Carolina. The Union

Army cut them off. Lee launched an attack at the Appomattox Court House, but his plans ended in surrender."

"What else did it say?" Logan's desire was etched on his face.

"Would you like to borrow my paper?"

"Very much." Logan rubbed his palms together; his hazel eyes sparkled with anticipation.

Garth passed the paper to Logan and then addressed his brother-in-law. "Besides the war news, there's a one-year anniversary article on the passing of the Coinage Act of 1864. I thought you'd be interested in reading that."

"I'll take a gander at it as soon as Logan finishes with the paper. Let's light a shuck for home and check on our womenfolk."

Logan was unsure which appealed more: reading a paper or seeing Penny. When the thought struck him that he could do both, his pace quickened. For the first time in years Logan Mayfield felt like whistling. He puckered up and blew out a cheerful rendition of *Ole Dan Tucker.*

"Where does a university educated, wellborn young man like yourself learn a song like that?"

Logan stopped whistling and tried to place the song. He conjured forth the memory of fiddle music drifting across the grounds of their family's Connecticut property. "When I was a boy, I used to hear it played by the gardener in the evening. He often played his fiddle when the workday was over."

"That's a plucky tune, indeed."

"I never knew the words, just the melody."

"Well, there are many renditions," said Zion, "with more being written all the time."

"It's not offensive, is it?" Logan recalled his father's disapproval of the dancing game the workers sometimes played when the gardener fiddled.

"That depends on the rendition you're singing." Zion laughed as memories of his old friend Balim flooded his senses like a quick spring rain filled the furrows around the farm.

"Balim was forever making up new lyrics. Of course, he always got some gospel message in there somehow."

"Was Balim your minister?"

"Balim was my slave."

The revelation astonished Logan. "Really? I never pictured you as a slave owner."

"It's a long story." Zion didn't feel like going into a drawn out narrative of his family's history. Not that he was ashamed; his father had always treated their slaves more like valued employees—family even.

"I'll tell you about it sometime, Logan. Suffice it to say that no Coldwells have purchased a slave for over two decades, and Balim's been free for over five years. He's married and lives in Canada with his wife, Minnie, and a couple of kids."

Zion's smile revealed the tender relationship between the two men. "Balim was my best friend. I hated to see him go—Penny, too."

"Penny and Balim were close?" The mention of his "provincial pixie" spiked Logan's interest in an already engaging conversation.

"Yes, they were. Balim was always there for Penny, especially after our parents died. He supported her in ways I just couldn't bring myself to."

"I'm sure you did your best by her."

"Oh, I took care of her physical needs as well as I could, but to tell you the truth, my faith went through the mill."

Zion's confession caught Logan by surprise. His faith seemed bedrock—the foundation on which everything else in his life rested and built upon. It was like his mother's had always been and like his father's shortly before he passed.

"About Penny . . ." Zion interrupted Logan's musings.

"Yes?" Logan's every faculty roused to attention.

"I plan to talk to her about what she did. She owes you an apology."

"For what?" Logan had no idea what Zion was talking about. As far as he knew, Penny had no reason to owe him an apology.

"It's pretty clear she was the only one who had the opportunity to put that burr under West's saddle." Zion shook his head, dismayed and puzzled by his sister's apparent lack of judgment. "And for some reason she's been as flustered as a nesting bird whenever you come around. She gets to fluttering and squawking. I've never seen her carry on so."

"Is that a fact?"

"It is. I'm befuddled by it. She's my sister. I've known her all her life."

"Perhaps she's just upset by all that's been going on with the attack and your injury." Logan offered an excuse for the girl who looked so innocent, but evidently had a bit of what Marigold called "Kilkenny cat."

"I'd like to credit it to some pardonable grounds, but it started before that, and I'm at sea as to why."

"Just when did she start acting peculiar?" Logan held his breath, afraid to hear the answer.

"Right after she met you."

CHAPTER 19

Logan said goodnight to Zion and hastily retreated into the barn. He gave Lucy a quick check as he had promised. Zion had been so engrossed in barn plans he had paid little attention to Logan's sunken demeanor as the two parted for the night.

There was no denying Lucy was replete with foal, but the mare's condition seemed unchanged to Logan. "Goodnight, Lucy. Sleep well."

With slow steps Logan climbed the ladder to the haymow. The joy of reading the newspaper, almost tangible a few short minutes before, dissipated into a fine mist and then lifted altogether like the dew on a hot summer day.

Conflicted, that's what he was. Of course he knew he and Penny had gotten off to a rocky start, and he never imagined falling for her. Still, could she really despise him so as to sabotage him in such a way that either he or her brother's prized stallion could have been seriously injured?

It just didn't make sense. How could the same girl who stood paralyzed beside the mint barrel looking so ready to be kissed do anything so dubious? Had he been wrong about the look on her exquisite face? Was it his desire he had projected into her beautiful blue eyes? Could he have only imagined the lingering touch of her hand against his?

The memory of Penny's golden head bent over his feet further complicated the young man's miry thoughts. How tenderly she had removed his boots after his fall. She seemed so sincere. She seemed to have cared. *Have I been played for a fool? Was it a feigned act of concern—a malicious twist as she watched me suffer as a result of her seedy actions?*

Logan's thoughts moved like dancers doing the Virginia Reel. Once at the head of the line and then at the bottom, swinging, reeling down, casting off, and sashaying here and there until he was lost in the dance.

All the talk about faith and God and providence rattled in Logan's brain along with thoughts of Penny, but Logan knew something had changed in his heart. Logic, his faithful companion for so many years, refused to reconcile with the growing awareness of his spiritual need.

His studies at Wesleyan University had been enlightening in many ways. Logan was well versed on the validity of the Scripture. Prophetic words spoken centuries before their fulfillment were support enough to know the words of the Bible were not merely conjecture.

Logan found the continuity of Scripture amazing. It could not be mere happenstance that a book written by 40 authors from various walks of life and over a period of 1,500 years contained such unity of theme. The words of the writers complemented each other's messages. The accurate cross-references made between cultures and generations were impossible to ignore and agreed with historical record.

One of the most interesting things to Logan was the unearthing of evidence: locations and identities of people mentioned in Scripture verified by archeologists. Progress in science continually validated the Bible in areas like biology and astronomy. The more men learned about themselves, their world and their universe; the more they learned the Bible was true and trustworthy. In the past, men had believed the earth was flat. Job identified it as a sphere centuries before Magellan's 1522 expedition launched on God's Word and proved the earth was circular by sailing around it.

Logan knew the internal evidence, the archaeological evidence, the historical evidence, the scientific evidence. He was too educated to reject the Bible's credibility. Where he lacked was in its application.

As a young man, Logan had given little thought to the word *testament*; but at university, he had looked deeply at the origin and significance of words. His studies had revealed the true meaning of testament was a covenant. The Old Covenant and the New Covenant were mutual and binding agreements between God and His people.

Logan sat on a bale of hay in the crisp silence of the barn, broken intermittently by Clover's lowing. He was keenly aware that he had never personally entered into the covenant offered to him through Jesus.

"God, I just don't know where to start, so I think I'll start again tomorrow after a good night's sleep."

Logan picked up the newspaper Garth had loaned him in an effort to focus his swirling thoughts on something he could understand. He unfolded the *Lexington Observer and Reporter* and scanned the article on the imminent end of the terrible civil war that had wrought such havoc on the nation. *At least this terrible war is almost over.*

The newsprint rustled as Logan flipped the page and found the guest editorial Garth had mentioned.

"The introduction of the two-cent coin passed one year ago on April 22, 1864, brought with it the first issuance of national currency bearing the inscription 'In God We Trust.' Less than one year subsequent, March 3, 1865, Congress passed another act in which James Pollock, the Mint Director, received approval to place the phrase on all gold and silver coins.

"Amidst the tragedy of our great civil war that has set brother against brother, countryman against fellow countryman, the unifying inscription 'In God we 'Trust' imprinted on our most recent coinage testifies to the true source of hope for our country.

"Salmon Chase, Secretary of the Treasury, wrote in his missive to Pollock directing the development of the two-cent coin and its motto, 'No nation can be strong except in the strength of God, or safe except in His defense. The trust of our people in God should be declared on our national coins.'

"'In God we trust,' declares each newly minted coin, coinciding with the words 'In God is our trust' in the fourth stanza of our national anthem written by Francis Scott Key during the War of 1812. 'In God we trust' cried the men of the 125th Pennsylvania Infantry as they engaged in the Battle of Antietam, what became the bloodiest single day in American military history.

"It is in times of conflict men become acutely aware of the only true source of strength and safety. As I lingered on these words uttered by great men in dire circumstances, my eyes continually fell upon the smallest in the phrase.

"'In' is comprised of only two letters, yet this humble word provides the key to applying our noble motto. The word 'in' indicates inclusion, location and means. If we are to trust God, and realize healing for our nation, we must first be 'in God.' To be 'in God' means to be in covenant with Him through faith. The Holy Writ expounds in the Second Book of Corinthians, Chapter 2 and Verse 14, that God causes man to triumph 'in Christ.'

"At Gettysburg, President Abraham Lincoln spoke of a nation 'under God' and a new birth of freedom. Again, a seemingly insignificant preposition gives the key to the phrase. 'Under' betokens location and covering.

"If our 36 states are to unite as one nation, the strength of that nation will come from and as a result of its citizenry, including its citizen-leaders in government, who position themselves and remain 'in God' and 'under God.' –Submitted by Reverend L.K. Wagner of Paducah."

Logan folded the paper in half, stunned by the timing in which it had come to him. Could God be so intimately involved with humanity that He would order minute details for individuals—like his reception of this article? His mother, Zion, Rosalie . . . Logan was sure each of them would answer yes.

"I've been a fool." With hands tightly clasped on his lap, Logan lifted his eyes to the ceiling. "How can a man know so much and then fail to act on it? I've know Your Word to be true for many years, but I've never responded to Your invitation to 'come unto Me.'

"I know I need you, Lord. I know I'm an imperfect man— yes, a sinner in need of Your grace and mercy; and I know that knowing about You isn't enough. I want to know You, to walk with You, to be 'in You' in covenant relationship.

"Forgive me, Lord, for walking in my own desires and making my own plans. Thank You for directing me to this place where I could hear Your voice through the faith of others.

"Oh, Jesus, wash me and make me clean. Fill me with Your Spirit." As soon as the words were spoken, Logan felt a great heaviness lift from deep inside his chest. A sweet presence entered the room. "Oh, God, You are here. I feel You. Thank You, Jesus. Thank You!"

Logan fell to his knees and raised his hands as he entered into true worship. The Spirit of the Living God filled him with a joy unspeakable within the limitations of human vocabulary. Utterances unlearned gave tongue to divine communication between the spirit of man and the Spirit of the Eternal God.

Logan leapt to his feet. "I've got to be baptized!" he announced to the rafters and then scurried down the ladder. "It's real, Lucy! It's real!" Logan shouted to the drowsy mare. "The Holy Ghost is real!"

Logan quickly closed the distance between the barn and the cabin. Light poured from the window as he approached and rapped on the door.

"Who could that be this time of night?" Zion rose and hurried to the door.

"I hope it's not the sheriff." Penny shifted in her chair and clasped her hands tightly in her lap."

The persistent rap sounded again before Zion reached the door. "Who is it?"

"It's me, Logan Mayfield," a breathy reply came through the closed door.

Zion opened the latch. Logan stood on the threshold, hazel eyes sparkling. "Guess what!?!"

"Come inside before the mosquitoes have us for a bedtime snack and you can tell us." Zion moved from the entrance and Logan rushed inside.

"Yes, sir!" Logan scanned the room and took a quick inventory of the people who had not yet retired for the evening. Besides Zion, Rosalie and Penny sat next to each other at the table with strips of fabric between them. "Where's Mother?"

Before Zion had a chance to answer, Logan spanned the floor to Penny's room with long strides and knocked on the door. "Mother, can I talk to you?"

Millicent cracked open the bedroom door. "Logan, is everything all right?"

"Fine as cream gravy!" The words practically bubbled forth from a jubilant internal fountain.

Zion thumbed his nose and grinned. "Listen to you, Logan Mayfield. Sounds like you've been taking vocabulary lessons from Mariogold."

Logan laughed out loud. "Oh, the things I've been saying you wouldn't believe!"

"What is it, Son?" Millicent tied a wrap around her waist as she stepped into the living area.

"I've got it, Mother! I've got it!"

"Got what?" Millicent had no idea what could have brought her son to such a level of excitement. She hadn't seen him carry on like this since he was a little boy.

"The Holy Ghost!" Logan grabbed his mother's delicate hands and calmed himself enough to stand still and look at her sweet face. "I can't believe it; but I can; I mean, I do; I mean, I've got it!"

"Oh, Logan, I'm so pleased and happy for you!" Millicent's porcelain face shone with gladness.

"Congratulations, brother." Zion stretched out his hand. Logan gave it a hearty shake and then slapped his employer on the back.

"And I'm ready to get baptized in Jesus' name!" Logan turned to Rosalie. "Does Reverend Dryfus baptize every Sunday?"

"He'll baptize any time Limestone Creek's not frozen over." Rosalie's jade-green eyes sparkled with unshed tears.

"We can see him right after breakfast, if you like," said Zion.

"I'd like."

Words failed Penny, but a cherubic expression graced her face as she observed the joyful exchange. Logan smiled at her and moved to her side.

"Penny, I want you to know I forgive you."

Penny studied Logan's face, her eyebrows knit as she attempted to call up the reason for his magnanimous proclamation. "You forgive me?"

"Yes." Logan grabbed her hand and looked deeply in her expressive blue eyes. "I'm sure you didn't intend for me or West to get hurt. And I don't need to know why you did it. I just want you to know I have no bad feelings."

Penny's speech faltered. She stared at Logan and then at her brother. Zion smiled and nodded. Logan looked so sincere. Valiantly, Penny struggled to keep her composure, but a dubious snicker shimmied through her pursed lips.

Rosalie watched the interplay. There was obviously a broken thread in this conversation. "Penny, what's so amusing?" She could hardly believe the girl was laughing at Logan when he was clearly speaking in earnest.

Penny covered her mouth with her fingertips. When she gained control of her vocal eruptions she shook her head to clear her thoughts. "I'm sorry, Logan." Penny placed her small hand on his sleeve. "I didn't mean to laugh. It's just that you were so great-hearted to forgive me for something I didn't do."

Penny looked at her brother. "You thought the same thing, and I can hardly believe it. You've known me my whole life, Zion. Have you ever seen me hurt any living thing?"

"Well, no, I haven't." Zion scrutinized his sister's expression. Her wide eyes and unpretentious countenance declared her innocence to the one who had known her since the day of her birth, her father figure the past five years. "I guess I have to apologize myself, Buttercup. It's just the only summation that figured." Zion stroked his chin and pondered the factors.

"It seemed to me you were the only person to have the opportunity to put that cocklebur under West's saddle. I admit, it is out of character, but you have to hold that you have been acting a bit out of sorts lately."

"That's true, Zion." Penny rose and stood next to her brother. She threaded her small hand through his elbow and patted his shoulder with the other. "Everything's been out of sorts lately. I'm sorry my behavior added vexation to an already trying time for our family." Penny leaned in to her brother's shoulder, and Zion cupped her oval face in his good hand.

"I should have known better myself. A house divided against itself cannot stand," said Zion.

"Wise words from our dear president, God rest his soul." Millicent exhaled a negligible sigh.

"Yes. Wise words from a brave and noble man." Rosalie folded her arms and scanned the faces of dear ones round about her. "We need to stick together, family."

Gratitude swept over Millicent, mingled with importunity. "There's so much to be thankful for, and at the same time so many unanswered questions."

"That's true, Mother." Logan wrapped an arm around his mother's waist in a side hug. "I'm just grateful the biggest question of my life has finally been answered."

"So am I, Logan." A tender smile played across Millicent's delicate face. "So am I."

CHAPTER 20

L.C. Yates lay in eerie stillness on a bed inside Dr. Byerly's Washington medical office. His wife Cordelia kept watch at his side. From her covered seat in the platform rocker, the woman's gaze lingered over a set of Currier and Ives lithographs flanking the window. In "The Road, Winter," a couple bundled in a sleigh drawn by two horses were out for a ride on a snow-covered lane. "The Road, Summer" portrayed a lone male driving a horse and buggy along a river.

"Oh, Lars," Cordelia whispered, "Come back to me. Don't ride away and leave me here alone."

Over the past three decades, Mrs. Yates' life with her husband had been all a wife could want. The couple had maintained a loving, intimate relationship; and although they were childless, they had been blessed with health and prosperity.

Memories of sleigh rides past filled Cordelia's thoughts. As she stared at the winter scene in the colorful print, she imagined herself and her husband only a few short months ago visiting friends and neighbors after a deep snowfall. Freshly fallen snow was the best for sleighing, L.C. always said.

In Cordelia's estimation, there were no bells that sounded sweeter than those ringing from her husband's team as they swished over the snow. She pictured herself wrapped in blankets and furs with hot bricks packed at her feet. Nestled safely beside her husband in their robin-egg blue bobsled, every sense was satisfied. She thrilled at the feel of the cold against her face. She admired the horses' arched necks as they curvetted and pranced in delightful motion. She enjoyed every facet of the ride: the intonation of the dancing bells, the incredible beauty of the team moving in unison, and the soft sound of the runners whispering through the snow. Most of all she treasured the time with her husband. He had so many demands on his time, but he always made a special effort to spend time with her.

The sight of her pale husband stretched out on the bed brought tears to Cordelia's eyes. Imagining a sleigh ride without him by her side was more than she wanted to think about.

"Jesus, I'm not ready to say goodbye to him yet. Please, Lord, touch his body with your healing power and wake him from this long sleep."

Harley listened from where he stood in the hallway outside the door where Mr. Yates lay. Curiosity had gotten the better of him, so he had snuck into the doctor's office to see how his victim was faring.

The better part of Harley's conscience hoped the banker would recover; but on the other hand, if Yates did move on to Beulah land, he would not be around to identify him. No one in Washington had seen him except his dolly girl; and since he was going to shuttle her out of this berg as quickly as possible, that should not pose a problem. No, all would be fine if he just kept his wits about him and played things cool and careful.

"Can I help you, sir?" Dr. Byerly's wife, Lou, examined the man with the mutton chop beard. His cheeks were unusually red, and a bulbous roseate nose protruded over barely visible thin lips. She looked into his eyes set in deep sockets and easily read consternation on the stranger's jaundiced face.

Harley tried to remain calm, but his breath refused to come without a struggle. With a shaky hand he lifted a filthy kerchief to muffle the cough that accompanied the familiar tightness in his chest.

"The doctor stepped over to the mercantile on a quick errand. He'll be right back." Lou's would-be patient was obviously in a state of respiratory distress. "Why don't you sit down and I'll get you something to ease your breathing."

The wheezing and tightening of Harley's air passages were undeniable. Although never welcome, this time they offered Harley an out. If he played along with the nurse, she would not suspect the true reason behind his visit.

"Sit here." Lou indicated a chair in a small examination room. "Now, close your mouth and take slow breaths through your nose. Try to relax."

The nurse in Lou set to work. She poured water from a pitcher into a pan on a small gas burner and then added ten drops of peppermint oil. "I know you're uncomfortable now, but this remedy will saturate the air and ease your breathing. All you have to do is relax for about an hour."

Lou smiled at Harley. He nodded his head in return. "I'm going to shut the door to keep the vapors in, and I'll have the doctor see you as soon as he's back. Is there anything I can get you?"

Harley shook his head and pointed to his nose.

"That's good. You just keep breathing through your nose. If you'd like to stretch out, feel free to move to the bed."

"I'm pleased to do it for you, young man." Reverend Dryfus beamed at the gathering in the parsonage parlor.

"Can we do it today?" asked Logan.

"We usually do baptisms on special days and invite the church family, but I don't see why not. When a fellow's ready, he's ready. Let me just make sure you know the reasons you're doing this first."

"Oh, I know, Reverend; but by all means, ask whatever you want."

"Baptism is a burial of sorts. Romans 6:4 says 'therefore we are buried with him by baptism into death.'"

"I'm ready to bury the old man, Reverend."

"Good, Son." Reverend Dryfus was pleased with Logan's enthusiasm. At the same time, he wanted to ensure the young man's comprehension of what was about to take place. Without truly turning from his sins and devoting himself to God, Logan would come out of the creek nothing more than a wet sinner.

"I've repented and been filled with the Holy Ghost already, sir. With all my heart I'm ready to be free from sin and walk with God."

"I believe you are, Logan. Let me just say this: The gospel of Jesus Christ is his death, burial and resurrection. When you repented, you identified with the death of Christ. Baptism identifies us with His burial. You've already been filled with the Holy Ghost that identifies you with Jesus' resurrection."

"Yes, I understand what Peter said when the people cried out 'what shall we do?' My mother has been telling me about it since I was knee high to a grasshopper." Logan chuckled at the recent expansion of his folksy vocabulary. He winked at his mother, and then composed himself to answer the minister's question with sincerity.

"Then Peter said unto them, repent and be baptized every one of you in the name of Jesus Christ for the remission of sins, and ye shall receive the gift of the Holy Ghost. For the promise is unto you, and to your children, and to all that are afar off, even as many as the Lord our God shall call."

Reverend Dryfus stood to his feet and extended a hand for a hearty shake. "I see no need to postpone the pardoning. Let's take this party to Limestone Creek."

Almira Dryfus surveyed the room filled with joy for what had already happened, and excitement for what was yet to come. "Charity, will you fetch a couple of towels?" she asked her daughter.

"No, need, Mrs. Dryfus," said Penny. "We brought some from home."

The party filed out of the parsonage. Logan assisted the Briar Hollow ladies into the wagon while Reverend Dryfus brought his buggy from the barn for his family.

"How is Mr. Yates?" Zion asked the minister as he pulled his buggy alongside the wagon.

"I haven't heard anything new today. Would you like to stop by Doc Byerly's and get a quick report?"

"If that's ok with our baptismal candidate." Zion winked at Logan.

"Of course." Logan jumped inside the wagon bed. "I'd love to hear how he's doing."

The wagon and buggy filled with animated travelers moved down Main Street to Dr. Byerly's office. "Whoa," Zion called to the team.

"Let's not choke the good doctor's office with visitors." Warren Dryfus handed the reins to his wife. "I'll just pop in and get an update. I'll be right back."

"Could I please come?" Penny asked. "I've been so concerned about him."

"Of course, Penny," said the reverend.

Logan leapt from the wagon bed and assisted Penny to the ground. He recognized that his emotions were heightened with all that had transpired in the past few hours. Still, there was no denying the swell in his heart when he put his hands around Penny's narrow waist and lifted her from the wagon.

The couple briefly locked eyes. Penny's were filled with apprehension for Mr. Yates. Logan smiled and gave both of her hands a quick squeeze.

A squeak from the spring of the screened door announced the visitors' entrance. Lou turned from the cabinet she was checking to greet them.

"Hello, Reverend, and Penny. What can I do for you today?"

"Is your husband around?" Warren Dryfus noted the closed examination room door.

"He's gone to the mercantile. I expect him directly. Is someone ill?"

"I hope not." Reverend Dryfus grinned at his friend and parishioner. "We just stopped by to check on L.C. Are there any changes?"

Lou shook her head, her lips pursed in a slight frown. Concern flitted behind her kind eyes. "Cordelia is with him now," Lou spoke in a hushed tone, "he's still unconscious."

"Could I see him?" Penny trembled at the thought, but compassion drove her past her discomfiture.

Lou smiled at the girl. "Let me check with Mrs. Yates. I'll be back quick as a wink."

Penny watched Mrs. Byerly disappear into one of the patient rooms and close the door behind her.

"I'm scared, Reverend," Penny confessed.

"You're scared to see Mr. Yates?"

"I'm scared of a lot of things." Penny wrapped her arms around her waist in a self-administered hug. "I'm feeling some better, but when I first witnessed the attack, I just kept seeing it replay over and over in my mind. It was so disturbing."

"I'm sure it was a hard thing to see."

"It happened so fast. It was a beautiful day and I was taking a walk through town. I heard a noise in the alley. I looked down it, and everything froze. Mr. Yates was there and this man. They both looked at me and then the man lifted his gun and hit Mr. Yates." Penny shook her head at the memory of the sight and the sound. "The noise from the impact was sickening, and then poor Mr. Yates slumped to the ground."

"I can't imagine the trauma you've experienced."

"It was nothing compared to what Mr. Yates went through . . . what he's going through now."

"Did you recognize the man with the gun?" asked Reverend Dryfus.

"I can't place him, but I know I've seen him before." Penny closed her eyes and attempted once more to conjure up details. Music played in her memory.

Penny's eyes popped open. "I remembered something." Breathless with excitement she almost whispered. "I keep hearing music. It's getting clearer, a repeating song, but I can't recall where I've heard it before."

"What kind of music, Penny? Singing? Guitar? Piano?"

Penny shook her head. "No. It's more of an organ sound. Nothing from church, but there's more. I remembered a new detail about the man."

"That's great. Can you share it with me, or do you want me to get the sheriff?"

"It's nothing big, just a bit more detail about his whiskers. The man that attacked Mr. Yates had sideburns that grew from his ear down the sides of his cheeks. There was no mustache or hair on his chin, but he had big sideboards."

Reverend Dryfus nodded. "I'm sure that's important information, Penny. We can stop by Nash's office when we're done here and you can let him know what you remembered. Maybe by then you'll have a full description of the curly wolf."

Above the sound of the water burbling in the pot, Harley heard the conversation taking place outside the examination room door. He did not know the voices, but it was obvious from the conversation that one of them belonged to his fair-haired darling.

From the safety of his chamber, he heard Mrs. Byerly usher the visitors into Yates' room. *I have to get out of here before my whole plan is a wash. If I'm caught, I'll be up the creek: in the calaboose for sure; or a noose, depending on the man's recovery or lack thereof.*

Harley slowly turned the knob and opened the door enough to peek into the parlor. All was clear. As quietly as possible, he slipped out of the room and eased the door shut behind him.

Steps away from making a clean escape, Mrs. Byerly entered the room and discovered her patient reaching for the door knob.

"Mister . . ." Lou realized she had neglected to get the man's name.

"Sorry, ma'am. I have to go. Thanks for your help." Harley bustled out the door with his head lowered. A wagon and a buggy filled with chattering people were parked outside the doctor's office. Harley did not take the time to see if he recognized anyone or they recognized him. He mashed his hat down on his head and hurried down Main Street where he disappeared in the alley by the Paxton Inn.

"That's strange." Lou mumbled to herself, shook her head and turned to greet Reverend Dryfus and Penny as they exited Mr. Yates' room.

"What's that, Lou?" asked Reverend Dryfus.

"Nothing, I guess. There was a man here to see my husband. He was having breathing problems, and I was giving him a treatment to ease his respiration until my husband returned. He left before he saw the doctor."

Penny watched the man pass by her brother's wagon. From her position she saw only his backside. He was a bit hunched over and wore a dark brown waistcoat and a low, brown topper. "Who was it?"

"I didn't get his name," said Lou. "He was in distress, so I started him on a treatment right away."

"That's odd," said Reverend Dryfus. "Well, we have a baptism to attend to. We best get going."

Penny reached for Lou's hand and grasped it between both her own. "Thank you for letting me see Mr. Yates. It's awful to see him in such a condition, but I know you and your husband are taking good care of him."

"There's not much we can do at this point but keep him hydrated and pray."

"We're all praying with you," said Revered Dryfus, "and we'll all keep doing that until the good Lord sees fit to wake our friend out of his slumber."

CHAPTER 21

"Well that was a hoot and a holler." Marigold jumped from the wagon without assistance, the last person to disembark at Briar Hollow.

"A great day," said Rosalie with a smile. "I'm so happy for you, Logan."

"Thank you." Logan clasped his hands together. His experience in the creek had touched him deeply. The presence of God had been so rich he had started shaking, and even now he had to concentrate to keep his hands still.

"It's been a miraculous day!" Millicent beamed at her son. "Your father would have been so pleased, Logan."

"And the day's just about half over." Zion rubbed his belly with his good hand. "I'm plumb starved, woman. Do you have any vittles in there for your hard working man?" Zion winked at his wife.

"Hard working?" Penny wrinkled her nose at her brother.

"I'd say more like a coffee boiler." Marigold threw the words over her shoulder with a chuckle as she made her way to the path between Coldwell Farms and her home. "I have to help Pa get some apricots to town. See you later."

"I think everyone's hungry," said Rosalie. "Let me get Mattie fed and down for a nap. "The beans have been on since this morning and I already made the cornbread. It won't take long to pull things together."

Dahlia tugged on Rosalie's skirt and looked up at her mother's face. "I'll help, Momma."

"Thank you, sweet girl."

"Me, too," said Penny. "I'll set the table while you take care of the baby."

"What can I do to help?" Millicent joined in, determined not to give in to frail health. She was a frontier woman now, and she was determined to do her fair share of the work.

Zion watched the womenfolk disappear inside the cabin. A peaceful stillness swept into the hollow broken only by the chirps and gurgles of a tree swallow singing from its perch near the stream. Fragrance from the last of the lilacs mingled with the sweet nectar of the honeysuckle and filled the yard with sweet smells of the season.

Logan breathed deeply, content to bask in the beauty of this place and soak in the serenity that filled his soul. "What a beautiful place you have, Zion. You are a blessed man."

"That I am." Zion clapped Logan on the shoulder and grinned from ear to ear. "What do you say we check on Lucy before the ladies call us for dinner?"

"That sounds good."

The two men made their way to the barn. "I'm looking forward to seeing the drawings Garth is working up for the new barn," said Zion.

"Me, too." Logan meandered next to Zion in a comfortable stroll. "I've been thinking about the barn and how it could advance the image of Coldwell Horse Farms."

"How so?" Zion's interest was piqued, pleased that someone beside himself was mindful of his enterprise. Raising horses had been his passion since childhood. Rosalie was involved on a peripheral level, but did not partake in the particulars of building the business.

"I was thinking that since you are still in the developing stages of your commerce and making a name for yourself in Kentucky, it could be beneficial to develop a trademark of sorts."

"What do you mean?"

"Trademarks are words and symbols that identify a product; horses in your case, and distinguish them from someone else's. The combination of a good trademark and a good product can build a great business."

"Tell me more." Zion caught his chin between his thumb and forefinger. Logan had his full attention.

"I was thinking that since round barns are a newer idea, especially in this area, using a picture of one on your sign and papers and any advertising you might do, could build recognition for Coldwell Horse Farm. When people see the same name and image over time it conveys reliability and reputability that give confidence to potential and returning customers. A good trademark can give you an identity among your competitors. And trademarks also make it easier for your clients to identify you, refer you, and bring you return business."

"In the past, I've just relied on my good name. Scripture says it's better than treasure."

Logan nodded. "That's true, but the Bible doesn't say you can't have both: a good name and treasure.

"Think of it like this. Your wife does laundry with a washboard, right?"

"Every week, sometimes more often when Mattie soaks through his diapers."

"If you wanted to get Rosalie a new washboard, you would have many to choose from: wood, metal, rubber-coated, and so on."

"You sure know a heap about washing."

"Mostly from articles and advertisements—but that's my point. If you bought her one that she really loved and she couldn't remember the name of it, how could she recommend it to others? And what if she wanted to get another one down the road?'

"I guess she'd go to the mercantile."

"And I'm guessing there are several to choose from."

"I haven't studied up on them, but mayhap, especially if she was going to order one."

"What if the washboard she used before and liked had a name printed on it?"

"Then she'd know just what to ask for, wouldn't she?" Zion's blue eyes lit up with understanding.

"Right, but what if she forgot the name, but remembered the way the name looked or a certain picture associated with it? That would build her recall."

"I get your point," said Zion. "A good name with a good image: sounds like a good plan."

"If we connect Coldwell Horse Farm with innovative ideas and quality stock, I believe it can set you at a place of prominence in your field."

"I like it, Logan." Zion's enthusiasm was building and he nodded his head with pluck. "Let's talk to Garth about that, too.

"Now we better get out of this 'field' and check on the 'quality stock' before eating time." Zion opened the barn door. "I was thinking of lunging her to get her blood circulating. She's so big I haven't had the heart to ride her, but some exercise would be good."

"Good afternoon, Lucy." Logan admired the mare's sculpted head and deep chest while Zion scratched her on the back.

"What's this, little lady?" Zion examined the straw beneath the horse and then checked her underside. "She's leaking milk. It looks like we'll be foaling soon."

"How exciting. Is there anything we need to do?"

"We can double check the foaling kit after dinner," said Zion. "I'm glad you're staying in the barn. A good many births happen between midnight and the wee hours before dawn. I'm hoping she'll let us know when it's time. There's nothing like watching new life come into the world."

Logan smiled remembering the feel of bursting through the surface of the creek just a short time ago. The weight of all his wrongdoing had lifted off faster than a peregrine falcon in a dive. He finally knew for himself the feeling of new life, and it was feeling mighty fine indeed.

"Good news, girls!" Zion burst through the cabin door.

"What, Daddy? What?" Dahlia jumped up and down.

Zion patted his excited girl on the top of her braids and then stooped to draw her into a one-armed embrace. "It's Lucy, baby. It looks like she's ready to have her foal in the next day or so— maybe even tonight."

"That *is* good news." Penny set the platter of cornbread she was carrying on the table. "It seems like she's been expecting forever."

"No longer than normal," said Zion. "Eleven months and eleven days is average. She's a bit shy of that yet."

"That does sound like forever." Rosalie recalled her last days of pregnancy and empathized with the animal.

"Let's eat before the beans get cold." Penny helped Dahlia into her seat while the others arranged themselves in front of bowls filled with Zion's favorite bean dish; tangy legumes cooked with onions and seasoned ground beef.

"Cowboy beans! It looks good enough to eat, Wife." Zion grinned and turned to Logan. "Would you like to offer the blessing, brother?"

"I'd be honored." Logan extended his hands, palms up. Everyone held hands, as much as was possible with one of Zion's still in the sling. Sweet satisfaction swept through Logan as he held his mother's hand to his right and Penny's to his left.

"Lord, this is a day of new beginnings. I thank You for new life and the good people You bring to us to share the precious gift of life with. I ask Your blessing on this meal and Your continued covering and provision on everyone gathered around this table and on Coldwell Horse Farm, too. In Jesus' name, amen."

The corners of Logan's mouth turned up in a pleasant expression. He squeezed the hands of both the ladies, but his gaze lingered on Penny's profile. Porcelain skin, exquisite blue eyes, lovely cheeks, and delicate pink lips; Logan found the combination perfectly attractive. Her hair was up. It was pretty in a loose knot with soft tendrils playing around her elegant neck. Logan recalled the times he had seen the dark golden tresses unbound and flowing over her shoulders and down her back.

Penny was manifestly aware of the press of Logan's hand and the feel of his visual caress. Her pulse quickened and a magnetism she had never known compelled her to turn to his handsome face. She wanted to look into his hazel eyes and see if today their amber flecks were light brown or golden-green. Most of all she wanted to read his soul through their windows and see if he was sensing as much as she at his nearness.

With determination, Penny kept her head facing forward and studied the cowboy beans on her spoon.

Zion stabbed a piece of cornbread with his fork and then passed the platter to Rosalie. "Speaking of the farm, Logan has some ideas on ways to build up our recognition in the area."

"Let's not talk business at the table." Rosalie served herself and cut a half-piece of cornbread for her daughter.

"All right, I'll give for now, but after dinner Logan and I are meeting up with Garth to go over the plans. Penny, when we get back, I'd like you to work with Logan on his idea for a trademark for our operation."

Penny seized the opportunity to peek at Logan. His eyes sparkled beneath bushy brows, and his tawny hair reminded her of the color of hazelnuts. It was in charming disarray, and she wondered how it would feel to brush the errant strands off his forehead like she had done for baby Mattie so many times.

To Penny's disappointment, she did not have the wherewithal to make substantial eye contact. Instead her gaze scanned his face top to bottom and landed on his dimpled chin before dropping back to her hands clasped in her lap.

"Sure, Zion. I'd be happy to."

"We can work on the quilt tomorrow if you run long," said Rosalie. "It's coming together nicely."

"Now, now, isn't that work you're talking about?" Zion teased his wife.

"Working with fabric is not work at all," said Millicent, "at least when it is as pleasant a venture as quilting or needlework."

"Perhaps you can take Penny's place tonight?" Rosalie had been looking for an opportunity to include Mrs. Mayfield in the quilting project, but she had been unsure if her guest would be pleased or insulted. Rosalie had been hesitant, wondering if working with scraps of fabric collected from her family's worn out items or leftovers from old sewing projects would be beneath the genteel lady.

Millicent beamed. "I was hoping you would ask, but I didn't want to intrude on your family project. The Goheen sisters gave me my own sewing basket, and I can't wait to use it."

"Women can be so silly sometimes." Rosalie chuckled. "I wanted to ask and you wanted to be asked, but neither of us said a word."

"I love needlework," said Millicent. "I've never quilted though. I hope you'll be patient with me."

"If you can do embroidery, you are definitely capable of piecing *Flying Geese*. It's really a beginner pattern, but it has some interesting history."

"I'd love to hear it."

"*Flying Geese* is actually one of the oldest and simplest piecework designs. It's all triangles and strips with the geese flying in long straight lines from one edge of the strip to the other. I like to alternate the geese pattern with stripes of solid colors."

"I noticed you had a variety of colors you're working with," said Millicent. "I'm so looking forward to the feel of a needle and thread and fabric. But what were you saying about an historical element?"

"What's interesting about the history of the pattern is that it was used by runaway slaves as a signal on the Underground Railroad."

"Oh, that is fascinating," said Millicent. "How did it work?"

"First of all, keep in mind most runaways couldn't read. They got their cues from signals and word of mouth. Think about this: what direction would they be heading?"

"North, I suppose."

"Right, and when do geese fly north?"

"In the spring, of course."

"Yes, and spring was the best time to attempt an escape. Runaways followed nature's cues: the timing, the honking noises, and flight paths overhead directed their way to Canada. Underground Railroad conductors used *Flying Geese* quilts to help escaping slaves navigate their journeys. The pattern created a large, graphic arrow that could be displayed to mark a path to freedom."

"Incredible." Millicent nodded her head as the pieces connected in her mind. "Of course, I've heard of the Underground Railroad, but I never knew any of the details. How clever, and they even called their benefactors conductors like on a real train."

"They did," Rosalie nodded, "and I have to say I'm so glad the season of slavery is coming to an end in our nation."

"Amen to that," said Logan.

Millicent smiled at her son. She could not remember the last time he had said "amen" and meant it. "Seasons do change, don't they? Birds fly south, then north, then south again. We've experienced seasonal changes in our lives as well, haven't we, Logan?"

"We certainly have, Mother."

"Through my life's journey I've learned some things that have helped me," said Millicent. "Not only do I trust God for eternity, I've learned to trust Him in each season life brings. Each season has its own unique trials and treasures, and I want to embrace the blessings each brings."

"That's so true," said Rosalie. "Each of us faces situations that are out of our control, and we have to trust God to give us the direction we need to move on with our lives."

"That must be true freedom," said Logan, "when we learn to look to the Lord for direction."

Zion washed down the last of his beans with a long drink from a tall tumbler. "I don't know about you good folks, but sometimes I'd like to hear an obnoxious honking overhead to show me the way to go. I can be downright thick-skulled."

"You know what I've been thinking?" Penny looked into the faces of the people gathered around the table.

Zion could tell from his sister's countenance she was about to share something worth hearing. "What's that, Penny-girl?"

"As Rosalie and I have been working on the quilt, I noticed that for every triangle of goose there are two triangles of sky. When we finish the quilt, we're going to see lots of little geese, but one immense sky. We serve a big God, and He knows right where we are."

"That's beautiful, Penny." Millicent admired the young girl's tender insight.

"That's right, Buttercup," said Zion. "We just have to remember to look up."

"True." Penny smiled at her brother. "And when I'm looking for the way to take, I have to remind myself that God guides my steps one day and decision at a time."

Zion pushed back from the table. "Speaking of decisions, it's time for us menfolk to commence with the barn planning. Let's head over to Garth's."

CHAPTER 22

"Garth said he's given it a lot of thought, and he believes that not only is it faster and easier to build a round barn over a post-and-beam barn, it's cheaper." Zion sat up in the front porch rocker and dunked the edge of his molasses cookie in his coffee.

"Why is it cheaper?" Rosalie rocked the baby while her husband alternately ate sopped bits of cookie and told of his meeting with their brother-in-law.

"Round barns use lumber that is one-inch thick instead of foot-thick beams; and we can use nails instead of pegs."

"I can't think of a reason not to move ahead with your plans," said Rosalie. "I'm excited for you, Zion. When you hurt your arm, it felt like it was the beginning of so many things going so wrong; but it seems your accident stopped us long enough to get redirected in a positive way."

"I can't disagree," said Zion, "but I'd like to think I would have listened if the Lord had just given me a little tap on the shoulder instead of allowing a break in my arm."

"I can't disagree with that, myself."

"I have some ideas, but I'm no good at sketching." Logan confessed his inadequacy to Penny who sat adjacent to him at the table.

"That's fine. I'll see what I can do." Penny picked up a pencil and held it at the ready.

"Why don't we put down in words some thoughts before you start drawing?" Logan was delighted with the opportunity to spend time with Penny. Even though it was on assignment, it was a chance to be with her and get to know her better.

"Begin." Penny smiled and put the pencil tip to paper.

"First, a trademark should be simple, memorable, and appropriate. The goal is to boost your recognition and help clients recognize Coldwell Horse Farm over the competition."

"Very clever."

"I can't take credit for the idea, but let's see how we can implement it."

"What did you have in mind?"

"You and I know your brother has amazing inventory and getting better all the time. Who else knows will determine the success of the operation. We need to draw buyers from a larger region than just Mason County."

"That seems like a good approach. His horses aren't your typical farm-working, carriage-pulling variety."

"Thoroughbreds are from the purest and best bloodlines. We want to develop an image that says 'quality' to potential buyers. A great logo will give a great impression to build on."

"Any specific details you can give me?"

Logan placed an elbow on the table and leaned his chin on the back of his hand. "I see three elements: a beautiful horse standing on his hind legs and kicking his front legs in the air."

"Rearing." Penny lifted her eyes from the paper and looked at Logan.

"Yes," Logan allowed himself for a moment to get lost in a set of cornflower blue irises, "rearing."

Penny's lips curved upward in an engaging smile. "And the second element, Mr. Mayfield?"

Logan shook himself from his fanciful musings and forced his thoughts back on track. "The second item, Miss Coldwell, ma'am, would be your name."

"Would you use the entire thing? Coldwell Horse Farm?"

"I think if we have an image of a horse, we can just use the name Coldwell. It will be easier to remember one word than three."

"Ok. Just Coldwell, then. And the third item?"

"This is what I think will make the logo stand out—a silhouette of the barn. Let me show you Garth's drawings." Logan unrolled the paper Garth had sent home with Zion. "See the outline of the building?"

"It is a unique shape. I'm seeing something. Let me try to sketch it out."

Logan watched as Penny first drew the outline of a barn with a distinctive round shape and cupola on a vaulted roof. Instead of a building foundation, she drew a slightly curved banner with ribbon-type ends and printed "Coldwell" in large block letters inside. In the barn she sketched a silhouette of a horse in a majestic rear.

"Wow."

"Wait right here." Penny slipped into her bedroom and swiftly returned with a box of colored pencils. "This definitely needs color."

Alternating between red, brown, and black, Penny created the perfect blend of barn red for the building. "I think the ribbon should be blue, don't you?"

"Blue ribbons say quality. I think that's a winner." Logan watched as Penny bent intently over her work. Her head tipped to the right and then to the left as she enlivened her sketch with a vibrant royal hue.

"What about the lettering? White or black?"

"Either one would work," said Logan. "Would it be possible to draw it up both ways?"

"I like the way you think."

"Does that mean I think the way you like?" A delightful grin played across Penny's face.

Logan smiled, captivated by the conversation and the comely conversationalist. "I think so; if you like, that is."

"I'd like to think so—I think."

Reluctantly, Logan pushed away from the table. "I need to get out to the barn and check on Lucy, and your brother wanted to do a last check on the foaling kit."

"All right. I'll finish these drawings and we can show them around—get some opinions from Zion and Rosalie, maybe even the Erlangers. They have good business sense."

"I can't wait to see the finished designs." Logan opened the cabin door and looked back for a final goodbye. "See you later, Penny."

"See you later, Logan."

Logan pulled the door to a close and greeted his employer. "Are you ready to check out the foaling kit, boss?"

"Aren't you the taskmaster, now?" Zion winked at his wife, reluctantly raised himself from his seat, and plodded down the porch steps with Logan.

"How's the trademark coming?"

"I think you'll be pleased," said Logan. "Your sister is quite talented. She's making two samples for you to choose from."

"I'm looking forward to seeing what the two of you have come up with."

Logan pondered Zion's words and wondered about the possibilities of additional future collaborations with his sister. He had longed to hold her hand as they sat next to each other at the table. They were close enough that he could smell the rosewater she used on her fair skin.

"Let's check on Lucy first and see if she's progressed."

Zion examined the mare's rump and tailhead muscles for signs of softening. "She doesn't look much different, but she seems a bit nervous."

Logan noted the level of roughage in the feeding trough was unchanged. "Her appetite seems down."

"That's a good sign, too. Before bed, would you put out some dry, clean straw? And we'll want to wrap her tail. The supplies are in the foaling kit."

Logan pulled down the wooden crate from the shelf Zion indicated and opened it on the work bench.

"Most foals are born within ten minutes of their forelegs emerging from the birth canal. That's why it's important to keep a well stocked foaling kit close at hand. Let's see what we have here."

Logan pulled out two clean buckets stacked together, the top one loaded with large and small towels. "Those are used to get a hold on the foal's feet and legs if needed, and of course to clean up afterwards. Let's see what else is in there."

Logan retrieved the items from the wooden crate as Zion called them out. "A pair of gloves, sharp scissors, a knife, suture material, clamps, a heavy canvas, lubricant, iodine, a roll of cotton, a clyster syringe, soap and the tail wrap. It looks like everything's in apple pie order. Let's take care of the tail wrap right now."

Logan retrieved the long roll of fabric. "It's important not to put this on too tight. The horse's tail is alive, and we don't want to cut off her circulation. Start at the dock of the tail and gently wrap it tight enough to keep it on, but loose enough to maintain blood flow."

Carefully following Zion's directions, Logan wrapped in a downward motion until he reached the end. "Birthing is a miracle, but it's a mucky miracle. Wrapping Lucy's tail will save us a heap of work cleaning blood, urine, feces, and bedding out of it the day after foaling."

Logan stepped back to inspect his work. "Fine job," said Zion. "If you'll take care of that clean bedding, I think everything is ready."

Harley's difficult breathing escalated to a full-fledged wheeze as he hurried down the alley. His plan had been to return to his lean-to refuge, but as he ducked behind buildings and trees, he realized that what he initially considered bad luck was actually a stroke of good fortune. All he had to do was follow the little lady. She would eventually lead him to her home.

Thankfully, the traveling party made a couple of stops, and Harley was able to keep up. Standing near the sheriff's office had been a bit unnerving, and the baptism was disconcerting to a sinner such as he.

Harley stayed hidden among the juniper trees until nightfall. Many conversations took place around the hollow that he could not make out, but he knew his dolly girl was inside the cabin. Now that it was dark he desperately wanted to peek in the window, but the two dogs patrolling the property dissuaded him. He had hoped they would be taken inside for the night, but they flopped down on the porch.

Just as Harley decided to return to the lean-to and finalize his plans to clean out the bank vault, the cabin door opened. To his delight, his girl stepped outside. She looked like an angel. Light from inside the cabin shone all around her like a giant halo.

Everything in him wanted to grab her and run. He could do it, too. He would just have to keep her tied up until he could get the money and a horse.

Penny moved gracefully down the path to the barn. The lantern in her hand lit her way. Harley watched and decided if he was going to take her, he would wait until she left the barn. That would give him some time to devise the best approach.

"Hello, the barn," Penny called from outside the door.

"Hello, the fair lady," Logan opened the door to admit his visitor.

Penny wore a simple dress, a coral calico with a small, all-over floral print. The top buttoned down the front and had a stand-up collar. The waist was gathered and the drop sleeves were full with a cuff band. A tall ruffle skirted the bottom.

Logan had seen many women in fine apparel, from fashionable zouave and pagoda ensembles to elegant ball gowns. Penny's dress boasted no trim whatsoever, no piping, lace, or any contrasting color; yet her graceful carriage and arresting beauty made the common raiment seem regal in Logan's estimation.

The moon created a glowing wreath on her hair, and the lantern light on her face gave a stunning effect to her notable features. "And to what do I owe the pleasure of your call?"

"I didn't come to see you, silly." Penny's eyes danced. "I heard we might be expecting company tonight."

Harley listened to the exchange from the timberline. Did they know he was there? Had he been discovered, or was someone else going to be traveling through the junipers to visit the home of his intended? His chest tightened and he willed his pulse to slow so he could hear the conversation across the way.

"We might indeed," said Logan. "Would you care to come in?"

"No. I just thought I would stand outside and see if the mosquitoes were hungry."

Logan laughed. "We wouldn't want you to turn into a pincushion. I do believe Kentucky has more than its fair share of the mosquito population. Please come in."

Harley watched the girl slip inside the barn. He had decisions to make. Should he stay or go? If he stayed, he could rush the barn right now or nab her when she left; but there were variables to be concerned with either way. The first of which was what appeared to be a gun strapped to the young man's leg. There was no way to know if she would return to the house alone or with an armed escort.

Harley rubbed the handle of his pistol. He had never shot a man in cold blood. Did he want to take that risk now? If Yates died he would be wanted for murder no matter what he chose to do now. Still, his scruples had never taken him to such a low place.

On his journey to Pennsylvania he had worked odd jobs as he could find them, but not everyone looked favorably on an adolescent traveling alone. Their suspicions of his character drove him to become what they imagined him to be—a thief. At times Harley's hunger drove him to steal, but he only took enough to appease his need and then moved on.

Once he began working for Gustav Dentzel, he never stole again. He had been a good employee for the most part, so much so that Gustav trusted him to take the portable carousel out for the season. His poor health didn't deter him from keeping the carousel horses galloping on their rounds at the many fairs across the states.

Loneliness and loveliness bit Harley hard when he first laid eyes on Penny Coldwell at the Germantown Fair the summer of 1864 in Washington, Kentucky. The sting of it drove him to the unreasonable. For months he spent his evenings carving and creating a music box. As he worked, he thought of her. He pictured himself giving the music box to her and the look of pleasure that would be on her sweet face.

Irrational, but hopeful, Harley dreamed his dreams while beams of reality shot through his conscience from time to time. They disturbed his imaginations and caused him to worry about details he would rather ignore.

How would he support them? He knew he did not have the means. He also had his doubts about the girl coming with him willingly, although he was certain she could learn to love him in time. After all, he loved her. He would cherish her and treat her like a princess—his princess.

Harley considered that having the girl watch him gun down the man in the barn, a man who was either a relative or a friend, might not be a good foundation to build a marriage on. And he still needed money. He could "borrow" a horse to ride to Maysville, but only money would buy the tickets for the steamboat and provide the resources they would need to live.

He already had some of the elements in place. He had picked up an entire widow's ensemble. With the help of some ether and the wheeled chair he planned to "borrow" from the doctor's office, he was sure he could pull it off. He could belt her into the chair and cover her up with the dark clothes and veiled hat. No one on the boat would question a veiled widow woman staying in her cabin. He could bring her meals and take care of her, and when it was time, they would disembark in the same manner they boarded.

The boat's destination made no difference. Harley's goal was to get as far away as possible. Anywhere would do for them to start their life together, at least anywhere there were not a lot of people around. He would need to pay for a place for them to live. He simply had to have money to make his plan work. As much as he wanted to take Penny with him, Harley turned from the hollow and began the walk back to the lean-to.

CHAPTER 23

"How's she doing?" Penny patted Lucy's neck.

"She seems restless," said Logan. "She's been pacing, getting up and down—even nipping at her flanks."

"She's sweaty. Poor Lucy-girl."

"Zion thinks she's close to delivering. I don't have the heart to go to bed and leave her."

"It could be hours yet. It might be a good idea to get some rest." Penny opened the door to a storage compartment and pulled out a folding cot.

"This might not be as comfortable as the haymow, but you could take a little nap by the stall." Memories of her father filled Penny's mind. "Daddy used to keep a cot in the barn for occasions such as this."

"Did you ever see a foal born?"

"Oh, yes. It's the most wonderful thing. So many times in the middle of the night Daddy or Balim would come for me when a mare's water broke or she started circling her stall."

"You have a lot of good memories, don't you?"

"Yes, I do." Penny closed her eyes and breathed in a collection of sights, smells and senses. A horse barn was certainly not a glamorous place for a young girl to pass her time, but Mr. Coldwell wanted his children to appreciate the work done in the barn that provided their fine home. Penny had loved every moment shared with her father, Balim, and Zion as the Coldwell mares brought forth their young.

"I hope there are many more yet to be made." Logan resisted his temptation no longer. He reached out and ran the back of his index finger along her jaw line. It was softer than he imagined. The upturned corners of Penny's pink lips let him know she enjoyed his touch as much as he had enjoyed touching her.

Penny kept her eyes closed, afraid to open them and wake from what surely must be a dream. She had wondered what it would feel like to be touched by a man. Henry had declared his love by letter, but theirs had been a long distance affair.

As much as Penny had been disappointed by the way her relationship with Henry had waned, Henry had never stirred her the way Logan Mayfield now did. She could not even imagine sharing such a sensation with Henry Coventry. Theirs was a childhood friendship that had grown to familiarity and fondness. They were committed to each other. It had seemed natural to Penny that fondness and commitment would lead to marriage, but the current flowing through her now made her thankful she had not sailed the smooth waters.

Although Penny longed to lean into the man causing the delightful sensations, she gathered her wits and stepped back instead. The move was bitter-sweet for both of them, but the right thing to do. It would be so easy to let passion carry them away, but so wrong to compromise God's best plans for momentary pleasure.

Penny opened her eyes to find Logan staring at her. He had been scanning her features, but when she opened her cornflower blue eyes, he broke into a broad grin. They stood a foot apart, not touching, each with their hands to their sides. Motionless, they looked into each other's eyes, delving into one another's souls.

At first Penny was afraid to open herself to the probing man, but the affection she read in his expression made her feel safe— compelled her to respond. She allowed her emotional safeguards to come down, and before she knew what had happened, Logan Mayfield reached into her soul with his. A connection was made that felt so very right.

"Zion will be wondering what's taking so long. I told him I was coming to get a report on Lucy."

Logan took a step back to assist Penny in bringing the intimate moment to a comfortable close. "What are you going to tell him?" Logan grinned.

"What do you want me to tell him?"

Logan delighted in the sparkle he saw in Penny's eyes. "What you *should* tell him is that Lucy seems a bit agitated, but no other changes."

Logan walked Penny to the door and opened it for her. Penny took her lantern from the hook and crossed the threshold. "All right. That's what I'll tell him then."

"See you later."

"Good night."

Logan watched the girl's return to the cabin. Her coral dress swished with her steps, and the light from the lantern bounced along the path until she reached the cabin. Before she opened the door, she turned and waved, and then disappeared inside.

"Oh," Logan whispered, "and you can tell Zion that his sister is lovely and I'm really quite smitten."

Penny unsuccessfully masked her emotions. Zion and Rosalie looked at her and then at each other with a knowing exchange.

"How are things in the barn?" Zion studied Penny's face and watched the different expressions play across it.

"Logan says to tell you that Lucy seems a bit agitated, but there have been no other changes."

"Really? No changes?" Zion watched his baby sister. She was twitterpated for sure. Perhaps her strong reaction to Logan had been based on something other than she had realized.

Rosalie shushed her husband. She knew he was close to launching a magnificent teasing assault if she did not discharge a swift intervention.

Millicent sat next to Rosalie with a strip of *Flying Geese* blocks on her lap. She was sewing it to an equal-length strip of solid fabric. She recognized something new in the air, but decided to continue her observations in silence.

The cabin door burst open. Dripping, Logan stood wide-eyed across the threshold.

"What happened?" Rosalie grabbed a towel and rushed to Logan.

"It's time." Logan grinned from ear to ear. "I'm wearing her water."

"Her water broke?" Zion's eyes grew large as he took in the details.

"As sure as I'm standing here dripping." Logan gave a hearty laugh. How life had changed over the past few months. If someone had asked him last year how he thought it would feel to sleep in a barn, muck stalls, and be sprayed with amniotic fluid; his answer would surely have been sarcastic and negative. Today, it felt wonderful. Excitement for the upcoming birth raced through him. "Let's go, boss-man!"

"You want to come, ladies?" Zion scanned the room for responses.

"Of course!" said Penny. "I wouldn't miss it!"

"I'll make some coffee and come down in a bit." Rosalie reached for the coffee pot and began filling it with water.

"I'll help her bring the coffee down," said Millicent.

"Let's go, then." Zion led the threesome to the barn. When they arrived they found Lucy standing with a strip of fluid running along her back and over her croup. Zion touched it. "Amniotic fluid."

"Hi, Lucy," said Penny. "You're about to become a momma."
Lucy stood for the greeting and then lay down on the ground.

"It looks like she's been laboring for some time," said Zion.
"We could have a foal soon."

Lucy vocalized with a hard contraction.

"You can do it, girl." Logan paced and cheered the mare on.
In just a few minutes a smooth bluish-white sac began to protrude.

"She's got 70 to 90 pounds to push through the birth canal."
Zion watched as his mare worked up a sweat.

"Oh, look," Penny pointed at the sac, "a foot!"

The foal remained inside the sac, but because it was somewhat
transparent, one hoof could be seen through the membrane.

"And there's another one." Logan clapped his hands as a
second foot showed.

"Good girl, Lucy. Now for the head and shoulders. That's the
most difficult part. She may rest a bit before pushing."

The onlookers waited with anticipation. After a minute, Lucy
pushed, but no head came through. Zion waited a few minutes
more, but the mare was obviously having difficulty.

"She's really struggling, and this is her first delivery. Let's
help her. Logan, get a dry towel and use it to get a hold on the
front feet. Break the sac first and then pull the feet down toward
Lucy's hind feet. The angle will help rotate the head as it passes
through the canal."

It was hard for Zion to sit back and watch; but with a broken
arm, the best he could do was navigate Logan through the process.
Even with his inability to engage hands on in the birth, foaling
was always an exciting experience. Watching new life enter the
world always brought with it a sense of the miraculous.

"That's right." Zion encouraged Logan as he worked. The
foal's head and shoulders were through. "Now, pull straight along
the line of Lucy's backbone."

Logan strained at the effort of pulling the foal and thought how tired the momma must be. Lucy had little strength left to push out the rear feet.

"Help her, Logan. Pull the foal the rest of the way out, but make sure you keep it next to Lucy. The umbilical cord will still be attached, and we want to keep it that way for a few minutes. A large amount of blood will pass from the mare to the foal before it's detached."

Logan followed directions, and in seconds the colt was freed.

"It's a colt, Zion!" Penny clapped both palms against the sides of her cheeks. "Just look at him! He's beautiful."

"He is. He looks just like West."

The colt lifted his head and neck, rolled onto his chest, and then rested his head on his mother's rear hock. A few minutes of precious bonding passed before Lucy stood to her feet and the umbilical cord snapped.

"Perfect," said Zion. "There's no need for sutures, but we'll dip the little fellow's navel in iodine to keep out infection."

Logan reached for the iodine bottle at the same moment Lucy moved across the stall.

"What's that?" Penny pointed to a mass of tissue protruding from Lucy.

"I'm not sure. I hope it's not her uterus prolapsing," said Zion. "If it is, she could go into shock. And if the uterus is damaged, this could be her only pregnancy."

Zion studied the tissue. Something didn't seem right. As he rehearsed scenarios, Lucy dropped to the ground and pushed.

"Zion, look!" Penny's eyes grew as large as saucers when a foot became visible in the sac.

"Twins! Dear God, she's having twins!" Zion was stunned. Goosebumps jumped all over his arms. In a matter of moments the front feet and nose were showing. It was clear the foal was in distress, and Lucy lay on the ground exhausted, too tired to push.

"Logan, pull the foal with the next contraction while I get the sack off its face." Logan worked with Lucy through one contraction, and then a second. Finally, the foal was free and gasping for air. Zion ripped the remainder of the sac from its nostrils.

The foal moved spasmodically as Zion checked her over. She was a bit smaller than her brother, but that was to be expected with a filly. She looked perfect: a beautiful chestnut with a blaze running from the top of her forehead to the end of her muzzle.

The filly exhaled and then stopped breathing. Zion held his breath waiting for her to take in air. The seconds passed in long stretches.

"Logan, grab her by the hind legs, hold her vertically and shake her." Logan did as Zion directed. The foal remained lifeless, but fluid began draining from her lungs.

"Once more and harder, like cracking a dish towel," barked Zion.

Logan mustered his strength and shook the foal with all his might.

"Now lay her on her side. Compress her chest with your hands. Hold her mouth closed and cup your mouth over her nostrils, then blow."

Logan gently laid the filly down on the straw and followed Zion's directions. Penny watched, dumbfounded, as Logan breathed life back into the filly. The shaking had apparently restarted her heart and expelled the fluid from her lungs that had been drowning her. She was limp, but breathing.

"Penny, towel her off. Rough her up a bit." Zion threw one of the large towels at her. She caught it, and as she began toweling her off, the filly snaked her neck, flattened her ears, and nipped at her.

"Look at that." Zion admired the filly's spunk. "I think she's going to be ok."

Penny grinned and finished her job, murmuring sweet nonsense to the foal.

"Perfect," said Zion. "Now let's get this little girl over to her momma and brother."

CHAPTER 24

Rosalie poured coffee for the delivery crew who sat on makeshift benches around the barn. "I still can't believe it," she said. "What are the odds?"

"My father was in the business for three decades," said Zion, "and as far as I know he only successfully delivered one set of twins. I'm not sure what the actual odds are, but there are easily thousands of single births to one set of twins."

"I knew it was unusual." Rosalie handed a cup of steaming coffee to Penny.

"It's nothing short of miraculous." Millicent stared at the horses and then at Logan covered in yuck and smiling from ear to ear.

"You missed all the excitement." Zion patted Logan on the shoulder. "You would have been proud of your son. I don't know what I would have done without his help."

"That's not another one, is it?" Millicent was taken aback by a large mass of red and white tissue emerging from Lucy's backside.

"That's the afterbirth," said Zion. "We want to make sure she passes all of it. If she doesn't within the next hour or so, I'm going to need your help again, Logan. For now we'll just let it hang and hope the weight of it pulls it away from her uterus."

"Happy to oblige, boss."

"Would you stop calling me that? It feels more like family sharing an occasion like this. You're practically an uncle."

"That reminds me," Penny's eyes brightened, "you haven't named them."

"You're right," said Zion. "I'm plumb taken by surprise. I'm going to have to think on it a bit. Gifts like these need fitting monikers."

Rosalie smiled at her husband. "I know you'll come up with something appropriate."

"Look there." Zion puffed up like a proud daddy. "The afterbirth's out. Lucy, you're doing a great job for a maiden."

A large, shiny, grayish-whitish sac lay on the ground under Lucy's rear legs. "Logan, will you spread that out? We need to make sure no little pieces are still inside."

The inside of the sac was a velvety red. Logan followed Zion's direction, checking for tears and abnormalities, and then measured the umbilical cord.

"Will they nurse soon?" asked Millicent.

"Any time. They just need to get up on their feet first." Zion watched Lucy nickering at her newborns. The colt was very active, but did not try to stand. "Look at the legs on him. They're almost as long as his momma's."

The filly pushed up on trembling front legs and fell back down. Without stopping for a break, she raised herself again. The second time, the front legs planted in the ground, quickly followed by the back legs. The filly wobbled, but won the race to stand driven by a sucking impulse that set her on a search for her first taste of colostrum.

"She is spunky." Penny admired the foal. "Maybe that would be a good name for her?"

"She's going to need that spunk. Lucy has two teats, but it's unlikely she will produce enough milk for two healthy foals."

"Can you supplement with something?" asked Logan.

"We're blessed to have three nannies in milk," said Zion. "Goat milk is a good second to horse milk. I've even seen a foal trained to nurse right from the goat. They had to set up a platform, but it got the foal through a rough spot."

"Are we going to do that?" Penny furrowed her brow at the picture she imagined.

"We're milking the goats anyway," said Rosalie. "Would bottle feeding work since it's just a supplement?"

"I think that will be fine." Zion watched his filly take her first steps. She was unsteady, constantly shifting her head, neck, and feet in her attempt to keep her balance.

"Should we help her?" asked Logan.

"No. It's good to let them stand by themselves. Lifting her to her feet before her legs are strong enough to support her weight can strain her tendons and ligaments. It can also interfere with the bonding process."

The foal remained standing and instinctively searched between her mother's legs. She nosed around until she found what she was looking for, and Lucy graciously accepted her foal's first nursing attempt.

"See how natural she took her?" said Zion. "The handling we've done over the past few days paid off."

"I'm surprised she got up first," said Millicent. "She seemed so weak and her brother so strong."

"There's no rhyme or reason." Zion accepted a coffee refill from Rosalie. "As long as the colt is up in the next couple of hours, there's nothing to be concerned about."

"I'm so happy for you, Zion." Rosalie squeezed her husband's arm and lifted a bright smile. "If you don't mind, I'm going to call it a night. Mattie and Dahlia will be up early."

"That's fine. Penny, you and Mrs. Mayfield should go to bed, too. There's not much else happening here tonight."

"All right, big brother. I'll see you in the morning."

"Goodnight." The ladies took the path to the house and disappeared inside. The door to the barn remained open and a gentle breeze carried sweet scents inside.

"Why don't you go lie down, too, Logan? You've got to be tired."

"I am at that, but it's the best tired I've ever experienced."

"I know what you mean." The two men sat in silence for a few minutes. The filly finished nursing and lay down. In seconds she was fast asleep.

"I think I'll wash up a bit more and change my clothes." Logan stripped off his shirt and picked up a washcloth. He dipped it in a bucket of clean water and used soap from the foaling kit to remove the last traces of blood and amniotic fluid.

Slowly he took the rungs of the ladder and hoisted himself into the haymow. He took a clean shirt from a peg on the wall and sat down on the bed he had made from bales and blankets. His arms felt like lead.

I'll just close my eyes for a second.

When his lids dropped over his tired globes, the burning sensation in his eyes eased. Short seconds passed before his shoulders slumped and his chin dropped to his chest.

I'll just lie down for a minute.

Zion chuckled when he heard the sounds of Logan's deep breathing drift down from the loft. "Thank You, Lord."

Zion studied his foals in the still, quiet barn. As he pondered his blessings, the colt struggled to his feet and found his way to his mother. The dam received him as well as she had his sister, and Zion watched the little one suckle.

"What a surprise, Lord." Zion ruffled his hair and grinned. "I mean, of course, it's not a surprise to You; but You really caught me off guard."

222

Zion stood and stretched. It felt good to move around. With long strides he spanned the length of the barn and back, and then stopped at the corner of the barn he used as a small office. He reached inside the cabinet on the wall and pulled out a worn leather Bible.

The lamp had been on low for the birthing. Zion turned the key to the burner to increase the light. A slip of paper marked his place in the eighth chapter of Ecclesiastes. He read the first few verses and noticed two words were repeated in both verses five and six.

"Whoso keepeth the commandment shall feel no evil thing: and a wise man's heart discerneth both time and judgment. Because to every purpose there is time and judgment . . . ."

"Time and judgment." Zion rolled the words over in his mind. "A wise man's heart understands both time and judgment; and to every purpose there is time and judgment."

Zion smiled. "I like that, Lord, but those don't seem fitting names for horses." He looked at his colt and watched him sleeping beside his mother. "You were right on time, weren't you? You are the one we planned for and hoped for. I like the concept of 'time,' but that sounds odd for a name. Let's see. Time is based on seasons, but Season doesn't seem like a good name, either. Seasons are based on the equinoxes of the sun and moon. How about Equinox for you? That has a nice ring to it, doesn't it? Equinox, I like it."

Zion turned his attention to the filly that had been such a surprise and given them such a scare. "That would leave judgment for you, little lady. Prudence would work, or Providence, but I think I like Equity the best. That's a good word for judgment, don't you think? What about you, girl? Is Equity good with you?"

A sweet peace swept over Zion's spirit. He was physically and emotionally drained, but a blissful calm filled his soul. "Yes, Lord, that's what we'll name them: Equinox and Equity. It feels right."

Zion kept watch over his little herd to ensure both of the foals continued to nurse well, and each passed meconium. Satisfied that neither was constipated nor had diarrhea, Zion lowered the flame in the lamp, stretched out on the cot, and fell fast asleep with a smile on his face.

Roo's morning ruckus roused Logan from sleep. The fuzzies in his thoughts mingled with the dust dancing in the shaft of light that shone through the window of the haymow.

"What's this?" Logan wondered aloud. His hand rested on the bare skin of his exposed chest. "Where's my shirt?" A quick perusal told the tale. His shirt had fallen to the ground when he fell into sleep a few short hours ago.

Logan sat up and reached for the shirt. His arms ached, but he rushed to put it on and hurry down the ladder. Zion was awake, stretched out on the old cot.

"Aren't you the lazy fellow, this morning?" Zion's eyes sparkled with humor.

"I guess so." Logan chuckled. "How are they?"

"Very good. Everyone's doing what they are supposed to, and done what they needed to. Lucy's a great mom, and both Equinox and Equity are fit as a fiddle."

"You named them."

"I sure did. What do you think?"

"Equinox and Equity: as a man who loves words I would say those are some fine names. I'd love to hear how you came up with them."

"I'll tell everyone over breakfast," said Zion. "I sure hope my wife has some vittles ready, because I'm about near starved to death."

"What about the bottle feeding?"

"We can start that this afternoon. I want them to get all the colostrum they can, and that won't last more than the first day."

224

"Why is that so important? What's the difference between colostrum and regular milk?"

"It is different. You can tell just by looking at it, and it's important because it gives the newborns protection against bacteria."

"Pa! Pa!" Dahlia called as she hurried from the cabin to the barn. She burst through the door and into her father's good arm. "Momma said you had a surprise for me."

"That I do, little girl. Look there." Zion nodded in the direction of the birthing stall.

"A baby!" Dahlia jumped up and down and clapped her hands.

"Yes, a baby," said Zion. "That's a colt, a baby boy named Equinox. Now go peek around Lucy and see what else you find."

Dahlia tiptoed to the stall for a better look and sucked in air when she saw the second foal. "Another baby?"

"Yes, ma'am. That's a filly, a baby girl named Equity."

Dahlia's hands clung to the side of the stall as she stared in wonder at the foals. "Can I touch them, Pa?"

"A little later today, baby girl, you sure can. Let's let them sleep for now and have something to eat. I'm guessing since your Ma sent you down she's up and working on some breakfast. Is that right?"

"Yes, sir, Pa: eggs and bacon and grits."

"That sounds like a feast. I'm hungry. Let's go on up to the house and fill this empty spot." Zion pointed to his belly and made a funny face.

Dahlia giggled and thrust her small hand in her father's large one. She skipped alongside Zion, and Logan followed behind grinning.

"After I read that Scripture, I felt drawn to the words 'timing' and 'judgment,' but they didn't seem like good names for horses." Zion took a piece of thick, crispy bacon as the serving dish made its way around the table. "So I thought of other words that meant close to the same thing. I have to say I was pretty pleased with Equinox and Equity."

"I like them, too." Penny held her coffee cup in both hands, intent on her brother's news.

"Not only are they great names individually, they also work together," said Logan. "And I like the alliteration."

"The what?" Zion's eyes turned to slits, and he gave Logan a sideways glance.

Logan laughed. "Their first sounds, they even match with equine. You're a horse farmer and a wordsmith."

"Oh, I get it," said Zion. "It's like 'good gracious, grab the grub.'"

"You've got it."

"You two are silly together." Rosalie laughed. "I do like the passage you took the names from. Every purpose of God has both its timing and its plan."

"It's important to have a good name," Millicent smiled and turned to Zion, "and I can't think of a better place to find one than in the Bible."

Zion nodded and took a bite of grits. An incident from years ago came to mind and made him smile.

"Sometimes names happen by accident." Zion took a sip of coffee and waited to make sure he had everyone's full attention. "When Penny was born, I wasn't allowed anywhere near the house. I kept pestering Pa to go in. I wanted to check on Ma and the baby. Pa had a tough time keeping me occupied. He said we should pick some flowers for the new baby, so he took me on a long walk. There were all kinds of flowers along the lane, but the only ones I wanted to pick were buttercups. They just seemed so cheerful."

"Oh, no." Penny moaned and shook her head. "Not this again."

Zion ignored his sister and continued his story. "When I brought them into the house, Penny was tucked in Ma's arm

226

while she rested on the bed. I handed Ma the flowers and said, 'Here, buttercups.'"

Penny laughed and finished the tale. "Momma was so done in she must have thought Zion called me Buttercup, but he was really telling her about the flowers he picked."

"And with that yellow hair of hers, well, it just stuck. Buttercup's been her pet name ever since."

"Only for a select few." Penny wiped her mouth and picked up an empty platter. "Don't you have work to do, brother?"

CHAPTER 25

"Which one do you think they'll like best?" Penny asked Logan as they headed toward the road bound for Garth and Pansy Joy's place.

"They are both excellent," said Logan. "I'm very impressed."

"Really?"

"Really." A soft smile lifted the corners of Logan's mouth. Tenderness filled his hazel eyes. "Very."

Pink traveled up Penny's throat and perched on her high cheekbones.

"I love how you used classic red for the barn and blue for the ribbon. The rearing horse brings action and even a bit of majesty to the design. I think it's the perfect combination of classic symbolism and avant-garde."

"Avant what?"

"Forward thinking. Creative and innovative."

"You do know your words."

"I love words—reading, writing, and good conversation. Words have been my friends all my life." Logan paused, his heart filled with more than he was able to express. "I've recently discovered, however, that words don't always come through for me."

Penny glanced into Logan's face, and then stepped into the tree-lined lane that spanned the distance between Briar Hollow and the main road. "I know what you mean."

Logan walked beside her. The couple continued in silence. Penny studied the leaves overhead, and then the ferns on the ground. The sound of a tinkling chime caught her attention.

"Come with me." Penny slipped between two junipers and into a three-foot mushroom circle surrounded by a ring of flowers. "Do you know what this is?"

"I have no idea." Logan smiled at Penny's animation and obvious delight. "Would you care to enlighten me, Miss Coldwell?"

"Why, yes, Mr. Mayfield. Stand next to me."

Logan joined Penny in the circle. "You are standing in the middle of a fairy ring," Penny picked up the glass jar from the center and placed it in his hands, "and this is a wishing jar."

"So fanciful, Miss Coldwell." Logan smiled at the girl he had once called a pixie and restrained himself from speaking the name again. "Do you believe in fairies?"

"I remember the first time I saw this place. It was when Zion and I came five years ago. I told him then that I didn't really believe in fairies, but if I did, I think they would like it here."

Logan nodded and considered her words. "What about wishing jars? Do you believe in them?"

"This is a magical place, you have to admit." Penny scanned the scenic beauty of the woodlands. A slight breeze continued to play the chimes and shafts of light pierced the thick canopy. "I do know this particular wishing jar has been tested and proven," said Penny in her best school teacher voice.

"Really? How so?" Logan enjoyed the banter and was happy to learn more about the girl who occupied so many of his thoughts.

"A few years ago Pansy Joy put a wish in there. She wrote that she wanted to marry Garth, and look at her now. She's Mrs. Garth Eldridge."

"Is that right?" Logan smiled with his lips, but skepticism marked his expression.

"It's undeniable history." Penny put a hand on her hip, indignantly supporting her case.

Logan studied the girl. He never tired of looking at her porcelain skin and beautiful features. He thoroughly enjoyed her mannerisms and mien. "Did you ever put a wish inside?"

"No. I never did." Penny shook her head and smiled. "I don't believe a blue Mason jar has any magic in it, but I do believe the Lord hears the longings of the heart. If you had seen Pansy Joy and Garth when they were betrothed, you would know they were very much in love."

"I've seen them now, and it looks like they still are . . . very much so," said Logan, pleased to have the occasion to speak of matters of the heart.

"What does love look like to you?" Logan wanted to reach for her hand, but instead reached for her heart. He believed a lady's virtue deserved to be cherished and treated with dignity. As much as he wanted to connect with Penny through physical touch, he wanted to make sure his behavior was above reproach.

Penny pondered Logan's words. Images came to mind and feelings breezed into her heightened emotions. She saw Pansy Joy and Garth on their wedding day, and then Zion and Rosalie. She thought about the blissful moments of their special days, and then her thoughts turned to the everyday matters of life.

"Love is so many things, don't you think?" Penny took the jar from Logan and placed it back in the middle of the fairy ring. "I mean, of course it's the feelings people have for each other, but I think love is about relationships. There are many components to relationships."

"Such as?"

"Rosalie loves Zion, and Zion loves Rosalie. You can see it in the way they look at each other and talk to each other. There's evidence of it by the children they share; but you asked what love looks like. To me, it looks like Zion chopping firewood and Rosalie making Zion's favorite dish. It's Zion taking the baby when Rosalie is exhausted on wash day and Rosalie scratching an itch on Zion's back he can't reach."

"So you are saying loving is serving?"

"I think I'm saying that loving is a lot of things, but one of the surest ways to *see* it is in serving." Penny cocked her head and lifted her eyes to the sky. She thought for a moment before speaking again. "Think about this. Rosalie doesn't do Garth's wash. Sure she loves him, and she would in an emergency, but because of her relationship with Zion, she serves his daily needs, not her brother-in-law's."

"I see," said Logan. "That doesn't sound very romantic."

Penny laughed. "Romance is part of love, but it's not what love is all about. True love means giving, not just getting."

"So you're saying giving is loving?"

"Not at all." Penny smiled brightly, tickled by the confused look in Logan's hazel eyes.

"Then exactly what are you saying, Professor Coldwell?"

"I'm hardly a professor, but a very wise man once told me, 'Missy Penny, yous can give without loving, but yous cain't love without giving.'"

Logan watched Penny's expression turn warm. "You must be talking about Balim."

Penny ticked her head. A quizzical look played across her face.

"Zion told me about him."

"Oh." The slight girl folded her arms across herself in a hug. "It's been five years, and I still miss him."

"Of course you do." Logan searched for a way to bring the twinkle back to Penny's blue eyes. An idea came to mind. "Let me see that paper."

"This one?" Penny retrieved the paper with the trademark drawings from her bag, and lifted it for Logan to see.

"Unless you have another one in your reticule."

"That's the only one." Penny handed the paper to Logan. She watched as he ripped a strip from the bottom. She felt to protest, but her curiosity got the better of her. Logan withdrew a stub of pencil from his shirt pocket and began writing.

"The lovely Penny Coldwell wishes she could see Balim." Logan read the words as he wrote them. When he finished, he winked at Penny and then reached for the wishing jar. After tucking the paper inside, he sealed the lid and definitively placed the jar back in the center of the fairy ring.

"Did you really write that? The lovely Penny Coldwell?"

"It's true." Logan envied the hat that sat on the girl's golden tresses. He thought back to the evening before in the barn and how he had swept a tendril from her silken forehead. "At least, it's quite true in my estimation; and I'm a very well educated man, you know."

Penny giggled. "Well then how could I argue with you, oh great scholar?"

"I guess it's in your best interest to agree with me."

"Then I must say thank you, kind sir." Penny curtsied before the fine gentleman. When she lifted her head, the humor in her eyes had changed to a wistful expression. "I would like to agree with your wish."

"As the Good Book says, 'where two or more agree . . . .'"

Penny brightened at his encouraging words. "You're right." She gave a firm nod of her head. "I do believe I'll see Balim again—someday."

"And I believe with you."

Logan and Penny finished the half mile walk to Garth and Pansy Joy's place in comfortable silence. When they turned in the lane at the Eldridge farm, Logan returned the sketches to Penny.

"Why don't you do the honors of presenting your handiwork?"

Penny smiled, thought for a moment, and then ripped the paper in half. She gave one of the drawings to Logan. "I just sketched your ideas. How about we present them together?"

"Garth liked elements of both designs," Penny reported to Zion. "He likes the white lettering in the ribbon, but black outlines around the outside."

"And he suggested adding the location under the ribbon," Logan chimed in.

Zion stood at the corral with one foot on the lowest rail. With a heart full of admiration, he watched Lucy and her foals in the enclosure. Equinox rubbed his head against his mother's flank while Equity frolicked a few feet away.

"I think he's got a good idea there," Zion repositioned his hat on his head to block the bright Kentucky sun from his eyes, "especially since we're going to be a multi-state operation."

Logan smiled. "Now you're talking."

"I've been doing a lot of thinking, actually."

"About the farm?" asked Penny.

"Yes, about the farm and life in general." Zion turned to face his companions and leaned his back against the rail. "I've been thinking about how the farrier works on a horse's foot before putting on a new shoe. After the old shoe is off, the farrier picks out the muck: all the compacted dirt and manure. Then he trims off the excess growth and cleans the sole and frog of the hoof. By the time the filing is done, what was dirty and possibly a danger to the animal, is white as a pearl and ready for new shoes.

"If the excess hoof isn't trimmed, bones can misalign, and that places stress on a horse's legs. Without proper care and shoes, a horse's foot can spread and even split. As the saying goes, 'no foot, no horse.'"

"What about in the wild?" asked Logan. "Feral horses, like mustangs, don't have shoes."

"That's true," said Zion, "but in the wild, conditions are different than they are for domesticated animals. Think about it. You have over a thousand pounds of horse flesh on four spindly legs and comparatively tiny feet. When they gallop, or jump, or pull heavy weight, having their feet shod protects the walls of their hooves and their toes—sometimes even muscles, bones, and tendons, depending on the type of work they do."

"I never thought about that," said Logan.

"Improper shoeing or not shoeing a horse that needs it, can make a horse permanently lame. One of the most important things that happens during the shoeing process is checking for signs of disease or other health concerns. During the shoeing, a good farrier checks for potential lameness issues and intervenes before problems occur."

"That's interesting, and important for horses," said Penny, "but what does it have to do with life in general?"

"I've been thinking about how breaking my arm has been like getting shoed. It certainly stopped me in my tracks."

"It did slow you down," said Penny.

"I know we've talked some about it before, but I've gone a bit deeper with my thinking." Zion sat down on a stump beside the corral and crossed his long legs at the ankles. He stared at his work boots as he spoke. "I know my thoughts might seem like a jackrabbit on the run, but I was reading Psalm 23 and thinking about how the Lord is the Good Shepherd. Being that I'm building a herd of my own of a different sort of four-legged critters, I naturally wondered if the Lord is like a good horseman."

"I see." Penny smiled at her brother.

"Part of being a good horseman is tending to your animals' physical needs, like shoeing. Like I said, a good farrier takes care to examine his horse when the shoe is off. It's during the re-shoeing process that it's the best time to detect any issues that need to be corrected that could cause real problems down the line."

Logan listened intently as Zion shared his heart. The big man's transparency and insight drew his full attention.

"This arm of mine has been like having a shoe off." Zion raised his cast arm captured in its sling. "As long as I'm wearing this, I'm like a horse with his hoof between the farrier's knees. And while I've been stopped, I've been asking the Lord to examine my feet, the paths I've been taking, and make sure there's nothing hidden in me that could make me halt or lame down the road."

Penny knelt in the grass and grabbed Zion's large hand between both of hers. "What have you been hearing?"

"It's like this, Buttercup, I believe I've had things a bit backwards." Zion looked toward his cabin and thought of the family inside. They were so dear to his heart, and he wanted to do his best for them. "I've been coming up with plans and asking God to bless them instead of asking Him for His plans, what He's blessing, and jumping in with that."

Zion turned his blue eyes to the matching pair in his sister's upturned face. "I'm not saying I've been in sin or anything. It's just that if I truly want to walk with God, I need to ask His direction first, not for His blessing on my ideas. Does that make sense?"

"Of course it does," said Penny. "What a beautiful concept. I think we could all learn from your lesson."

"Without the broken arm, I hope," said Logan. "Who would get all the work done around here?"

"I don't rightly know about that." Zion released Penny's hand and raised his tall frame from his seat on the stump. Penny stood beside him. "I do know one more thing, however."

"What's that?" asked Logan.

"When it comes to shoeing horses, before the new shoe gets put on and the horse is ready to run again, growth gets clipped off. What happens to the excess?"

"I guess it gets thrown away. Is it good for composting or something?"

"Actually, my friend, I throw it to the dogs. They love it."

"They eat it?" Logan wrinkled his brow and frowned.

"They do," said Zion. "When the shoeing gets done, it's like an Easter egg hunt around here. We have to keep Micah tied up so he doesn't get in the way; but when the farrier's job is done, he races over and snorts around like a truffle hog on a hunt."

"It's true." Penny laughed. "He goes crazy for them."

"Why is that significant?" asked Logan.

"Dogs are mentioned many times in the Scripture, and mostly in reference to folks who aren't walking with the Lord. When it's shoeing time, and the excess is cut off and thrown to the dogs; it reminds me that sometimes there's excess in me. I don't want to keep that for myself. I don't rightly know how to explain it without sounding offish. I'm not meaning a slight to anyone who doesn't know the Lord. It's just that there are things 'dogs' enjoy that I'm not supposed to have attached to me. There are things that can hinder my walk, and I need to throw them off. There may be some that think what I'm throwing off is fine, even enjoyable, like the dogs and the hoof trimmings; but God wants me to let them go."

"Oh, Zion." Penny gave her brother a squeeze. "You are sounding more and more like Balim every day."

CHAPTER 26

"It's just like the Erlangers to do something sweet like this." Rosalie tied Dahlia's braids together with one green ribbon. "That matches your dress to perfection, baby girl."

"A pahdy! A pahdy!" Dahlia jumped up and down in the chair. "We'e going to a pahdy!"

"Calm down, sweet pea." Penny drew the little girl to her side and then onto her lap as she plopped into the rocking chair. "You're wearing me out before the party starts."

"Daddy! Daddy!"

Zion watched his little girl squirm on Penny's lap. Her excitement filled the house and sparked some livelihood in the Coldwell cabin that had been missing since his accident. "Yes, angel?"

"Daddy, can I bwing one of your big hankies?"

"Are you expecting to catch a cold at the Lodge?"

"Oh, Daddy, it's not for bwowing my nose." Dahlia shook her head at her father and gave him a condescending look. "It's for games! We need it for Bwind Man's Bwuff and Dwop the Hank'chief."

"By all means you shall have a handkerchief!" Zion declared with a majestic bow. "Are we ready to go?"

"I believe so," said Rosalie. "Let me just cover this fried chicken; and Millie's dish needs to be covered, too. I can hardly wait for her to show off her mulberry sauce."

"Me, too," said Penny. "We walked all the way to town for her secret ingredient. She wouldn't tell me what it was until we got there. I couldn't believe it was orange rind. I'm glad Mrs. Matheny had some at the mercantile, or she would have been disappointed."

Rosalie and Penny had watched Millicent make the sauce of mulberries, sugar, vanilla, orange rind, and thyme. It was a combination neither of them had fathomed in their days of working with mulberries, but the aroma was fabulous while Millicent prepared the sauce she planned to serve over crepes at the party.

After much hustling and bustling, everyone was finally ready for the walk to Comfort Lodge. The party passed the wildflower garden on the right of the property and entered the tree-canopied lane that led to the main road. Rosalie watched as Dahlia admired the fairyland of her childhood. Without stopping to admire the scenery, the party-goers exited the tree-covered passage and stepped out on the main road.

Comfort Lodge was a mile south of Briar Hollow and one mile from the Washington city line. When their group arrived at the Erlanger's place, Millicent and Logan learned firsthand that Comfort Lodge lived up to its name. The grounds seemed to welcome them, beginning with a weeping willow opposite the pond that waved and bid them down the lane. In the center of the pond edged with fuzzy cattails, a goose house perched on a little island complete with a family of white geese.

Beneath the willow tree, two benches beckoned guests to sit for a spell and enjoy the quiet surroundings. Down a bit from the pond stood a large barn painted a cheery red with white trim and a big white X on the door. It was capped with a black roof that arched over the haymow. A henhouse and springhouse completed the outbuildings, and across the lane, Comfort Lodge nestled in the shade of tall timbers.

Painted a deep green, the vastness of the lodge blended into a lovely scene. A large wraparound porch swung across the front and both sides of the first floor. Four ladder-backed rocking chairs wore the same floral cushions as the bench swing suspended from the porch ceiling. The black-shingled roof was adorned with eight gables, four facing front and four looking into the woods. Clusters of black-eyed Susans lined the flagstone path to the door that was decorated with a wreath of grapevine and dried wildflowers.

In front of the porch, saw horses supported cloth-covered planks that were being filled with food items brought for the impromptu potluck. The party had been Florence Erlanger's idea. At church that morning there had been no denying the stress etched on the pinched face of Cordelia Yates. Florence knew the after effects of the attack on Mr. Yates hovered over her dear Briar Hollow friends as well.

Her husband, James, had gone along with her spontaneous party plans and made the announcement after service. "Everyone bring what you were planning for your own dinner. We'll put it all out and have a potluck party on a lazy Sunday afternoon."

Millicent and Rosalie stopped at the makeshift tables to set out their food. Florence met them and offered to give the newcomers a tour of the Lodge. Logan and his mother filed in behind Florence, admiring the charming details of the home. A large room spanned the biggest portion of the lower level beneath the rental rooms above. "What a lovely place for your guests," said Millicent.

"It's come in handy for many a community event when the weather wasn't cooperating, or when love-struck young-uns wanted to get married at the stroke of midnight on a New Year's Day."

Millicent smiled. She had heard the tale of Garth and Pansy Joy's unique, middle-of-the night wedding at the Lodge.

Florence led the tour from the massive parlor to a large dining room that abutted the kitchen, the washroom, and the private quarters where she and James lived. In the dining room, four matching tables with walnut balloon-backed chairs sat atop a gleaming wood floor. Cream-colored basket-weave cloths covered the tables, each with red and cream cross-stitched embroidery around its fringed perimeters. Paned windows capped with ecru lace valances marched along the front wall that overlooked the porch. In the corner, the flat lid of a dormant wood stove held a crockery pitcher of burnt-red coneflowers and Queen Anne's lace, a colorful complement to the cheery tablecloths. Beside the wood stove stood a functional sideboard crafted in a simple rectangular style with a rich walnut finish.

"Everything is so inviting." Millicent appraised the room. "You've done a beautiful job of creating a warm feeling of home for your guests."

Florence beamed under Millicent's praise. Coming from a highborn lady like Mrs. Mayfield honeyed the accolades.

"Thank you, Mrs. Mayfield." Florence smoothed an invisible wrinkle from a tablecloth. "Well, it's too lovely outside to stay in. Let's see what everyone's brought for dinner."

Back out on the lawn, Penny, in her new periwinkle dress, was serving up cherry punch. Logan thought she looked pretty as a picture and used the excuse of a cold drink to talk to her.

"Punch, please?" Logan smiled at the girl across the table.

Penny considered the request for a moment, and then burst out in a cheerful laugh.

Logan wondered what had inspired her merriment, and decided if it was at his expense, it was worth the cost. "Is there something funny about my request for punch?"

Penny dropped her head and shook it from side to side. A giggle escaped and Logan could see the lift of her cheeks, though she tried to hide her broad smile from his view. With one delicate hand, she covered her mouth, and then took a deep breath before looking Logan in the eye.

"It just struck me funny, Logan, that you would ask me for punch. The way you and Zion thought I rigged West with that cocklebur . . . ." Penny giggled again at a picture she conjured up of Zion watching her throw a punch at Logan over the refreshment table. "I know you didn't mean a literal punch. I guess I just needed a laugh."

Logan loved the sound of her laughter and his name on her lips. "Well, if it makes you happy, by all means, punch away."

"I'm sorry," said Penny, "I've been overtaken by the giggles. You must think I'm a silly girl."

"Not at all." Logan's tone arrested Penny's attention. Her tittering morphed into a shy smile. "I was just thinking what a lovely girl you are, serving and smiling in your pretty new dress."

Color swept up Penny's cheeks. "Well, kind sir, such flattery will earn you a cup of Katie Eldridge's famous cherry punch." Penny dipped a ladle into the glass bowl and filled a cup for her patron. The exchange of the cup from one hand to the next lingered in a way that spoke volumes of words unspoken.

"Thank you." Logan lifted the cup to his lips and sipped the bright red liquid. It was as delicious as its reputation bode, and refreshingly cold thanks to a contribution from Matheny's Ice House.

"Oh, Logan." Penny whispered his name and leaned forward. "Let's start over. I'm so sorry for the way I acted when you first came to Briar Hollow."

"Oh, no," Logan was adamant, "I don't want to go back to not knowing you, Miss Penny. Let's just move forward from here. What do you say?"

A hush filled the space between the couple. Penny's heart was dancing and her spirit light for what seemed the first time in such a long time.

"I say . . ."

Evan and Ethan Matheny flanked Katie Eldridge, each with a firm grasp on one of her arms. Indecorously, the twins dragged the girl to the punch bowl with a boisterous interchange that interrupted Penny's response.

"Now you promised me you'd dip me up a cup of your famous cherry punch." Ethan pulled on Katie's right elbow.

"Well, she promised me too, Ethan Matheny, and I'm gonna be first," said Evan while he tugged on Katie's left arm.

The girl felt like a wishbone being pulled in two different directions. Katie, who usually looked fresh as a daisy, was being jostled and undone by her would-be suitors. Her glistening raven tresses fought against the hairpins she had carefully positioned in her coiffure. Consternation swam in her deep blue eyes.

Mild-mannered, sweet-hearted, beautiful Katie Eldridge was moments from losing her composure when Evan tripped his brother in a last-ditch effort to gain the first cup of punch. Like a stack of dominoes set into motion, first Katie was loosed, and then Ethan fell forward into Logan who bumped into Penny. Logan's cup of cherry punch spilled all over Penny's shirtwaist and splashed on his clothing, as well.

"Oh, my," Penny looked down at her new dress splattered with red.

"Oops." Evan hardly looked penitent. Triumphant for the moment over his brother, he flashed a big grin at Katie. "How about some punch, Katie-girl?"

Rosalie rushed to Penny's aid. She pressed the towel she had used to cover the fried chicken against Penny's soaked top. "Oh, what a shame, your new dress!"

"I know. I hope it's not ruined."

"Maybe Mrs. Erlanger has something you could wear, and we could rinse it out."

Penny smirked at the thought of wearing Florence's dress. "Oh, Rosalie, I don't think that would be safe. We're not even close to the same size. I would have to pin up the top, and that would look awful."

Rosalie could not argue with the girl's logic or desire to be modest. "Do you want me to see if someone will drive you home for a quick change? You could soak the dress and come back to the party."

As much as Penny had been enjoying her time at the Lodge, time alone sounded like a bit of heaven on earth. She had so many things to sort out. "I'll just run home and change. It won't take long, and a walk sounds so nice."

"Would you like me to accompany you?" Logan asked.

Part of Penny leapt at the idea, but she was drenched and knew it would be awkward walking next to a single gentleman with her dress clinging to her chest. "Thanks for the offer, but the party's just starting, and I don't want you to miss anything on my account. I won't be long."

Sunday morning had been the perfect time to break into the bank and clean out the vault. All the fine folks of Washington had been off to the gospel mill for worship service, and the benders were sleeping off their Saturday night fandangos.

The task had been easier than Harley imagined. Having the key had helped tremendously. After the heist, Harley made his way to the lean-to. He had everything ready except the wagon. The night before, he had lifted the wheeled chair from Dr. Byerly's office. The physician left one on the covered porch for emergencies, so that had come off without a fuss.

"I've got the bulge now." Harley adjusted the bag of money on his shoulder. When he arrived at the lean-to, he dropped the bag in a hole he had dug outside the shelter and covered it with his wash bucket.

"I'll give her the chance to come with me willingly first." Harley picked up the music box and turned the key that wound the tension on the spring motor. With a shaking hand, he opened the box. Pins on the cylinder plucked tuned teeth on a steel comb. A familiar melody chimed out; the song the calliope had played when his dolly-girl had ridden the carousel at the fair last year. *I'll Twine 'Mid the Ringlets* was the perfect song for her.

I'll twine 'mid the ringlets
Of my raven black hair,
The lilies so pale
And the roses so fair,
The myrtle so bright
With an emerald hue,
And the pale aronatus
With eyes of bright blue.

I'll sing and I'll dance,
My laugh shall be gay;
I'll cease this wild weeping–
Drive sorrow away,
He taught me to love him,
He call'd me his flower
That blossom'd for him
All the brighter each hour.

Of course, Harley's dolly was golden haired, not raven, but he changed the word when the lyrics played in his mind. *My frail, wildwood flower.* With high hopes, Harley closed the music box and started toward Briar Hollow. *Soon you'll be mine.*

CHAPTER 27

Despite the warmth of the day, a chill swept over Penny. She crossed both arms over her chest as she walked toward home.

An unusual quiet marked her way, and an uneasiness settled in her spirit. She tried to brush it off, but despite her best efforts to remain calm, her pulse quickened. The sound of a twig cracking broke the silence.

Penny wanted to run, but reminded herself there were lots of noises in the woods. *There's nothing to be afraid of. It's probably just a deer.* With purposeful, quiet steps she continued down the road.

What is that? That's definitely not an animal. Penny heard a chiming noise—not like the spontaneous tinkling of a wind chime, but something melodic.

To better discern the sound, Penny stopped. Motionless, she stood listening. The distant music competed with the pounding of her pulse in her ears. It seemed to be coming nearer.

The tune was familiar. At first she did not place it, but then she recognized it. It was the song from her dreams, but now it was coming to her in broad daylight. *I must be losing my mind! What is happening to me, Lord?*

Penny listened intently. Something was different. The melody was the same, but the song in her dreams had been more of an organ sound. This was a tinkly-chiming tone. Regardless, there was no denying the volume was getting louder.

"Can you help me?" A voice Penny did not recognize called from the edge of the woods.

A chill raced down her spine. She could not see the man and doubted her ability to outrun him. Penny squinted in the sunlight and tried to get a better look.

"Do I know you, sir?"

"Oh, please," said Harley, "don't call me sir."

Penny had trouble with the details of his features, but she clearly made out the man's silhouette. He was not overly tall and was wearing a low top hat.

The stranger emerged from the forest shadows and stepped into the light. Mutton chop beard, jaundiced skin, the same dark outfit—all confirmed Penny's foreboding. Her senses were beyond elevated. She was close to delirious as the revelation dawned. She was indeed face to face with Mr. Yates' attacker.

She trembled and simultaneously searched for the right response. She had seen this man's brutal attack on the banker. *I can't let him see that I know who he is.*

Penny decided to take a lighthearted approach until she could find a sure way of escape. Going into the woods with him did not seem a good option.

"You need help with something?"

Harley smiled. His plan was working perfectly. Soon his wildwood flower would be clay in his hands. "I do have a problem. Would you mind looking at this box for me?"

"Not at all." Penny feigned a smile. "If you'll just bring it to me, I'll be happy to."

Harley had hoped to get the girl out of sight as quickly as possible, but he did not want to frighten her away. "All right, m'lady."

Penny watched Harley look up and down the road before taking a cautious step from the edge of the woods. "Come closer, dear, and look."

The sound from the music box played on. "I dropped something in the box, and I can't seem to get it out. Perhaps with your small fingers you could get it for me."

Alarms rang in Penny. She did not want to go anywhere near the man, but she knew he had a gun. She had, after all, seen him clock poor Mr. Yates with it in the alley. If she ran now, she was an open target. She had to keep her cool and find the right time to make a break.

Penny took a trepid step forward. "Why don't we meet halfway?" She did her best to keep a pleasant expression on her face.

Harley stepped forward, wearing a crooked smile. "Another, shall we? It's almost like we're dancing."

Penny took another step.

The stranger did the same.

When he drew near enough to grab her, his lips contorted in a sneering grin. Penny could no longer hide her fear as she read the desire in his eyes. Petrified, she stood frozen in the middle of the road.

Harley lunged forward.

In his right hand, hidden under the music box, he held a rag soaked in ether. With a quick motion, he grabbed the girl, dropped the music box, and smashed the cloth against her face.

Penny tried to scream, but the cloth muffled the sound. Struggling, she took in deep breaths that only helped the ether deliver her to a state of unconsciousness.

Harley worked hard to drag the girl's dead weight off the road. He wished he had the strength to lift her, but with his limited lung capacity and poor health, he had little upper body strength.

Through the woods, Harley jolted his burden in a jagged path; moving and then stopping and then moving again. All the while, Penny remained unconscious.

When he reached the place he had stowed the wheeled chair, Harley dropped the girl in the seat and rolled her the rest of the way to the lean-to. To keep her from escaping while he went for a wagon, Harley tied her arms and feet to the chair. She was slumped over in an awkward position, so he gathered his bedroll and placed it on her lap to make her more comfortable. Before he left, he rolled the chair completely out of sight inside the triangular shelter.

Eagerly, Harley left on his mission to retrieve the wagon that would transport them to Maysville. The steamboat, *The Messenger*, was scheduled to leave first thing in the morning, and he was going to do everything possible to be on it.

In his hasty departure, Harley missed seeing the ether bottle knocked over on the ground beside the lean-to.

Logan had watched Penny as she walked past the pond and turned down the lane to Briar Hollow. He attempted to occupy himself with the party, but what had begun as disquiet in his spirit had grown to a blaring alert.

"Mother, I'm going to run back and change my shirt. It's sticky, and I don't want this to stain, either."

"Hurry back. We're going to start the games after the meal, and then the singing." Millicent smiled brightly. "Isn't it a beautiful day?"

"Yes, it is." Logan was pleased to see his mother's peaceful countenance, even in his distracted state. He placed a tender kiss on Millicent's cheek and waved goodbye to Zion. "I'll be back shortly."

Hurriedly, Logan traced Penny's steps. Driven by a strong impulse he could not explain, he scanned the road as he covered it with long strides. Halfway between the Eldridge place and Briar Hollow, a box in the road caught his eye.

Logan picked up his pace and ran to the spot where the music box sat on the ground. It was damaged, but still playing. He picked it up and recognized the smell instantly.

"Ether!"

Harley headed back to the road to retrieve the music box before going in search of a wagon and team. The sound of someone crashing through the woods sent him scurrying back to his camp. With the wheeled chair inside, there was no room for him, so he hid behind the shelter and hoped whoever was in the woods would go a different direction.

The path was plain. Someone had been dragged into the woods, and based on the riot of emotions coursing through Logan, he felt certain it was Penny. He realized he was making a lot of noise and slowed his steps to a more cautious pace.

Following the trail was no problem. It led him a half-mile into the woods to a lean-to and then stopped. *Dear Lord, show me what to do.*

Logan found cover behind a large tree and waited. He didn't know what he was waiting for, but he knew he didn't want to press into a dangerous situation without a plan.

Plagued by a host of scenarios, Harley searched for a strategy that might divert his visitor. There was no way he was going to outrun a healthy man. His best option, he considered, was playing innocent. He picked up the pan he had warmed beans in earlier in the day and stepped away from the lean-to.

Logan watched as the man walked out in the open. Whistling while he worked, he scraped the pan and dipped it in a bucket of water. He turned toward Logan who tucked his head behind the tree. The trunk successfully hid his narrow silhouette with the exception of his hat brim that jutted out and gave him away.

"Hello, the tree," Harley called. "Can I help you, stranger?"

"Hello, the . . . the . . ." Logan didn't know what to call the small shelter.

Harley cackled. "It's a lean-to, for hunting. What brings you out here in the woods?"

The hair on the back of Logan's neck rose to attention. The man was playing it cool. Logan indeed was a stranger in these woods. As far as he knew, this man might be standing on his own property. Logan could be trespassing. Those were the facts; but something in Logan screamed otherwise.

He knew it was a risk, but for Penny's sake, he had to take it. Logan drew on the man.

Harley shook his head. "What's this? Are you here to rob a poor hunter?"

"No. Not at all." Logan kept a steely gaze on the man. "I'm looking for someone, and I'd like to take a peek in that lean-to."

"That's tomfoolery." Harley took a step to the lean-to. "There's nobody here except me and the coons."

"That may be, but I will have a look in there. I'd thank you to step back out of the way while I do."

Harley took a protective step towards the shelter. "A man's got a right to some privacy, now. You move along and mind your own business."

Logan weighed his options. He didn't want to risk hurting the man, but he had to follow his heart. He aimed his Beaumont-Adams at the ground by Harley's feet and pulled the trigger.

Flames erupted when the bullet struck near the ether spill. The lean-to caught fire.

"No!" Harley screamed. "She's going to burn!"

"Oh, God!" Logan watched in horror as the fire moved rapidly. If Penny was inside, it would take a miracle to get her out.

Harley ran into the fiery cave. It was not tall enough for him to stand erect, so he hunched over and shoved the wheeled chair with all his strength. Relief flooded Logan when Penny rolled out the open side. Harley fell to the ground inside the burning structure.

Logan rushed to pull Penny to safety. The dried timbers of the lean-to, aided by the ignition of the ether, had created an instantaneous, full-fledged blaze. The two sides of the shelter collapsed on top of Harley who was trapped under the burning wood.

Once Penny was out of harm's way, Logan ran to see what he could do for the man. His feet protruded from beneath the wood, but the rest of his body was covered. Logan summoned all his strength and pulled the man out from the fire. When Logan pulled, the man's hat was caught inside, but it had protected his hair from catching fire. His clothes, however, were ablaze on his backside from the burning wood that had fallen on him.

Logan pulled the man's arms out of his coat and forcefully struck it against the ground. Once the flames were extinguished, he used it to beat down the man's trousers. Whoever he was, he was knocked out from either smoke inhalation or the impact of the lean-to that had collapsed on his head.

Logan assessed the situation. He had no idea how to treat Penny or the unconscious man. *What should I do, Lord?*

Run! Logan heard the word impressed on his spirit.

What Logan lacked in muscular build, he made up for in long legs. The young man vaulted into motion and pumped hard, racing back to the party as fast his legs could carry him.

The sound of Logan's feet thudding on the road arrived before he came into view. The wild look on his face as he searched the crowd let everyone know something was terribly wrong.

Zion hurried to his side. "What is it, Logan?"

"Penny. A man. A fire." Logan panted between the words as he struggled for air. "Doctor."

Zion took charge. "Garth, ride to town for Doc Byerly!" He turned to James Erlanger. "Can I borrow a horse?"

"Of course. I'll get Dorcas." James started for the barn.

"No, use mine. Black is saddled and ready to go." Jim Cooper ran for his horse.

"Where are they?" Zion asked Logan.

"Down the road. There's a music box in the street. Turn left. The path is easy to follow."

"You got that?" Garth nodded to Zion and took off for town. Cooper returned with his horse. Zion remembered his broken arm and moaned.

"You've got this, Zion." Cooper sidled the horse next to a stump that served as a stand for a basket overflowing with petunias. He removed the flowers, and Zion moved quickly to his side.

"Grab the reins and mount. Black will work with you."

"Wait a minute!" Logan made his presence known. "You're not leaving me here."

"All right." Zion looked down from the horse. "Hop up here behind the saddle and hang on to the cantle."

Logan used the stump to climb up behind Zion. "Don't hang on to me. If I fall, we'll both be on the ground. And make sure you don't grip the flanks. Keep your feet as forward as possible." Zion closed his legs and clucked the horse into motion. Black handled the weight of the two riders with ease and sped down the road.

CHAPTER 28

Logan dismounted first, followed quickly by Zion. Still unconscious, Penny hunched over the bedroll in her lap. She looked unharmed, but Zion could hardly contain the outrage that boiled in his chest.

In his angry state, he had little compassion for the moaning man lying on the ground at a distance; but he moved to check on him regardless of his emotions. He was breathing, but it was labored. Since the man had fallen face down, his hat and clothing had protected most of his body. His hands were badly burned.

Zion wanted to roll him over and get a look at his face, but he didn't know if it would worsen his condition. He had nothing to treat the man with, so he offered a quick prayer and returned to his sister's side. "Better hurry, Doc."

By the time Zion reached Penny, Logan had untied her hands and feet from the chair and stretched her out on the bedroll. Her breathing was normal. Zion was relieved to see no visible signs of injury.

"It's ether." Logan pushed the hair back from Penny's face with the tips of his fingers. "I smelled it on the music box. He must have used it to knock her out. It's what started the fire, too."

"You don't think he hurt her?"

Logan shook his head. "He dove in the fire to save her. She's just sleeping. She'll be fine."

"Ah, Buttercup." Zion looked over Penny's still form. She was dirty, but did look unharmed. He wished she would wake up so he could be sure. Her features were peaceful and her chest was moving in a solid breathing pattern. It looked like he would have to wait for the doctor to find out for sure.

Garth arrived at the scene with Dr. Byerly. "Check him first," said Zion. "We think Penny's ok. She was knocked out with ether, but he's hurt bad."

The doctor moved to the man's side and gently opened his clothing. The injury to the skin on his backside was minimal, but his hands were in rough shape. The first layer of skin had completely burned through with damage into the second layer. "That's going to hurt." The doctor pulled strips of clean fabric from his case and wrapped them around the injured hands. "This will keep him until we can get him back to my office."

Rosalie hurried through the woods with a large basket. "Oh, my. Zion, is Penny alright?"

"We think so. She's passed out, but it doesn't look like she's been injured."

"Thank God."

"Yes, thank God." Zion offered a strained smile to his wife. "That fellow over there's not faring as well."

With quick steps, Rosalie moved to the doctor's side. "Oh, his poor back."

"It's bad, but not as bad as his hands. I'm going to need to get him back to town."

"There's a wheeled chair right here," said Zion.

Dr. Byerly stood and looked at the conveyance. "That's my chair. It's been missing since yesterday. Someone took it off the porch."

"I'll bet he never thought he'd be the one sitting in it," said Logan.

Rosalie reached in her basket and drew out a large sheet. "Would you like to wrap his back in this?"

"That's perfect." The doctor reached in his bag and pulled out a vial of laudanum. "Let me get some of this into his system in case he starts to wake up."

A retching sound called everyone's attention to Penny. She rolled to her side and vomited. "That's a good sign," said the doctor.

Images of people and trees were fuzzy and swirling. Penny's head pounded as she tried to focus.

"You're ok, Buttercup." Zion knelt beside his woozy sister and stroked her face with the back of his good hand.

"Zion," Penny blinked hard several times, "what happened?"

"You can tell us when you're feeling better, but I'm glad to see you're waking up."

Zion moved to make room for Dr. Byerly. "Penny, it's Dr. Byerly."

"Dr. Byerly? Yes?"

"You don't appear to have sustained any injuries, although I'm sure you're not feeling too spry right now." The doctor manipulated Penny's eyelids and checked her pulse.

"What's your full name?"

"Penny Hope Coldwell."

"Do you know the date?"

"April 30, 1865."

"How old are you?"

"That's not a polite question to ask a lady, Dr. Byerly."

An assortment of chortles and laughs filled the air.

"Oh, Penny." Zion shook his head. "She'll be fine. She's already playing to the gallery."

"I'm going to see this man into town and treat his injuries. I'll be back to check on you later. I know you're in good hands with Rosalie."

The doctor settled his patient in a room. His shoulders and back were flushed; his lower legs a deeper red, but only the top layer of skin affected. His hands, however were moist, completely red and covered in clear blisters.

"His back is superficial," said the doctor. "I'm concerned about his hands."

"Is he in shock?" Lou watched her husband work to cool the patient's burns.

"The unaffected skin is a normal color, a bit jaundiced, but not bad. His pulse is slightly elevated. He's obviously unconscious, but that could be from the laudanum I gave him in the woods."

"That's good. We don't need two patients in comas."

"Help me roll him onto his side so I can check his lungs." The couple worked together and rolled their patient up on his side. Lou bent the knee that wasn't touching the bed and tucked a pillow between his legs. She sucked in a breath when she saw his face for the first time.

"It's him."

"Who?"

"The man I told you about who left in the middle of a breathing treatment. He was the oddest fellow."

"Peculiar." The doctor listened to his lungs. "He's wheezing badly." With practiced fingers, the doctor checked the lymph nodes around his neck. "Swollen, too."

"I don't like the looks of this," said the doctor. "This is not a healthy man. With the smoke he breathed in, I'd say he's quite susceptible to infection—in his lungs, hands or both."

Penny stretched out across the quilt on her bed. Nausea and relief do-si-doed, each taking their turns at the lead in a sporadic twist as she processed physically, mentally, and emotionally all that had happened.

Rosalie sponged her pale face with a cool cloth while Dahlia stood at her bedside and held her fingertips in her small hand.

"It happened so fast," said Penny. "One moment I was standing in the road and the next everything was spinning and turning to black."

"I'm so sorry, sweetheart." Rosalie dipped the cloth in water and wringed out the excess. Tenderly, she continued the soothing ministrations. "It's over now, and at least you didn't get burned or injured."

"There are benefits to being unconscious, I guess." Penny studied the ceiling, and then the picture hanging on the wall. She didn't want to close her eyes. It was behind closed eyes the memories so vividly replayed.

A rap at the bedroom door announced a visitor. Logan stood at the threshold. "May I come in?"

"Of course," Rosalie nodded towards a chair, "please sit down and keep us company."

"How are the foals?" Penny offered a feeble smile.

"They're fine. I just gave Equity some goat milk, and I'll give Equinox a feeding later."

"Did she like it?"

"They both do. Zion said we'll be able to get them off the bottles and using a bucket next week. Putting a bucket in a creep area where they can get to it themselves will save a lot of time bottle feeding."

"At least it's not their only source of food," said Rosalie. "Lucy's making a good amount of milk, and she's being a good momma."

"It's nice to get a little mothering from time to time." Logan watched Rosalie's comforting care generously poured out by loving hands. Penny lay still on the bed, but it was clear to Logan that much activity was taking place below the surface.

"If you're ok for now, I'm going to check on Mattie. I can hear him waking up, and I know he's hungry." Rosalie dropped the cloth in the bowl and stood. "Come with Mommy, Dahlia. You can help me change your little brother, and I'll tell you a story while I nurse him." A happy story might be just what her little one needed to get her mind of the happenings of the day.

Logan pushed his chair next to the bed. His heart was doing crazy things. How could this slip of a girl come to mean so much to him in such a short time? The thought that she could have been hurt got his adrenalin pumping. The realization that she could have been whisked away, never to be seen again, spurred feelings of anger and grief.

The light in Penny's blue eyes had shined in the dark places of Logan's heart. He wanted to tell her how much he cared for her, but it didn't seem the right time.

"Did I tell you how much I enjoyed the punch?"

Penny grinned. "You enjoyed drinking it or wearing it?"

"Both." Logan matched the girl's grin with one of his own. "If I recall correctly, you and I were having a most pleasant conversation before Katie's admirers made their grand entrance."

"Yes."

"I believe we were talking about moving forward, isn't that right, Miss Coldwell? You didn't get to give me your thoughts on that." Logan studied Penny's lovely oval face. He was in no hurry for her reply. The change in her expression revealed her answer before she spoke one word.

"My thoughts." Penny lifted a finger to her chin. "Hm. I think . . ."

The front door of the cabin opened and Marigold marched directly to Penny's bedside. "Sister-sister!" She noted Logan's near presence to Penny, but kept her thoughts to herself. "How are you feeling?"

"Actually, I'm a bit nauseous, but it's so nice to be home."

"So you're not up to a game of horseshoes?" Marigold winked and then crinkled her freckled nosed.

"I don't think so."

"Blind Man's Bluff? You can be 'it' first."

"Oh no, thank you." Penny clamped her eyes shut and shook her head. The thought of being blindfolded and spun around in circles sent a wave of nausea through her.

"Oh, all right." Remorse shot through Marigold at the girl's obvious discomfiture. "I'll shut my big bazoo. I was just fooling around, you know."

"I know," Penny chuckled, "it's ok."

"I really came by to see how you were doing and if you needed anything."

Penny turned her head on the pillow and smiled softly at Logan before looking at her concerned friend. "I'm being well taken care of, Marigold."

"It looks to be so." Uncomfortable with the vibrations in the atmosphere, Marigold plopped down on the bed next to Penny. "What about the fellow who did this? I hope Zion cleans his plow."

"He may have done his own 'plow cleaning,'" said Logan. "He was burnt pretty bad and still unconscious when the doctor took him to town."

"Do you know who he is?"

As much as Penny wished she could connect the pieces of the puzzle, she had not yet been able to do so. "I know I've seen him before, but I don't know where."

"Well I bet Zion will find out who that deadbeat is." Marigold jumped to her feet and headed toward the door. "I'm going to go talk to him. I'll see you later." Marigold's expression softened. "You take care of yourself now, y'hear?"

"That's a good looking set of foals you have there, Zion." Sheriff Nash stood next to the corral watching the twins frolic around their mother's legs.

"Thank you. They came as quit a surprise, I have to say."

"It seems you've been getting more than your share of surprises lately."

"At least this one was of the agreeable sort." Zion gave a lopsided grin and patted his arm. "This one on the other hand . . . ."

"I hear you. It's hard to run a farm with a bum arm."

"That it is."

"Speaking of bum," said Sheriff Nash, "do you have any idea the identity of the man who shanghaied your sister?"

"Not a clue, Sheriff. Penny remembers seeing him before, but not where. I'm still hoping it will come to her in time and clear up this mystery."

"Doc's not sure we'll get the chance to question the chiseler. He's still unconscious, just like Yates. I'm plumb fed up with the not-knowing."

"If the Good Lord wants us to know, then He'll make a way. If not, well, I'm just choosing to be thankful Penny's home and safe." The heat of the day raised a sweat on Zion's brow. He lifted his hat, wiped his forehead with the back of his hand, and then repositioned his hat on his head. "And I'm praying for healing for Mr. Yates . . . this stranger, too."

"That's big of you."

"It wasn't big *of* me, it was big *for* me. God somehow gave me the gumption to forgive him. As a Christian, I don't have the option to hang on to hate, but that doesn't mean it's easy to pray for a man who hurt people I care about."

"You take your Bible to heart, Zion." The sheriff clapped Zion's beefy shoulder and then mounted his horse. "It's refreshing to see." Nash clucked his gelding to motion. "I'll let you know if I hear anything."

"I'll do the same. Thanks for coming by."

Marigold burst through the cabin door and swiftly moved across the yard, waving to the sheriff as his horse ambled toward the lane.

"Hey, Zion." Marigold hopped up on the top fence post. Her bare feet dangled from beneath the ruffle of her calico dress. "What did the sheriff have to say?"

"Not much. He was hoping we had some news for him."

"Oh." Marigold watched Zion pump water into a bucket and then dump it in the horse trough. "Do you think they'll hang him?"

"I'm not sure, Marigold. Sheriff Nash said the bank was robbed Sunday. He can't be certain there's a connection, but it's likely. If there is, this fellow's future isn't too promising."

"I told Penny you were going to 'clean his plow.'"

"I wanted to, that's for sure, but after I wrestled down my flesh, I came to the conclusion that justice will be served. I'm just waiting to see how things play out."

"You're pretty calm."

"I wasn't. I'm actually a bit restless right now. I want to go to town and get a look at this man. If Penny saw him before, then I might have, too."

"When you gonna go?"

"Since our dinner went up the flume, I think I'll have a bite to eat and head on over afterwards."

"Can I come?" Marigold hopped down from the fence and brushed her skirt into place.

"Next time," said Zion. "Let me get a gander at him, check out his condition and all first."

Marigold nodded her golden head in reluctant agreement. "All right, Zion. I'll just head back then and let Pa and Lucas know what's going on."

"I'll send word if anything develops."

"Thanks."

CHAPTER 29

"I'm going with you." Penny grabbed her hat from its peg on the wall.

"Are you sure you're up to this?" Rosalie stopped sweeping, leaned on the broom handle and studied her sister-in-law.

"Absolutely." Penny's resolve showed through in her countenance. She tied the ribbons of her hat and opened the door for her brother.

"I guess that settles it then." Zion grinned at the determined girl.

Logan met the siblings as they neared the barn and lifted Penny into the wagon. Zion hoisted himself in and sat next to her on the bench seat. "I'll be praying for you," said Logan.

"Thank you." Penny peeked out from her straw poke bonnet.

"I appreciate that." Zion tipped his head and signaled the team to move out.

Once they were on the main road, Zion stole a glance at Penny's profile. From the set of her chin, he could tell she was in earnest about meeting her kidnapper.

"What are you thinking about?" asked Zion.

"I'm wondering what drives a person to such drastic deeds." Penny sighed and relaxed her rigid shoulders.

"You know, Zion, when it first happened, I kept wondering, 'why me?' Somehow something switched in my thoughts, and now I keep wondering about the man who did this. What was his motive? What were his thoughts? And what's the connection with the music I keep hearing."

"Those are all good questions." The wagon neared the site of the confrontation. Penny slipped her left hand through Zion's bent arm and then covered it with her right hand. The passengers continued down the road in silence.

"Mr. Yates has regained consciousness." Lou beamed as she escorted the Coldwells into the parlor. "The doctor said he has a contusion, a bruised brain from the impact of the gun. The good news is that the skull wasn't broken, and he's going to be fine."

"I'm so glad." A wave of relief flooded through Penny. "When I saw him slump to the ground, I was so afraid he would never get up again."

"He will." Lou spoke with confidence. "He has normal feeling in his hands and feet. No bones were broken. His brain just put him to sleep for awhile so his body could work on healing from the trauma."

"What about the other fellow?" asked Zion. "Has he roused at all?"

"He was moaning with pain, so the doctor gave him laudanum that knocked him out. He hasn't wakened yet."

"I'd like to see him, if I may." Penny's firm gaze masked the symphony of emotions playing behind her blue eyes.

Lou looked at Zion. He nodded his approval. "I'll check with my husband."

The nurse disappeared behind a door. Only a moment passed before she returned. "He says you are welcome. This way."

Penny followed Lou Byerly into the room, and Zion entered behind her. The doctor blocked Penny's view of the man's upper body, including his head. Motionless, he lay on his stomach with loose bandages over his back and a sheet covering his lower limbs.

Penny moved next to the doctor. She wanted to get a good look at the man, but his head faced the opposite wall. Slowly, she circled around the bed, more nervous with each step.

"Are you ok, Penny?" Zion watched the color drain from his sister's face.

"Yes," she nodded, but kept her gaze on the face that was coming into view, "thanks."

"He's not that old," she said with surprise. "In his thirties, would you say?"

"I'd say that's a good guess," said the doctor. "Do you know him?"

"That's what has been puzzling me so." Penny studied the gaunt face surprised at the compassion that stirred for her attacker. "I know I've seen him, but I haven't been able to place when or where."

A pain- and opium-induced fog held Harley in a state of suspension. He heard the conversation taking place around him, unable to respond. Although his pain was great and breathing laborious, a joy swept over him that he had never experienced in his lonely life. Thrilling in the wonder that the girl of his dreams had come to see him, Harley willed his leaden eyes to open. *She's here! She's come!*

His eyelids were heavy, so heavy. First they fluttered, and then slits formed at the bottom, opening just enough for him to see his blue-eyed dolly standing before him.

Unbidden, Penny's hands flew to cover her heart. Her mouth parted in a gasp. The shock of seeing him awaken from unconsciousness took the girl off guard for a moment, but she drew in a deep breath and settled herself. Consciously, she lifted the corners of her mouth in a slight smile. Questions danced behind her cornflower blue eyes. She wanted answers.

Penny looked to Zion, and then back to the man. "Hi."

The effort to open his eyes had taken much of Harley's energy, but he determined with everything in him to seize this miraculous opportunity. In addition to the misery inflicted by the burns on his back, legs and hands; internally his chest burned and his throat ached from the smoke he had inhaled.

"Hi," he croaked and then wheezed in as much air as his inflamed bronchioles allowed.

The raspy, weak voice startled Penny. It was clear the man was miserable and struggling to breathe. "I'm sorry you're hurting." Tears sparkled in Penny's eyes. Harley reveled in her concern.

"You came." A cough racked Harley's ravaged body and he winced in pain.

"I had to see you." Penny cocked her head and tried to read the soul of her abductor. Something broke within her at what she saw. He reminded her of Dahlia when Rosalie said 'no more cookies,' or Lucas on Christmas Eve longing to open a present that was not yet his.

"What's your name?"

"Harley. Harley Crawford. What's yours?"

"Penny."

"Ah. That's right purty." Harley managed a quasi-smile.

Zion was not at all happy with the direction the conversation was taking. He wanted to interrogate the malefactor, but he allowed Penny to continue. She was, after all, the one who had been accosted.

Lou picked up a pad of paper and began scratching down notes.

"I know I've seen you before."

Harley was pleased. She remembered him. He thought of how many times visions of Penny had filled his thoughts. "The fair. Last year. At the carousel."

Finally, Penny's memory brought forth the long-awaited image of their previous encounter. She saw him now, helping her from the carousel. Dahlia had enjoyed the ride so much she had taken three turns on it. She remembered the painted horses galloping on their posts, and then it came to her—the music.

"I remember." Penny felt weak enough to lose her footing, but maintained her composure. The relief of finally remembering was both sweet and exhausting.

Zion watched her fade and circled around the table. He captured Penny's elbow in his hand for support.

"The music," Penny lifted her face to Zion's, "the music I kept hearing was from the calliope that played at the carousel."

Zion was relieved as well, but still had a quiver full of unanswered questions. "So you were here last year at the Germantown Fair?"

Without diverting his gaze from Penny's face, Harley answered Zion with a brief nod. He fought to remain awake, to savor Penny's sweet presence, but the mixture of pain, drugs, and exhaustion swept him back into unconsciousness.

"That will have to be enough for now," Dr. Byerly said. "Hopefully he'll wake back up and we can get more information."

"Hopefully?" Penny asked.

"His lungs were in bad shape before he took in the smoke. By the looks of his swollen glands, it appears his body was already fighting some sort of infection before the incident. The burns aren't life threatening, but I just don't have a prognosis right now."

"I got the eggs for you," said Rosalie.

"Thank you." Penny took a sandwich from the plate and passed it. "How was Lavinia? She's been broody lately."

"She didn't want to give up her egg," said Rosalie.

Penny laughed. It felt good to have a conversation about everyday things. Rosalie always seemed to have a sense of just what she needed. "I'm going for more coffee." Penny bounced to her feet and retrieved the pot from the stove.

"Anyone else?"

"I'd love some. Thanks, Buttercup." Zion pushed his cup forward, pleased to see the lightness in Penny's step and countenance. "I think we should have us a singing tonight."

"That would be nice," said Rosalie. "I was looking forward to it at the Erlangers."

"We can have our own after our bit of supper here. What's everybody say?" Zion scanned the faces at the table. Everyone was in agreement. "It won't be the same without your Pa and Marigold. That girl sings like an angel."

"Really?" Logan had a hard time connecting Marigold with angelic beings.

"Really," said Zion. "Will you play your violin, Penny?"

"If you'll play your harmonica."

"I don't think this one-winged bird will be able to fly on that one, Buttercup—at least not very well. I use both my hands when I blow my mouth organ."

"Balim always loved to hear you play." Penny rose to get her instrument.

"Are you ready to quilt tonight?" asked Rosalie. "I can't believe how quickly the top pieced together with Millie's help."

"I am." Penny nodded and smiled at Mrs. Mayfield. "It's been nice working with you on the project."

"I've enjoyed every minute, dear. I'm going to miss our evening sewing and quilting bees."

"Miss them? Are you going somewhere?" Dismayed, Penny plopped down in her chair and dropped the violin case on her lap.

"You've been so gracious in our time of need, but I can't displace you from your room forever. As soon as Logan earns enough money, we will return your home back to you with hearts full of thanks for your kindness and hospitality."

The thought of the Mayfields leaving Briar Hollow dismayed Penny. Yes, she had despised their coming, but the idea of them leaving was far from her thoughts now, and most definitely from her wishes.

"Where will you go?" Penny turned bright eyes on Logan.

"Let's not think of such things tonight." Zion slapped his knee and motioned for Dahlia to jump on his lap. "According to Dr. Byerly, I've got at least four more weeks in this cast, and I'll need help for some time following. You don't have to make any moving plans in the near future."

"That works for me," said Logan. "It's my goal to get your barn ready as soon as possible. Maybe you'll get that stock from the Belle Meade yearling sale yet."

"Mayhap, my friend." Zion jostled Dahlia on his knee. "Are you ready to commence with the singing, little one?"

"Yes, Pa!" Dahlia clapped her hands.

Penny plucked the strings to check their pitch and then raised her bow. "Are you sure?"

"Yes, Auntie Penny! What will you pway first?"

"Before we begin," said Penny in a matter-of-fact voice, "I would like to thank West for his contribution to the singing tonight."

"Daddy's horsey?"

"Yes, Daddy's horsey." Penny picked up her bow and turned the end screw to adjust the tension on the bow hair. "See this part here that runs over the strings? That's about 150 to 200 of West's tail hairs. Your daddy collected them and made a new bow for me."

Dahlia's eyes grew wide, and she turned to her father for verification. "It's true. Penny needed a bow, and West didn't mind at all. I think he's got about a million tail hairs, anyhow."

Penny used a piece of paper to apply rosin to the bow and then tucked the violin under her chin. She placed the flat side of the bow between the bridge and fingerboard and pulled it straight across the string. With a mixture of short and long strokes she played the winsome melody of *Sweet Hour of Prayer*.

When Penny started the verse a second time, Rosalie began singing. Everyone joined in.

Sweet hour of prayer! Sweet hour of prayer!
That calls me from a world of care,
And bids me at my Father's throne
Make all my wants and wishes known.
In seasons of distress and grief,
My soul has often found relief,
And oft escaped the tempter's snare,
By thy return, sweet hour of prayer!

The atmosphere in the cabin filled with a peaceful presence. When the final note played, after a moment of silence, Penny began another of her favorite hymns. Millicent and Rosalie sang the verses in two-part harmony.

Abide with me; fast falls the eventide;
The darkness deepens; Lord, with me abide;
When other helpers fail and comforts flee,
Help of the helpless, oh, abide with me.

Penny stopped playing after the first verse, her eyes brilliant with unshed tears. "Can we pray for Mr. Crawford? I know what he did was wrong, but if you could have looked into his eyes today and seen the emptiness inside." Words failed Penny.

"Of course we can." Zion held both of Dahlia's small hands in his and bowed his head. "Lord, Jesus, we are so privileged to know You. We are so blessed to be part of a loving family. We don't know this Harley Crawford's story, but You do. With all that's happened, and how intimately you are involved in our lives, I'm wondering if You allowed him to come to Washington for a reason.

"I pray that you would touch him, Lord. Touch his body, touch his mind, and touch his spirit. If it's Your will, raise him up. I don't know what you have in mind, Lord, but I do know it is Your will that every man would be saved. So that's my prayer, Lord. Above all else, I ask that You would give us the opportunity to speak to his soul.

"You are a God of restoration, and I pray right now in the precious name of Jesus, that Harley Crawford's spirit would be restored to You in this world and prepared for the next."

A chorus of amens filled the room. Logan stood to his feet. "It's past time for a feeding. I better get out to the corral and check on the twins."

"I'll come with you."

The men left and Rosalie stood with her sleepy daughter in her arms. Dahlia's head lolled on her mother's shoulder, and Rosalie patted her softly on the back. "Time for bed, little one."

"I'll get the quilting supplies," said Penny.

CHAPTER 30

The women made quick work of pinning the quilt top, batting and backing together. "We'll baste these thicknesses together," said Rosalie. "That way everything will stay in place during the quilting."

Millicent smiled and clasped her hands in anticipation. "Will we have time to get it in the hoop tonight?"

"With the three of us running loose basting stitches, there's a good chance we might. Then everything will be ready to start the quilting."

"This pattern moves very quickly," said Millicent.

"The long strips between the rows help. Less piecework saves a lot of time cutting and sewing," said Penny.

"I love how the different patterns have names. *Flying Geese* is perfect for this one." Millicent pulled a needle from her sewing basket, threaded it, and began running basting stitches from one end of the quilt top to the other.

"I do, too," said Rosalie, "and this is just one arrangement. There are many ways to configure *Flying Geese*. They can fly back and forth in strips, point in all four directions, and even point inward in little blocks or one big pattern. "

"This seems best to me," said Millicent. "Geese migrate with the seasons. That means they would all be flying in the same direction."

"That's true," said Penny. "Some of those layouts might look more along the lines of a flying poultry square dance than a migration."

"Aren't you the clever one?" Millicent laughed. "What's the pattern on your bed, dear? It's simple, but lovely."

"Can you guess?" asked Rosalie.

"It's obviously a flower of sorts."

"And what is Zion's pet name for his sister?"

Understanding shone in Millicent's eyes. "Oh, it's *Buttercup*, isn't it?"

"Yes. Rosalie made it for me the first year she and Zion were married. I love the cheery yellow, red and green on the light background."

"Guess what's on my bed?" Rosalie looked up from her stitching.

"It must be roses." Millicent gave a confident smile, certain she had solved the riddle.

"Of a sort," said Rosalie. "My mother's name was Sharon. When I was born she named me Rosalie and called me her little 'Rose of Sharon.' You probably know that's more of a flowering shrub than a rose bush."

"That it is. We had them on the grounds in Connecticut. The harsh winters were challenging, so the gardener took special care with them. They are lovely—like you, dear Rosalie. You must have been your mother's joy."

"Isn't every child?"

"I confess, Logan has a special place in my heart."

And mine, Penny silently acknowledged to herself.

"With all the crops in and the first haying done, Garth's able to help now." Zion watched as Logan bottle fed his filly. She was thriving, and he was pleased, especially given her rough start.

"Spring pruning's been done for some time, and now the fertilizing. I'm sure my father-in-law will be able to help some," said Zion.

"I'm not what you would call experienced with building tools, but you know I'll give it my best effort." Logan pulled the empty bottle from Equity's mouth and patted her on the flank. The lively filly gamboled across the moonlit yard to her brother. The men watched the foals in silence, each lost in his own thoughts.

The sound of a wagon coming through the lane broke the evening quiet. "Who could that be this time of night?" said Zion.

The rhythm of the turning wheels played background music for a deep baritone singing a familiar song:

King Jesus is a listnin' when I pray
King Jesus is a listnin' when I pray
Said if I'd just hold my peace
Then de Lawd will fight my battles
King Jesus is a listnin' when I pray

Zion stood in amazement. His brain could not assimilate what his ears and eyes were telling him. It was impossible, unreal, but it was. Balim was on the back of that wagon.

"Cat got yo tongue, Massa Zion?" Balim grinned from ear to ear, his white teeth gleaming in the moonlight.

"Balim." Zion's slow gait picked up, and he hurried to the tailgate. "A cat, you ask? More like a mountain lion. I can't believe you're here."

Balim jumped from the wagon and picked up his carpetbag. "Thanks for the ride, Jenkins."

"My pleasure." The postman tipped his hat. "I was picking up the mail from Maysville, and got to bring you a special delivery, Coldwell." Mr. Jenkins chuckled at his pun and signaled the team to move forward and then turn around. "See you in town."

At 5 foot 9 inches, Balim was a bundle of taut, bulky muscles. His strength could have been intimidating, but his gentle eyes and demeanor tempered his appearance.

Since childhood, Zion had found comfort with Balim. When he was little and fell from the swing, he had run to the stables where Balim tended his scratches. When he was five and got a fishing hook stuck in his thumb, Balim had pulled it out. As a boy, Zion liked to work alongside Balim. When he was yet an undeveloped youngster, he struggled to lift bales of hay that Balim moved with ease. Many times Balim reached a beefy arm over Zion's straining back, grabbed the cord on the bale, and helped him heave it into the feeder.

When his parents had died, Zion went to sea emotionally and spiritually. It was Balim's prayer and faith that held things together. All of Zion's life, Balim had been there for him—his rock, his helper, his friend.

Although Zion had legally given Balim his freedom after his father died, Balim had chosen to stay with Zion for a season before searching for his wife. Two years prior to the Coldwell's tragedy, Minnie's owners, the Coldwell's neighbors, planned to move to North Carolina. She reasoned that if she was going to be separated from the man she loved, she would try to escape and live as a free woman. She had succeeded, and Balim had found her when he left Zion five years ago.

"I, I . . . I just can't believe you're here."

"As soon as I got Miss Rozlee's wire, I took to praying, and the good Lawd sent me to ya. You's done gone through the mill, ain't ya?"

Zion lifted his sling. "Oh, we've had a few ups and downs for sure; but what about Minnie and the kids?"

"They's fine. Reverend Henson's looking out fo' them. Everything's in apple pie order on the settlement."

"You don't mean Reverend Josiah Henson and the Dawn Settlement?" Logan's astonishment got the better of his manners.

"That I do, young man. Uncle Tom hisself." Balim stuck out a beefy paw for a handshake. "I'm Balim Coldwell."

"Sorry, Balim. This is Logan Mayfield. He's been helping out around here since I broke my arm."

"Pleasure, suh."

"Nice to meet you. I've heard so much about you from Zion and Penny." The two men shook hands.

"How's Missy Penny, Massa?"

"Balim, I told you a long time ago not to call me Massa."

"I know. It's just what I's called you since you was a little tyke. It don't mean nothing to ole Balim."

"Well, it means something to me. We share the same last name. We're family. No need for titles here, especially a bygone, petered-out, no-longer-fitting title like that."

"I'll try to let slide, it just ain't easy to think of ya with a different name than I's called you yo whole life."

"Let's go inside," said Zion. "Penny is going to be happier than a June bug on a tomato plant."

The din inside the cabin was all Zion imagined. Rosalie and Penny both gave Balim big hugs, and then Penny nearly passed out when she stopped and stared at her lifetime friend. "I can't believe you're here, Balim. You look just the same."

"I ain't the same since I seen you, Missy Penny. I'm a pa now of my own two young-uns. And just look at yoself. Yous the spittin' image of yo momma."

Tears welled in Penny's eyes. "I'm so glad you came. I've been missing you so."

"It's true," said Logan. "She prayed you here at the wishing jar."

Balim threw his head back and gave a hearty laugh. "I was nigh on my way as soon as I got the news of yo troubles. As ya know, I was working at the sawmill for some time, but I's recently moved to the stables. Besides being a minister, a world traveler, and a farmer, Reverend Henson breeds fine hosses."

"Really?" Zion was pleased for Balim. "You've been working at the stables now?"

"Yes, suh, and if you'll pardon the pun, everythin's stable at the stables. I told the reverend about ya, and he said I should come and do fo you after all you done fo me and so many others."

Zion was touched by the kindness extended to him by a complete stranger, as well as Balim's sacrifice. "But what about Minnie and the kids?"

"She know'd you must be busier than a borrowed mule. She's at camp meeting most nights. She's not even gwanna miss me."

"How long are you able to stay?" asked Rosalie.

Balim paused and looked around the room. His eyes lit on the *Flying Geese* quilt in the frame in front of the fireplace. "I know that." Balim nodded towards the ladies' sewing. "*Flying Geese*, ain't so?"

Rosalie smiled. "It is."

"That there quilt picture done helped many a black man and woman on their way to freedom."

Millicent listened with rapt attention. "It's true, then," she asked, "about the quilts and the Underground Railroad?"

"Sho 'nough, Miss Mayfield." Balim blinked and tipped his head. "Look here at that, now. See how they's all flying in one direction?"

"Yes," said Millicent. "We were just discussing that earlier, weren't we, girls?"

Rosalie and Penny nodded.

"Well, it's like this." Balim walked to the quilt and turned the stand 180 degrees. The geese had been pointing toward the fireplace, but now they faced into the room. "When the seasons change, the geese fly home."

"Balim!" Zion jumped to his feet. Adrenalin shot through his body, and he grinned from ear to ear. "Are you saying what I think you're saying?"

"The season's changed, ain't it? The 'Mancipation Proclamation's done been read. Po Mr. Lincoln's dead and buried, along with countless others. On the train I heard men saying Lee's done surrendered his troops."

"It's true," said Rosalie. "The end of the war and slavery has finally come to our nation."

"If you can use a goose like me, I'd like to fly home, Zion." The atmosphere in the room was still. "Me and Minnie have had a good life in Dresden. They's good people there doing good things, but you's family. You and Missy Penny, and you too, Miss Rozlee."

With quick strides, Zion rushed to embrace Balim. "Your timing couldn't be better, my friend."

"I'm glad you think so." A round of excited chatter filled the room and then stopped as quickly as it started.

"We can talk over the details in the morning, if you like," said Zion.

"If'n ya don' mind," Balim's face split in his signature grin, "right now I'm about played out and as hungry as a tick on a turnip."

Rosalie set herself in motion. The shock of Balim's arrival had dulled her normally keen sense of hospitality. "Oh, I'm so sorry, Balim. I'll get you something to eat. It's too late for coffee. Would you like some tea or cold milk?"

"A glass of cold milk would go down the pipe right nice, Miss Rozlee."

"Good thing I didn't make the Indian pudding today. I saved some milk this morning and put it in the stream. It should be nice and cool." Rosalie turned to her sister-in-law. "Penny, will you get the milk?"

"Sure." Penny knew just where Rosalie stashed things in the bend of the stream to keep them cool.

"I hope you two don't mind sharing the haymow," said Zion.

"Absolutely not," said Logan. "I'll run out and get things ready while you have something to eat." Logan left the bright atmosphere of the cabin moments after Penny, his way lit by a silvery quarter moon.

Logan watched as Penny walked past the cordoned garden where a colorful variety of roses grew on bushes and trellises. Next to the rose garden, a vine-covered arbor marked the entrance to the orchards between Briar Hollow and the Johnson cabin. Beyond the arbor, a glistening stream meandered along the edge of Zion's property.

Moonlight shined on the smooth plane of flowing water. The surface was glasslike until it hit a shallow section where the water played over rocks. Light danced among the ripples. A whippoorwill sallied out from its perch to sweep up an evening meal. Logan didn't see it, but he heard when he began his chant, "whip-poor-will, whip-poor-will, whip-poor-will" in a repeating circular rhythm.

Logan had every intention of going straight to the barn and readying things for Balim, but the halo of moonlight on Penny's golden head drew him like a moth to a flame. He traced the girl's steps and joined her at the water's edge.

Penny wiped the jar she retrieved from the stream with the edge of a towel. She had heard the cabin door close and knew she was not alone. Without looking, she sensed Logan's presence. The sound of his steps walking toward her confirmed her feelings. With her head still bowed, she peeked over the jar at her visitor.

"Did you want some milk, Mr. Mayfield?" asked the demure young lady with the porcelain skin that looked absolutely iridescent in the moonlight.

"I do seem to have an unquenchable thirst," said Logan. "It's not for milk, however."

"Some cold water then? We have a dipper right here."

"No. Water won't quench my craving, Miss Coldwell." Hazel eyes locked with blue in a prolonged, silent exchange.

Logan saw his reflection in Penny's pupils. The corners of his mouth lifted in a sly smile. "I see I'm the apple of your eye."

"How presumptuous you are, Logan Mayfield." Penny stepped back, her mouth slightly agape.

"That's not presumption at all."

The stream gurgled by her side while Penny puzzled over Logan's words. The whippoorwill continued his song in the otherwise quiet evening. Logan seemed matter-of-fact, but he was not making sense to her. "Would you care to enlighten me?"

"I'm sure you've heard the phrase before—'the apple of God's eye.'"

"Of course. God said Israel was the apple of His eye, but what does that have to do with you and me?"

"The Hebrew word translated 'apple' is also the word for pupil—like the pupil in your eye. It refers to the reflection of one person in another's eyes. In other words, God is so intently focused on the object of His affection, His beloved, that if we could see His visible eye, we would see ourselves therein."

"That's beautiful. I've never heard it explained that way." Penny's features softened, and a slight smile played on her face. "So when God says we are the apple of His eye, it means we are the focus of His attention?"

"That's right, because we are His beloved." Logan caught Penny's chin in his hand and peered deeply in her eyes. "What do you see in my eyes, Miss Coldwell?"

A tremor shot through Penny at his touch, his words, his expression. She searched his face, and then studied his amber-flecked pupils. "I see me."

"Good. That makes you the apple of my eye, too." Logan smiled deeply and released Penny's chin. Both of the girl's arms were wrapped around the milk jar. Logan extended an open palm to her. She shifted the jar to one side, and freeing one hand, placed it gingerly in his.

Logan decorously bowed and brushed his lips over the back of Penny's hand. "Balim will be drinking warm milk if you don't get a wiggle on, Missy Penny."

Penny laughed. Logan's humor had broken the spell. "It sounds like you've been taking Kentucky vocabulary lessons from Marigold again."

"I've been learning much at Briar Hollow. Yes, indeed." An endearing smile spread across Logan's face. "Good night, Buttercup."

Penny pressed the back of her hand against her cheek as she watched Logan cross the yard and disappear inside the barn. "Good night."

CHAPTER 31

"Every path has its puddles, Missy Penny, that's fo sho and fo certain." Balim moved the team forward on the road to town. "I'm sorry things have been hard fo ya as of late."

"I'm just so glad you're here." Penny threaded her hand through Balim's arm. It was a beautiful day. The sun was shining and the tiger lilies stood at attention as the wagon passed. "Thank you for coming with me."

"I wanted to see this fella," said Balim. "I hope he's up to visitors."

"Me, too." A comfortable silence settled on the pair broken after a time by Balim's curiosity.

"So tell, me, Missy Penny, how's the townfolk? Is Miss Lark still as flashy as a rat with a gold tooth?"

Penny laughed. "You must be referring to Mrs. Lark Thalman. She married last year, but she's still the same old Lark.

"The Goheen sisters are still running the boarding house. They are in good health. Sheriff Nash has been busy with all that's been going on, but I'm sure he's resting easier these days. Effie Matheny is still the teacher at the school. All the family is well— Pansy Joy, Garth and the kids. You'll see everyone at church Sunday that we don't run into today."

"That Dahlia girl is cuter than a sack full o' puppies."

"She is. I just love her and Mattie. They fill the days with smiles."

"It's nice to see a smile on yo face, Missy. Ole Balim's thinkin' that's from mo than looking at young-uns."

Penny felt the flush rise up her neck. "What are you talking about Balim?"

"I might be a few years older, but my eyesight's jus' fine. I seen the way you and that Logan fella was a lookin' at each other."

Penny clamped her lips together. She untied and retied the ribbon on her bonnet as she searched for a means to redirect the conversation. "Oh, we'll see the Matheny twins, of course, when we stop by the ice house for Rosalie."

"Mmhm."

"Ain't that like finding a feather on a frog?" Marigold beamed at the news of Balim's arrival. Her big brown eyes danced in her round freckled face. Her hair, like spun honey, was caught in two braids that hung midway down her back.

"It was unexpected." Rosalie shook her head at her sister. "The good news is he's planning to stay, and he can help Zion and Logan and Garth get the new barn raised. Zion's so pleased and relieved."

"And I can tell you're feeling the same way." Marigold tied her netted hat on her head and slipped on her gloves.

"I'll bring you some honey."

"Thanks, Marigold." Rosalie smiled. "I never have to remind you to wear your hat when you're tending your bees."

"That's a fact." Marigold tipped her hat, and then stuck out her foot. "I remembered my shoes, too."

"That's a good thing."

"When Dahlia gets up from her nap, tell her we're going crawdaddying."

"I'm not sure she's as excited about it as you are," said Rosalie. "She's a bit unsure of the pinchers."

"Aw, the worst they will do is give you a little pinch. Even the big ones don't hurt none. If you move the rocks slow enough, they'll freeze right where they are, and you can grab them easy as huckleberry pie."

"That's easy for you to say, but maybe you should give her a cup to scoop them up in."

"If you say so."

Rosalie smiled at memories of times spent at the creek when she was a little girl. It had always been so refreshing to stick her bare feet in the water on a hot summer day. She, like her daughter, however, had been afraid of the crawdad's pinchers; so Matthias taught her to back them into a cup with a stick.

"I say so."

Balim and Penny left the doctor's office in high spirits. Harley had been alert enough to speak with them. He shared his sad history and sincerely apologized for his plan. He even told them the location of the money and sent his apologies to Mr. Yates.

The best part of their time together had been their talk about the Lord. Penny and Balim had been able to share the good news of salvation. Tears had spilled from Harley's eyes when he repented to them and to God. His breath had been labored as he prayed, and his pain great from the burns, so Balim and Penny had bid him goodbye and promised to return the next day.

Penny sat on the wagon bench with a silly smile plastered across her face, her hands tightly clasped together on her lap. "What a beautiful day," she said.

"On earth and in heaven. The angels are rejoicin', fo sho and fo certain."

"Whoa." Balim stopped the wagon outside Matheny's Ice House and set the brake. A ruckus could be heard from the outside as the twins exchanged verbal spars in the office.

"Boy, I'll smack you so hard your kids will come out behaving."

"Touch me, Ethan Matheny, and I'll put a knot on your head so tall you'll have to climb a ladder to comb your mangy hair."

"Oh, yeah? If you touch me, I'll skin you like a Georgia catfish."

"Oh hobble your lip, Ethan. The last time I saw a mouth like that it had a bit in it."

"Speaking of mouths, you've got tongue enough for ten rows of teeth."

Balim smiled like a possum eating fish. "Those two don't have the brains the good Lawd gave a bale o hay."

"Excuse me." Penny called and knocked loudly. "Could we get some ice, please?"

Ethan smoothed his hair and wiped his mouth with his palm. "Why sure. Just a bucket, or a block?"

"A block today. Balim's here to help." Penny motioned to her friend. "Have you met?"

"We've howdied, but we ain't shook yet," said Evan. "Pleased to know you."

"Pleased to know you," echoed Ethan.

Balim shook their hands and got straight to business. "Can I use your tongs?"

Ethan pulled the large metal tongs from their hook on the wall. "That's what they're here for."

As quickly as possible, Balim and Penny completed their transaction and boarded the wagon. Before Balim could signal the horses, Ethan started up where he had left off.

"You're uglier than a mud fence."

"You're so ugly you could stop a bucket of snot in mid-air," said Evan.

"Oh, yeah? You're so ugly you could knock a buzzard off a gut wagon."

"Well, you're so ugly you'd make a freight train take a dirt road."

"You think that's ugly? You look like you fell out of an ugly tree and hit every branch on the way down."

"Well, if you fell into a pond, we'd be skimming off ugly for a week."

The sound of the barbs faded as Balim and Penny moved down the road toward home. "Did ya ever hear the like of that afore?" asked Balim. "Them two is crazier than outhouse flies."

Penny burst into a giggle. "Do you know what the funniest thing is?"

"What's that?"

"They're identical twins—arguing about who is the ugliest."

Balim threw his head back and erupted in hearty laughter.

"Miss Coldwell! Oh, Miss Coldwell!" The postman ran into the street to stop the wagon. "There's someone looking for the Mayfields. They're staying at your place, aren't they?"

"Yes, they are, Mr. Jenkins."

"He's over at the mercantile right now. He's a big fellow wearing light grey pants, a burgundy vest and a dark slouch hat."

Balim pulled the wagon into Briar Hollow and tied the team to the hitching post. "I'll take care of the ice. You can take your guest up to the house."

Logan heard the wagon wheels pull down the lane and come to a stop outside the barn. He had been listening for the sound of Penny's return and hurried out to assist her from the wagon. To his disappointment another man beat him to the task. His back was to Logan, but something looked familiar about him. He watched as the man made sure Penny had her footing. When he turned, Logan could not believe his eyes.

One look at the man's face, and Logan's heart skipped a beat. How could it be? This was impossible. It was Angus, the man who

289

had taken his father's crops to market and never returned. What was he doing here?

Logan dashed into the barn for his pistol. "Hold it right there, Carver."

Angus Carver stared into the face of his employer's son and slowly raised his hands. "Mr. Logan," he said, "it's so good to see you."

"I can't imagine why. We have nothing left for you to steal."

"I understand why you feel that way, but you're wrong."

"I don't think so, and I'm not going to let you do to the Coldwells what you've done to my family. Balim, grab his arms."

"Now hold up, Son. Maybe you should hear him out."

"Hear him out? He cleaned us out."

"I know what you are thinking," said Angus, "and if I was you, I'd be thinking the same thing, but hear me out. You're going to like what I have to say."

"All right." Logan pointed to the cabin door with his gun. "I'll listen, but you'll forgive me if I reserve my judgment until the end of the tale."

Angus nodded. "That's fair."

Penny watched in shocked silence. She had never seen Logan act in such a way. When she had spoken to Mr. Carver in town she had no idea there was bad blood between him and the Mayfields.

Logan followed the troop into the cabin, his gun trained on Angus Carver's backside.

"Angus!" Millicent was just as shocked at the man's presence as Logan had been.

"Howdy, ma'am. It's sure nice to see you."

"Sit." Logan jerked his gun in the direction of the rocking chair.

"Don't mind if I do. It's been a long journey."

"Angus, tell us, what happened. What kept you? Are you all right?" Millicent plied the man with questions.

"First, let me tell you how sorry I am for the loss of your husband. Mr. Mayfield was a fine man."

"Thank you, Angus." Millicent stared, still unbelieving that the man presumed dead or far, far away was sitting in the same room as she.

"I got everything to market. We made a good profit, too. Your Andrew would have been right pleased."

"That's a bit of good news, at least. He worked so hard. What happened from there?" asked Millicent.

"I got sick, ma'am. I had the promissory note in hand, but couldn't get to the bank with it. Truth is, I was feeling lower than a bow-legged caterpillar.

"First it was the fever. I'd had a sore throat while traveling and been a bit uncomfortable, but on the way to the exchange I started up with the chills. I got a miserable coating on my tongue and the back of my throat.

"I got so weak I was afraid I wouldn't be able to make the exchange, but I didn't want to disappoint your husband, so I pressed through. Right after the sale, I started throwing up and noticed I was plumb covered in red rash."

"Oh, Angus, I'm sorry," Millicent's eyes filled with compassion, but Logan kept his pistol pointed at the man.

"Thank you, ma'am. It weren't pretty, that's for sure."

"Scarlet Fever usually runs its course in a matter of days," said Rosalie. "This was months ago."

"That it was, ma'am, but as the saying goes, 'when it rains it pours.' I passed out on the way from the exchange. A kindly farmer hauled me off to his house in his wagon and took care of me.

"That's not the bad part, of course. That part's good. Where it went bad was the fever turned to something worse. The farmer called in the doctor and he said I had acute hepatitis. It took me six months to get my strength back."

"Why didn't you contact us?" asked Logan.

"I was too sick at first, and by the time I was able, you were gone."

"It must have been after the house burned." Millicent nodded. "We lost everything."

"I was sorry to hear it, but Mrs. Mayfield, I'm happy to tell you that you haven't lost everything. I've got your promissory note right here, and there's no expiration date on it. You can take it to the bank today."

Logan stood to his feet and dropped his gun to his side. All the color drained from his face. *Could this be true?*

"Since you've put your weapon down, is it okay if I reach in my vest and pull it out for you?"

"Oh, yes, Angus." Millicent clapped her hands together. Her eyes sparkled. As she watched Angus retrieve the envelope, her look turned from excitement to confusion.

"This is Andrew's writing."

"Yes, it is." Angus handed the missive to the lady. "He was planning to go with me, you know. When at the last minute he stayed with you, he gave me over his bag and this letter was in it. I didn't read it, but I put the promissory note in there for you."

"Oh, Angus, it's too wonderful to be true. My heart is so full." Millicent clutched the letter to her chest.

"If it's ok with you, ma'am, I'd like to send a little something to the farmer and the doctor. You can take it out of my pay."

"Of course," Millicent eked out the words, overcome with emotion.

"Your husband made a fine choice raising corn. We got $1.40 a bushel, while oats were going for only 84 cents."

"How many bushels, Angus?"

"Are you sure you want to discuss it here, Mrs. Mayfield?"

"It's fine. Go ahead, please."

"Your husband bought 200 acres, but took 10 for the house. That left 190 acres to farm with an average yield of 70 bushels an acre."

Logan did some quick calculations. "Are you telling me you have a note there for over $18,000?" Logan asked, astonishment swam in his hazel eyes.

"That I do."

Logan dropped his gun on the table, astounded by Angus' disclosures. He held out his hand and Angus shook it. "I'm sorry I doubted you, Angus. My father held you in very high regard."

"That's understandable. I'm just glad to find you and make things right."

"Logan," Millicent held out the sheet of paper she had withdrawn from the envelope. "Look at this."

Logan took the paper from his mother. "It's a copy of his will. It must have been in with his business papers.

"To whom it may concern . . . ." Logan stopped reading aloud and scanned the document.

"Mother, this is unbelievable. There's a trust for me in Connecticut, and Father invested your inheritance in gold."

"Praise God! This is so wonderful. Angus, we are indebted to you. Thank you so much for finding us."

"If you don't have any prospects, and there are no hard feelings, I'd like to maintain your employment," said Logan. "I have some things in mind we could discuss after you've rested from your journey."

"I don't know what you have in mind," said Angus, "but I can assure you I haven't had any better offers."

CHAPTER 32

Logan walked back from town with a smile on his face. His pocket was deliciously fattened by a new bank book and the telegraph confirming his holdings in the East. His father had been wise to invest in gold, given the inflation of paper money due to the war. The future looked bright for the first time in a long time.

His visit to the doctor's office had gone well. Harley Crawford was on the decline, but there was a light of hope burning in his eyes. Logan was thankful he had the chance to talk to him. They talked about the Lord, and Logan was pleased to learn that as a young man Harley had been baptized during a brush arbor revival. He expressed his regret for not following through on a walk with God.

At the end of their visit, Logan prayed with the man for some time and left him still whispering undiscernable praise on his sick bed. Harley didn't have much of a future in this world. If he lived, he would face the law for his deeds. His hope was in the eternal, but for now, he had the strength and peace he had been searching for all his life.

Logan walked and hummed with a spry step.

O for a thousand tongues to sing
My great Redeemer's praise,

The glories of my God and King,
The triumphs of His grace!

Logan thought back to his stop at the Paxton Inn. He had set Angus up in a room until he sorted things out. Carver was willing to go along with his plans if everything worked out accordingly.

With confident steps, Logan plodded down the lane. When he spied the fairy ring, he was captured by sweet memories of a "provincial pixie" never far from his thoughts. As he circled the barn, he discovered Balim giving a bottle to Equity. "Hey, you're doing my job."

"T'aint a job to feed a young-un, Logan. 'Tis a pleasure, fo sho and fo certain."

"That it is." Logan smiled. "Has Zion told you about the plans for the barn?"

"Sho 'nough has." Balim scratched the filly's blaze where the hair started to swirl. She flickered her ears with pleasure.

"Are you in?"

"In on what, suh?"

"I'll give you all the details once I get them worked out. I need to ride into Maysville first."

Balim studied the eager face of the young man and liked what he read in his features. He gave a firm nod and a smile. "Why don't you ask Zion if'n you can take West? He's always up fo a run."

"I'll do it right now."

Balim watched the young man's light step. "You up to something, Lawd. Yes, You is." Balim smiled and went into the barn for West's saddle and tack. "I think I'm gwanna like it."

Zion leaned over his paper and reworked his numbers. "It looks like we're going to be ok, Rosalie."

"I never doubted that."

"I tried not to, but it was hard a time or two."

"I know." Rosalie placed the dried cup on the shelf, tucked the dish towel into her apron and gave Zion's broad shoulders a firm rub. "It's hard sometimes, when you're in the middle of a change or a challenge, to trust God's purpose and timing."

"That's what He's been trying to get through this thick head of mine."

"Did it take?" Rosalie ruffled her husband's hair with both of her hands and then thumped his nose with her forefinger.

"Equinox and Equity: timing and judgment. With each plan of God are both the timing of it and the right process. I won't forget this lesson for a long time.

Penny sat cross-legged on the front porch with piles of radishes all around. She separated plant roots from the leaves, lopped the top off the roots and put them in a pot. Then she split off the green leaves she would use for dinner from the yellow she planned to give the chickens.

"How's it going?" Logan bounded up the steps and leaned against the porch wall. He looked happy.

"I feel like a squash in a radish stew, but I'm pretty good."

"That's good. Well, I'll see you later." Logan reached for the handle and disappeared inside the cabin. He was gone for only a minute before he slipped back outside and dashed down the steps to the barn.

I guess things are different around here now that Mr. Mayfield's fortune has changed.

Penny cut and sorted a radish plant, and then stared at the barn. *What am I doing?* She berated herself for seeking him out, following his moves so attentively when he obviously had better things to do with his time than spend it with a lowly farm girl.

Logan led West out of the barn and mounted without incident. He set his brown bowler in place on his tawny hair before heading down the lane on the back of Zion's prized stallion.

Vacillating emotions dominated Penny's afternoon. She was up and then down like the painted pony on the carousel ride. One moment she made excuses for Logan's apparent disinterest, and the next she was chiding herself for the foolishness of thinking he would still be interested in her. She tried to keep herself busy, but by mid-afternoon, she was ready for a change of scenery.

"Rosalie, I'm going to walk to town and check on Mr. Crawford."

"Would you like me to go with you? I'm sure Pansy Joy would watch the kids."

"Oh, no. I'm fine. He's not a threat to me or anyone. Would you mind if I took some of the Indian pudding?"

"You are a good-hearted soul, Penny Coldwell." Rosalie smiled. "I'll get a nice-sized slice for you. Perhaps Dr. Byerly and his wife would enjoy some."

Penny hung her apron and smoothed her dress. She grabbed her straw poke-bonnet off its peg and waited while Rosalie wrapped the pudding.

She had hoped the walk to town would settle her a bit. She started out agitated, and by the time she arrived at the place of the fairy ring, she was close to stomping mad. She stalked into the trees and over to the Mason jar, and then kicked it off the ring. *Stupid wishes.*

The wind chimes mocked her. "Cheer up, cheer up, Buttercup!" they seemed to sing in an abhorrently chipper tone. Penny reached down for a rock to throw at the chimes, and then realized they would just sing louder if she made the hit. She heaved a sigh and dropped the rock to the ground.

I don't know what's gotten into me, Lord. Logan never promised me anything . . . at least not with words. She thought back to their moonlit encounter at the stream. The memory of his hazel eyes and the expression on his face taunted her vexed emotions.

There's nothing to do but move on, I guess. Penny took deliberate steps back to the lane and restarted her journey to town. *How am I going to be a light for Mr. Crawford when I'm barely twinkling enough to see the path in front of me?*

From within the fog of her confusion, a reminder plucked at the strings of her heart. *Praise.*

"Praise, that's what always helped me in the past, didn't it, Lord?"

Our God, our help in ages past,
Our hope for years to come,
Our shelter from the stormy blast,
And our eternal home.

Penny sang the words in time with her steps and smiled at the end of the first verse. Praise had lifted her once again. By the time she arrived at the Byerly's, she had sung all nine verses through twice and was feeling much lighter in spirit.

The sight of the coffin wagon parked outside the doctor's office drew her up short. Penny sucked in her breath and dropped the pudding to the ground.

Dr. Byerly stood on the covered porch speaking with the undertaker. He spied the girl standing in the street and motioned to her. "Penny, won't you come here?"

The last thing Penny wanted to do was move towards the coffin wagon and hear what Dr. Byerly had to say. "I'm sorry, dear, but Mr. Crawford passed just a short while ago."

Stricken, Penny shook her head and closed her eyes. "He had such an awful life. I felt so bad for him."

"I know, but I want to tell you something; and then I have something to give you. Let's go inside."

Penny followed the doctor into the parlor and sat next to him in one of the waiting chairs.

"Penny, I want you to know that Mr. Crawford is truly in a better place. Because of your kindness, the man who accosted you, left this life to spend eternity with God."

Penny clamped her lips to keep back a sob. Two tears dropped one after the other from her tightly closed eyes. "I wish I could know that's true."

Dr. Byerly covered Penny's clasped hands with one of his own and gave a soft squeeze. "I know it's true. If you had only heard him praying with Mr. Mayfield, you would be as confident as I."

Penny lifted her tear-stained face and read the sincerity in the doctor's eyes. "For two hours after Mr. Mayfield left, I heard him. He didn't have the strength for travail or anything like that, but every few minutes he would breathe out a heavenly praise."

Penny's shoulders shook with sobs of mingling relief and sorrow. Dr. Byerly stood and reached for something on his wife's desk. "He wanted you to have this."

The doctor placed the damaged music box in Penny's lap. "I'll leave you now, dear. Stay as long as you like."

Logan passed through the covered bridge. It was the double post and brace design used to protect the complex system of rigid trusses beneath. Like so many others that dotted the rough terrain, Logan thought again of the many reasons he was beginning to consider Kentucky a beautiful place to call home.

His visit to the county seat had been all he had hoped, evidenced by the thick envelope in West's saddlebag. The property across the stream from Briar Hollow was now his. He prayed Zion would be happy with his plan. He had the money to buy in as a partner and develop Coldwell Horse Farm into a successful, multi-state venture. He wanted nothing more than to call Briar Hollow home, if even from across the stream, as long as a certain blonde-haired, blue-eyed girl would share that home with him.

The sun was low in the sky as he neared the turn-in for Briar Hollow. "Whoa, West." Logan reined in the stallion and dismounted. He ground tied him like Zion had taught him and slipped through the trees to the fairy ring.

"What's this?" Logan spotted the Mason jar knocked over several feet from the ring. He picked it up, smiled, and carried the jar back to the lane. Holding West's leads, he walked the horse back to his corral.

"I'll be back to take that saddle off in a few minutes, boy. Thanks for the ride." Logan carried the jar into the barn, hid it behind a bail of hay, and then went in search of Zion.

"You seem in especially high spirits today, Zion." Penny stared at her brother. Something was up. She knew him too well to miss his peculiar behavior.

"Not much, Buttercup." Zion shoved a biscuit in his mouth and talked around the bite. "This is good, honey." His words were muffled around his meal and Rosalie misunderstood them.

"You want honey?"

Zion shook his head and chewed and smiled.

Supper couldn't get over fast enough for Penny. She hoped an evening quilting bee would calm her after her tumultuous day. Logan disappeared before the dishes were cleared, leaving Penny to wonder at his quick departure. *He doesn't want to be in the same room with me anymore.*

By the time the dishes were washed and the little ones tucked in, Penny was ready to wile away the evening in the quilting chair. The low, armless rocker had belonged to Rosalie's mother, and Penny always felt peaceful sitting in it.

"Penny, would you mind fetching some dried apples from the root cellar?" asked Rosalie. "I want to soak them for pies tomorrow."

"I guess it's best to do it now before we settle into the sewing." Penny opened the door and stepped outside. She took a lantern with her to light the inside of the root cellar, but outside the first quarter moon lit the evening with a lovely glow.

Penny sighed and moved around the cabin to the root cellar.

"Psst."

Penny turned her head to the direction of the sound.

"Psst."

Lifting the lamp high, she took a step forward.

"Who's there?" she whispered.

"Come see," Logan whispered back.

The sound of his voice sent a chill up Penny's spine. She was confused, but she couldn't stop the smile that demanded to be released.

Logan stepped into view. One hand was behind his back, and the other reached for the girl he had come to love.

"You are a presumptuous man, Mr. Mayfield." Penny allowed Logan to take her hand and followed him to the seat beneath the arbor. Instead of facing the rose gardens, he sat her facing the stream and the land he hoped to share with her.

Logan dropped to one knee. Penny blinked quickly several times in a row, confused by what was happening.

"Logan?"

Enraptured by the sound of his name on her lips, Logan smiled and brought forth the Mason jar hidden behind his back. Fireflies flickered inside, and there were other items in the jar Penny could not make out.

"What is this?"

"This, my dear, is a wishing jar."

She laughed and shook her head. "I know that, but what's inside."

"Just a little magic."

302

"Oh, really?" Penny took the jar and peered through the glass. A dozen or so fireflies blinked off and on lighting the contents in a haphazard fashion. "Are those my . . . ?"

"I have a confession to make with my profession." Logan assumed a humble posture. "If you will, please open the jar."

Relief and joy danced in Penny's heart. She looked at Logan and then at the jar, and then tilted her head back and reveled beneath the beautiful moon. Tears of happiness pooled in her blue eyes.

"Open it."

Logan watched as Penny focused on the jar in her hands. She removed the lid, and several fireflies escaped. With shaking fingers, she withdrew her missing blue ribbons.

"I can't believe you stole my ribbons."

"Neither can I. I've never stolen anything in my life," said Logan, "but you know you've stolen from me, as well."

Penny's eyes grew large at his false accusation. "I never have, Logan Mayfield."

"Oh, but you did. From the first moment I saw you, you stole my heart." Logan paused and thought of their meeting at the swimming hole. How his life had changed since that day. "There's something else. Look inside."

Penny reached in the jar once again and withdrew a piece of paper.

"You've heard my confession. That's my profession."

The folded paper held one of the season's first buttercups. Penny held the flower under her nose and breathed in its sweet fragrance. She smiled, laced the buttercup's stem between her fingers and unfolded the paper.

For a man of words, Logan's missive was short and to the point, but to Penny Coldwell, it could not have read any sweeter:

I love you, Buttercup.
Will you marry me?

Other Affirming Faith titles by Lori Wagner

The Rose of Sharon

Quilting Patches of Life

A Patchwork of Freedom

Gateway of the Son

Holy Intimacy: Dwelling with God in the Secret Place

The 8 Days of Christmas: Praying Through the Nativity

Insight on Ministry from a Christmas Tree Farm

Gates & Fences: Straight Talk in a Crooked World

Christian 101

www.ingramcontent.com/pod-product-compliance
Lightning Source LLC
Chambersburg PA
CBHW070109120726
47909CB00002B/542